Falling *for* Love

Falling for Love

A WEST VIRGINIA ROMANCE

ADDISON M. CONLEY

Falling for Love: A West Virginia Romance
© 2019 by Addison M. Conley
Published by: Cold Run Valley Publishing, LLC. Second Edition.

Paperback edition ISBN: 978-0-9980296-0-3
E-book edition ISBN: 978-0-9980296-1-0

This is a work of fiction - names, characters, places, and incidents are the product of the author's imagination or are used fictitiously. Any resemblance to actual persons living or dead, business, events or locales is entirely coincidental.

Credits:
Editor: Nikki Busch, nikkibuschediting.com
Book Design: Maureen Cutajar, Go Published, gopublished.com
Cover Design: Natasja Hellenthal, Beyond Book Covers, beyondbookcovers.com
Cover Photographer: Ervin-Edward, shutterstock.com/g/ervinedward

Dedication

To M&M. Thank you for helping me become my true self.

To Lisa – Alfred Lord Tennyson said, "'Tis better to have loved and lost than never to have loved at all." I think of you from time to time and miss the happy, wonderful piece of you. I wish you well in defeating your demons.

To the entire group of Mountain Mamas – Love you!!!

Acknowledgments

This novel would not have been possible without the assistance and kind support from many people.

The title of this second edition has been tweaked to *Falling for Love: A West Virginia Romance* since the story begins in the Fall of 2014 and ends in June 2015. Besides a romance, the story is built around the fight for equality and same-sex marriage and is more than a winter read. My real neck of the woods is an eclectic mix and is changing for the better. I'm fortunate to have several around me who have given lots of love and support.

For this second edition, Nikki Busch was again the editor, and Natasja Hellenthal was the cover artist. Thank you, ladies. Natasja was a joy to work with and extremely patient with me. The cover photography is from Ervin-Edward whose amazing work can be found on Shutterstock. I'd also like to thank Ann McMan who designed the cover for the first edition back in 2017. My apologies to the readers that that version was unavailable after November 2018.

Thanks to the Golden Crown Literary Society (GCLS) Writing Academy and the class of 2016-2017. It was a pleasure to work with everyone. A special thanks to the instructors and authors that volunteered their time and suggestions. You all were an inspiration. We may be from different parts of the country, the world, and professions, but our passion for writing unites us. Also, I never would have joined the writing academy if it had not been for Karen Richard talking up a storm and introducing me to the amazing Beth Burnett at the GCLS Washington DC 2016 conference.

To all the wonderful authors I've met along the way – too many to name – you all were the first to open my eyes to the broader world of LesFic. I've met many at GCLS conferences and at one of my favorite venues – Women's Fest in Rehoboth Beach, Delaware. Also, thanks to the numerous volunteers operating in the shadows that make conferences, events, and book fairs a success.

I would like to express my deep gratitude to the authors who gave me advice on becoming an Indie author, especially Caren Werlinger for exceptional tips over coffee and numerous text messages. Some wish to remain nameless, and I don't want to muddy the political waters of publishing. Therefore, you will become the unsung heroes. You know who you are.

Thank you to my beta readers Loretta HK, Tracy Silka, and Laure Dherbécourt. All the feedback was invaluable. Special thanks to Loretta HK for going the extra mile, having faith in my writing, and not sugar coating anything, but most of all, for being an Ally to myself and others at work. I wish I were still there, but as you know, my body wouldn't cooperate.

Thanks to those that have walked up to me at GCLS and book fairs, and those who have written to me in email or sent me a Facebook note; a special shout-out to Judith and Carol. I was touched by everyone's sincerity and thankful for the support.

To Kaitlyn and Justin, you're always in my heart.

Lastly, I want to thank the readers, especially those that wrote reviews on the first edition and posted to Goodreads or Amazon: Loek in the Netherlands. Laure Dherbécourt from Reunion Island, France; her review is on the French Amazon site. Rocío

Toboso F from Madrid, Spain. Kitty Kat from Scotland, UK. Mirtha Siblesz. Ameliah Faith. ELC in Washington DC, USA. Jo. Michele. Goofy 22. Reviewers that are simply identified as Amazon Customers. And R. who wrote the very first review on Goodreads then posted to Amazon. Also, thanks to those that just left a star rating on Goodreads. Every little bit helps! And cheers to everyone who posted wonderful comments on FB. Thank you all from the bottom of my heart!!!!!!!!

Chapter One

The dull throb in her head, a dry throat, and tired muscles made Jordan Simón feel like a cardboard figure going through the motions. Searching the desk drawer for her new menu, her fingers touched the book she had long ago forgotten. Gingerly pulling it out, a Polaroid picture fell to the floor. Her stomach clenched and her breathing stilled as she slowly picked it up. She wanted to cry but couldn't. No matter what level of success she had achieved, the screams of the past lurked in her brain, reminding her there was no running away.

She mindlessly caressed the faded picture with her thumb when the sound of a metal tray, rattling on the other side of the door, brought her back to the present. Tucking the picture back into the book, she carefully slid it from sight. After a few deep breaths, she left the office and displayed the best cheery persona she could muster.

After nodding to the staff, she strolled into the dining room where the harsh glare of the kitchen lighting gave way to the warm glow of candles. Laughter, the clanking of glasses, well wishes, and playful shouts echoed throughout. She smiled and glanced around then mingled with her customers. Conversations were long enough to be polite, but she rushed through a couple of encounters—the frequent patrons who either hit on her or tried to fix her up with a friend or relative. They never gave up, especially when fortified with alcohol. She changed direction after spotting a family friend.

"Good evening, Betty Jean. Pleased to see you're feeling better."

"Why thank you, dear. The canelones are incredible, but against the better judgment of my doctor, I ordered extra spices and garlic."

Jordan noticed a half-eaten bowl of her favorite chicken stew across from Betty Jean. It had been hours since she ate, no doubt adding to her fatigue and mood.

"Betty Jean, are you on a date?" She propped her hand on her hip, flicked her eyebrows up, and widened her smile.

Between a rumble of laughter, Betty Jean said, "Don't I wish."

Jordan caught the hint of lilac—springtime, wet blossoms. Her eyes briefly fluttered.

The touch of Betty Jean's hand snapped Jordan back to the present. "I'd like you to meet my niece, Emmy Russo. Honey, this is Jordan Simón, the chef and owner of the restaurant."

"Pleased to meet you, Ms. Simón. I never expected to find delicious authentic Spanish cuisine in the eastern panhandle of West Virginia. The dish was prepared to perfection."

"Welcome to La Vida Al Máximo, and the pleasure is mine." Jordan extended her hand. The woman's grip was firm yet gentle, and there was something about her accent, perhaps British. Jordan was instantly drawn to her and equally embarrassed that she noticed the low-cut neckline of the teal blouse, which revealed ample round breasts.

After several minutes of conversation, Jordan excused herself back to the kitchen. The smell of lilac lingered in her senses. Hesitating at the door, she glanced back. Emmy was watching her.

The woman had a gorgeous face, but Emmy savored the view as she walked away. The sway of the hips and the long black ponytail contrasting against the crisp white chef jacket were alluring.

"Your eyes seem to be popping out of your head, dear."

"Why, whatever do you mean, Auntie? And why the whisper?" Emmy turned and smirked over her teacup before taking a long sip.

Betty Jean eyed her before saying another word. "I think you're looking in the wrong direction."

"Looking doesn't hurt. Besides, you said yourself there's always been a liberal element in town. I'm merely interested as to how much Oakville has changed since my last visit a few years back."

"A few years. It's been almost ten." Betty Jean tore a bread-stick in half.

"Ouch. Guess I deserved that." She glanced over and saw Jordan paused at the kitchen door. Their gazes lingered a split second. Emmy smiled, but there was no hint of a similar return from the beautiful woman.

"So tell me, why haven't I met her before?"

"She moved to Spain after high school and returned about five years ago to open the restaurant."

"Does she have a partner?" The words were spoken out of curiosity and partially to tease her aunt.

"She's Gwyneth's daughter and Elizabeth's niece. You know, my best friends." Aunt Betty Jean's harsh glare silently seemed to say, *Don't even think about it.*

"I'm only admiring the positive change in this quaint town."

"And as I said, I think you're mistaken. Try to stay out of trouble while visiting."

"I promise to behave, but I have no intentions of hiding or avoiding anyone because of who I am."

Betty Jean leaned over, and her eyes softened. "I'm not asking you to. It's...some people around here have problems. Her older brother has become a religious radical. Be careful for everyone's sake."

The next morning, Jordan crawled out of bed half-asleep and stumbled toward the kitchen. Her body ached, almost like a hangover, even though she'd only had two glasses of wine the night before. Minutes later, curled up on the sofa next to the picture window and nursing a potent brew flavored with hazelnut, she gazed at the unique beauty of the forest.

The trees reached up to the gray sky. Their limbs were losing leaves fast this year. The landscape was scattered with boulders, and the mountain brook trickled by. It was beautiful, peaceful, and lonely at the same time. Soon winter would come. Just as nature had a way of turning, so did most things in life.

Her eyes fixated on the large solitary boulder. She was like that one: hard, isolated, and wearing down with the winds of time. No doubt to others, she appeared to have it all. If only they knew the truth. She was tired of the inner turmoil and the lies and half-truths piled around her, which were like landmines that required precise navigation.

Life in Madrid had afforded her freedom away from prying eyes and small-town prejudice. A space to grow. Returning home was an opportunity to fulfill her dream of opening her own restaurant, and a chance to reconnect with family and heal from the past. But after five years, she had not come out nor had she developed many friendships. And she never spoke to anyone about what really happened years ago on that awful day in May.

Jordan squeezed her eyes tight and took some deep breaths. "I have to take the last step," she murmured to the empty room. "Christ, I'll be freaking forty in three months." She raised her mug and shouted, "And happy birthday to you too, Cybill."

She thought back on those years watching the *Moonlighting* TV show. The lead actress, Cybill Shepherd, captivated her. At first, she didn't know why. Of course, having the same birthday as such a famous celebrity was part of the infatuation. And there was the cool detective work, jobs no other women she knew had.

Over time, Jordan discovered the real reason. She recalled those days when she first became aware that she was different.

On her twelfth birthday, her older brother Gerry had given her a couple vintage magazines with Cybill on the cover. She relished them alone in her bedroom and imagined what it would be like to kiss Cybill. The newly discovered emotions were a swirl of pleasure, guilt, and shame. She recalled someone saying that homosexuality was a sin. Classmates said, "those people were sickening freaks," while others called a few of the less popular kids lesbos or faggots. Was she a homosexual for wanting to kiss another girl? Why was it so bad?

One day, she was cleaning Gerry's room for some spending money and had been curious as to what his friend had hastily thrown under the bed the day before. After running the vacuum, she took a flashlight and looked. Stretching to grab something from the deep middle, she pulled out a couple of magazines. She gasped. Alongside the motorcycles and cars were scantily dressed women seductively proffered. Jordan's breath caught in her throat, her heart beat faster, and her body felt strange.

The unusual sensations rippling through her body told her to look more, but fear crushed her. She quickly hid the magazines back under the bed, and crept down the hallway in shame. She locked her door, drew the blinds, and lay in bed trying to forget what she had seen. She couldn't. A million thoughts raced through her head. One kept tumbling to the forefront. She was one of "those people." A sinner. Sad and confused, she vowed to bury this secret deep.

Then there was high school. Karen. Lilacs in the spring. Fun. Love. Loss. Even after many years, the joy and hurt lingered in the deepest pit of her soul.

Let it go. It wasn't your fault. The chill in the air caused goose bumps to cover Jordan's arms. But was it only the cold? The wounds of the past were sucking the life out of her.

Chapter Two

ordan squeezed down the grocery aisle, mumbling under her breath, "I can't believe I'm in the store the day before Thanksgiving, and there are no freakin' carts or baskets. Damn, what a zoo." Balancing ingredients in her arms, she swung around and almost collided with Betty Jean's niece.

"Um...sorry. It's been a busy week," Jordan mumbled.

A warm smile spread across the woman's face, giving Jordan enough time to notice her lips and hazel eyes.

"I'm Emmy, and you're Gwyneth's daughter Jordan. Looks like you're about ready to spill your booty."

The warmth of a blush crept up Jordan's neck and face. She had changed into her favorite comfy sweatpants before leaving the restaurant and now felt the fabric dip below her hips and the bottom of the T-shirt exposing a bit of her midriff. "Yeah. Kind of crazy to be in the store today."

"Please, share my basket with me."

"Thanks, but I don't want to slow you down."

"I insist, and I'd love the company."

Jordan smiled and began to place items in the cart when she lost control of a box of tea. With each attempt to grab it, the box danced through the air until Emmy caught it in front of her face.

"Good thing that was not a carton of eggs."

Jordan liked how Emmy's mouth turned into a wicked grin, and her eyes twinkled. They strolled along in no particular hurry, and Jordan began to relax with the light chitchat between them. Soon, they were standing in the monster checkout line.

"I'm a dual British and American citizen, but I find Thanksgiving to be a uniquely American holiday that's both happy and sad."

Jordan cocked an eyebrow. "Oh, in what way?"

"It's a day for everyone to enjoy family and friends. I'm driving Betty Jean to visit our cousins in Leestown tomorrow, which should be loads of fun. But if you think about history, the day essentially celebrates an Anglo-Saxon invasion of a country that already belonged to someone else."

Jordan's jaw dropped, and she glanced around to see if anyone had an adverse reaction to the statement. The town had always been a mix of city transplants, artists, and rednecks. Fortunately, no one was paying attention. That was good because somewhere in the store was the owner of the pickup truck parked in the lot, with a six-foot Confederate flag flying from a makeshift pole.

"True," she said, looking back into Emmy's eyes. "For sadness, I was thinking more of the pain-in-the-ass relatives."

Emmy's dead-serious face broke into a wry smile, followed by a chuckle. "What do you like about Thanksgiving, Jordan? Tell me the happy part."

"I donate to the food shelter. The holiday season is always a time to give a little more. As for the restaurant, we close early the day before and don't reopen until Saturday. For the past three years, I've allowed a couple of employees to host a dinner for their friends who don't have anywhere to go. I pick up the tab. In return, they clean up the restaurant afterward and volunteer at the shelter."

"That's generous. And your relatives? I know Betty Jean is close to your mum and aunt."

Jordan grinned. "Mom's large family gathers for dinner at Grammy and Poppa Lange's farmhouse. I'm close to my younger brother Carter and his family." She leaned in closer to Emmy. "Aunt Elizabeth is sweet, but her kids are a mixed bunch." Jordan bit her lip and stuffed her hands in her pockets. Her shoulders sagged. "My older brother Gerry turned obnoxious somewhere along the line. He and a few other relatives can't keep their mouths shut about religion and politics no matter what the occasion."

"Oh my, sounds like a challenging day."

Jordan nodded and was relieved by the distraction of the cashier greeting them. She did not want to discuss her family further; in fact, she'd probably already said too much. As they walked out into the parking lot, Jordan had that familiar twist of excitement and fear. When they reached Emmy's car, she began to panic. Emmy was making her goodbyes, but Jordan was frozen. *Say something.*

"Ah…I'll see you around. The restaurant gets crazy during the holidays, but please, stop by. We can chat longer. You're in town for a while, right?"

"Yes. I'm visiting for several months, and I'd love to."

Jordan hesitated, wrestling with the conundrum of what to do next. She had never been comfortable with hugging nonfamily members, and the Food Lion parking lot was not the place to begin snuggling with an attractive woman she barely knew.

"Sorry. I have to run."

Jordan's hand was barely in front of her when Emmy reached out as if to shake then instantly covered it with her other and did not let go. The warmth was inviting.

"The next time, we can exchange invasion stories," Emmy smirked.

Jordan released a small laugh and withdrew her hand. She waved and walked to her SUV.

The next day, Jordan arrived late for Thanksgiving dinner. She loved Grammy and Poppa Lange, but large family gatherings usually turned awkward. This holiday would be a particular challenge since the state's same-sex marriage ban had recently been ruled unconstitutional by the federal Fourth Circuit Court of Appeals. Expecting the worst with the rigid views of her brother Gerry and a few others, she braced herself and took a breath before walking into the house.

She was grateful when dinner finished on a pleasant note. After helping serve dessert, she joined her brother Carter and his wife, Angie, in the downstairs rec room with a few easygoing relatives. Her grandparents and mom remained upstairs. Unfortunately, the peacefulness did not last long when Gerry walked in with several conservative family members. She only acknowledged them with a slight nod.

The one who got under Jordan's skin the most was a lawyer who passed himself off as a good ole country boy. She cringed when he said, "Letting the lower courts uproot state marriage law is unjust. We're going to fight it."

Gerry agreed. "Yeah, this year's been a horrible disappointment. I'll be happy to see 2014 end."

The cousin slapped Gerry on the back. "With any luck, the US Supreme Court will come to their senses and uphold the constitution."

"Congress should pass an amendment to defend the sanctity of marriage, but I'm not sure I have much faith in the government."

"Don't worry, Gerry. You might want to join the Family Research Council. We have a chapter opening up nearby."

Jordan's stomach lurched, and her skin prickled as if a thousand nanometer-sized insects were crawling all over her. The

FRC was slick, but its extremist agenda had won them a spot on the Southern Poverty Law Group list of hate groups.

"Why do they have to publicly display that lifestyle? It's disgusting," another cousin said loudly. "I don't want to see it!" She casually sipped her coffee and took small bites of pie, either not realizing or not caring about the impact of her words.

"Yeah, it's unnatural," Gerry added. "People are turning away from God these days."

Out of the corner of her eye, Jordan saw the vein in Carter's neck bulging, and he looked as though he would explode. Carter said through gritted teeth, "Not everyone agrees with your views." Angie put her hand on his forearm, and he calmed. "I didn't come over for a sermon."

Jordan's mouth dropped when another cousin whose leanings were ambiguous said, "I think we have more important things to worry about in this country than who someone chooses to love."

Before the situation became worse, Angie stood. "I'm going to check on the kids."

Jordan jumped up to take advantage of the opening. "I'll join you. Besides, I promised to drop by the employee dinner."

"Yeah, I think I'll leave too." Disdain rolled off Carter's tongue as the two brothers glared at one another.

Before they could make their exit, Aunt Elizabeth stood in the doorframe. They faced her like three ducks in a row, but her scowl fell upon the others.

"What the heck is going on in here? This isn't a political rally. Change the topic. For heaven's sake, can't you talk football or something happy? What about music?"

Jordan suppressed a smile and thought, *Yeah, I could talk about Taylor Swift and imagine her singing to me.* Instead, she said, "I really do have to get going. Take care, everyone." She waved and tried to edge past, but Aunt Elizabeth wasn't budging.

"Your mother's not going to be happy that you're sneaking away to work."

"It's not work. It's just some friends who have nowhere else to go, and this is Jo's first Thanksgiving since her mom died last year. You all have each other."

"We gotta check on the kids, and I promised to build a Lego spaceship," Carter rattled off.

Elizabeth stepped aside. "You three go. The rest of you, tone it down!"

When Jordan made her final round of goodbyes, she expected an earful, but Mom, Grammy, and Poppa let her go without much grief. Hopping into the vehicle, she cranked up the radio. Despite the distraction, her muscles remained tense, and her pulse thumped more rapidly than the beat. Speeding down the gravel road, a plume of dust swirled behind her. She couldn't get out of there fast enough.

Part of her original plan in returning home had been to eventually come out. Delaying it was more than an unwillingness to move outside her comfort zone. Living in this part of the country meant picking your fights. The fear of possible vandalism and memories of Karen were unshakable. But the damned balancing act was getting old, and lately, her internal panic attacks threatened to spill over into public view. She needed and wanted to change. It was simply a matter of timing. At least, that's what she told herself.

Chapter Three

Relaxing in the coffeehouse, Jordan was in no hurry this morning as pleasant thoughts of Emmy filled her head. Two weeks had passed since they spoke. Despite brief encounters or the casual wave as they drove past each other, Jordan wanted more. *Does Emmy feel the same attraction?* Since returning home, anxiety had virtually wiped out Jordan's gaydar and making the wrong assumption could be a disaster, but every fiber of her body and mind screamed, *Take the chance.*

"Got any answers for me today, coffeehouse?" Jordan mumbled as she rotated her cup. Her eyes blinked several times as she read each quote. The words of William Ernest Henley read, "I am the master of my fate. I am the captain of my soul." The other side was from Ralph Waldo Emerson, "Once you make a decision, the universe conspires to make it happen." The ding of the door made her glance up. Emmy and her aunt strolled to the counter.

Betty Jean grabbed a to-go cup, placed a peck on her niece's cheek, and left. Seemingly unaware of Jordan's presence, Emmy removed her coat and scrolled through her phone while waiting for her order, giving Jordan time to get lost in thoughts of admiration.

Jordan's pulse quickened as Emmy's slender fingers tucked a piece of wavy blond hair behind her ear, and when Emmy responded to the barista with a soft laugh, warmth spread through Jordan. She watched Emmy carefully balance a full cup in one hand and her coat and a couple of books in the other while making her way to a table. Jordan jumped up to assist.

"Looks like you need some help."

"Fancy meeting you here," Emmy said with a mischievous glint in her eye.

"Please, join me." She took Emmy's cup and managed to not spill a drop despite the zing that went through her body when their fingers brushed together. As Emmy settled into the seat, she noted the light makeup over Emmy's creamy skin followed by lovely hazel eyes. They appeared greener today.

Jordan held out the plate. "Scone? It's delicious, but I probably shouldn't have another."

"Thank you. How did your invasion celebration go?" Emmy winked, and a small crinkle appeared on the edge of her mouth before bursting into a full gleaming smile.

Emmy's gesture immediately dashed away Jordan's bad feelings about her bigoted relatives. "Good with some relatives, but I finished the evening at the employee dinner with plenty of laughter."

"Laughter's good for the soul." Emmy took a bite of the scone, and her hand flew up to catch some crumbs. With her hand over her mouth, she giggled and pushed her cup across the table. "The quote appears to suit your night of merriment."

"Ah, George Bernard Shaw: 'If you want to tell people the truth, make them laugh, otherwise they'll kill you.' Good one. And how were your relatives?"

Emmy tried to cover a smirk. "Enjoyable. Although, Betty Jean wasn't pleased that we had to spend the night. I drank too much. Nothing crazy, but we killed a bottle of Irish whiskey that I had brought them."

"Sounds like a good time. You mentioned dual citizenship the other day. Will you go back to the UK after your visit?"

"I'll be working in Washington DC for a couple of years since snagging a part-time position at our US headquarters. Most of my career was spent in London, but I recently completed three years in India. I'm sick of traveling, and honestly, work. Part of the deal was the bank allowing me a four-month sabbatical. I also do private consulting."

I wonder if she's available, zipped through Jordan's mind, followed by, *Oh God, I'm in so much trouble.*

"You look surprised." When Jordan didn't respond immediately, Emmy said, "Is that a good thing or a bad thing?"

"Oh...I...um...good." She wanted to crawl under the table as Emmy intently studied her over the coffee cup rim. Finally, Jordan found her voice. "Your aunt will be happy, and I would love to see you again." *Did I really just say that out loud?* A flush ran through her, and she hurried to change the topic. "Tell me about your parents."

"As you know my father was Auntie's brother-in-law. He went to university in England and became a British citizen. My mum was a teacher from Leestown and met my father on holiday in London." Emmy dabbed the corner of her mouth as her eyes lit up. "Well, she never went home. A year later, I was born in London. We lived throughout Europe, and I spent occasional summers in America with relatives. So, you can see my background is different from most people's." Emmy's broad smile faded. "Unfortunately, my mother died over twenty years ago, and my father passed last year."

"I'm sorry. My dad died when I was a little girl."

"Was your father from Spain? Betty Jean said you lived there for several years after graduating from culinary school."

Jordan bit her lip. "Yes." She reached for her cup and accidentally knocked it over. The last dribbles of the coffee spilled over Emmy's books. "Shit."

They both grabbed napkins, sopping up the liquid frantically.

"No harm," Emmy said. "The smell of coffee will remind me of you while reading."

Jordan froze when she saw Philip Simmons's book. While Emmy continued to wipe down the books, Jordan softly said, "Have you read it?"

"I just bought the mystery."

"No, I meant *Learning to Fall: The Blessings of An Imperfect Life.*"

"Oh, almost finished. What an inspirational and spiritual work of art. Simmons's humor and ability to stop and point out the beauty in life were a gift that he left for us all. I'm not sure I could be brave in his position."

After a few silent seconds, Jordan looked up. "The essays he wrote were nothing short of amazing. Lots of lessons to live by." She swallowed hard and quoted from the book. "'When we learn to fall, we learn that only by letting go...we find, ultimately, the most profound freedom.'"

Emmy reached out and placed her hand on top of Jordan's. In that instant, Jordan wanted to crumble. The gentle warmth of Emmy's hand felt good, and her eyes revealed trust, but fear caused Jordan to retract. Leaning back in the seat and sipping her coffee, she recalled the night she first met Emmy. The night she found her missing copy with the Polaroid tucked in the middle.

The awkward silence was soon interrupted by Betty Jean's booming voice. She sauntered to the table, carrying a shopping bag, and wrapped Jordan in a big hug.

"Well, twice in one month. That's a record. We should come here with your mom and Aunt Elizabeth. We don't get to see one another as much as we used to."

Betty Jean's jovial character usually lightened everyone's mood. Jordan only felt relief that Emmy didn't have time to pepper her with questions. She heard herself say, "Yes, it would be fun," and hoped the lack of enthusiasm went unnoticed.

"So, you two getting to know one another?"

"Gradually but surely," Emmy said.

As Betty Jean rattled on, Jordan found it impossible to pay attention. She stood. "Betty Jean, why don't you sit closer to the fire? I have to get over to the restaurant."

"Oh, but so soon? It's early. Won't you stay for a few minutes longer?" Betty Jean pleaded.

"I'm sorry. We're extremely busy this time of year. Christmas is right around the corner. It's been lovely seeing you." She hugged Betty Jean again and held out her hand to Emmy. "And nice to enjoy your company again."

"Likewise." Emmy wrapped both hands around Jordan's. "I enjoy our discussions. We'll have to get together again. Soon, I hope."

Jordan sensed strength and determination in Emmy's touch and saw the sincerity in her smile and eyes, but she had to get out of there. "Yes. Well, enjoy your day, ladies." She slid her hand out from Emmy's and waved goodbye.

Somehow, Jordan managed to walk out of the coffeehouse. Glancing back inside, she saw Emmy once again watching her. Instead of the devilish smile like the night before, the smile seemed to acknowledge the vulnerable moment they had shared.

Emmy's mind was on Jordan despite her aunt's efforts to drag her into a conversation. The tall, dark woman was a mystery. Beautiful and talented with a killer smile. Yet, that smile and the sparkle in her eyes sometimes clouded over with worry and sadness. Shortly after the coffee spill, Jordan looked hurt and was aimlessly turning her pinky ring over and over while staring at the book cover.

Learning to Fall was one of the most powerful and uplifting books Emmy had ever read but impossible to complete without crying because it was written while Simmons was dying of Lou Gehrig's disease.

Emmy was drawn physically and emotionally to Jordan. Hopefully, whatever made Jordan sad was in the past.

Chapter Four

The town was strangely quiet for mid-December, and lunchtime had slowed to a crawl. Jordan needed to loosen up.

"Robby, I'm heading off to the gym."

"How about working out for me, too?" He grinned.

"You should get a membership. Thirty minutes a day, three days a week to become healthier."

"I walk. Sorry, never been into lifting weights or working on any machines. You enjoy." Scolding, he shook his finger at her. "Also, you might want to take a long weekend or vacation. There's got to be more than work and doing gym time."

"Has my mother been coaching you?"

"Nope. Just want you to know I care, too." He kissed the top of her head before continuing with dinner preps.

Jordan had met Robby shortly after the opening of her restaurant. His connections to wealthy and influential people helped the struggling restaurant thrive even with the heavy competition from Sherry's Café and the Lost Dog Saloon. Snagging him as her sous chef was a lucky break. Fortunately for her, Robby was sick of the Washington DC traffic, and his wife wanted to be closer to her aging parents.

"You could walk with me for some exercise." Jordan poked

him in the ribs. "Come on. The sun is peeking out of the clouds. Jo can handle things on her own until you get back."

"No, thanks. Besides, I'm waiting until you're gone to eat some leftover dessert."

If there was one thing Robby overindulged in, it was sweets. She laughed and jokingly shook her finger at him while heading out the door.

Jordan breathed in the crisp air along the way. The gym improved her mood like a minivacation. She liked the peace and quiet from Monday through Thursday and avoided other busy times. The attendant waved at her as she scanned her card. Fiddling with her earbuds in one hand and her iPhone and bag in the other, she entered the locker room and collided with someone.

"Pardon me." Jordan looked up, right into Emmy's eyes. Her breath caught in her throat.

"No, my apologies. I was rushing."

Jordan eyed Emmy's tight-fitting T-shirt accentuating ample breasts and shorts that hugged nice hips. Embarrassed, she stepped aside. "I'm sorry," she mumbled. "Ah, I'll see you out there."

Emmy wasn't flustered in the least and nodded. As she glided past, their upper torsos touched. Jordan sucked air into her lungs and breathed in Emmy's scent. *Oh my God, she can have me any way she wants.* After putting her things into a locker, Jordan sat on the bench for a moment. She had always been the cool, calm, collected pursuer. Around Emmy, she felt like the prey. The kind that wanted to be gobbled up. She filled her lungs again then walked out to the machines. Emmy was waiting for her.

"How about we work together? I could use some encouragement and help with the equipment," Emmy pleaded.

"Sure."

After stretching, Jordan started at a fast pace. Emmy was no slouch. She had a muscular, stocky build that screamed strength, and Jordan shivered at the thought of feeling those arms and thighs wrapped around her.

Emmy must have picked up on Jordan's gaze. "Although I've been a serious tennis player most of my life, my thunder thighs and arms are courtesy of genetics from the women on my mum's side."

For a split second, the tennis reference brought memories of Karen to Jordan's mind. She brushed it aside. "You're beautiful."

"Why thank you, Ms. Simón. Did anyone ever tell you what a lovely, mischievous grin and cute legs you have?"

The open flirting left Jordan speechless.

"I'm sorry if I've made you uncomfortable." Emmy moved to the stationary bikes while casting a sly look over her shoulder.

After standing with a slack jaw, Jordan caught up to her and steered the conversation to a safe subject: movies. She was delighted to hear that Emmy liked sci-fi. Jordan's favorite was *The Matrix*; Emmy's was *Star Wars*.

Within no time, the gym hour flew by. "Okay. I can see you liking drama but never thought you'd be a sci-fi fan," Jordan said as they strolled toward the locker room.

"Why not? Lots of intelligent, cute, and take-charge women in sci-fi. Carrie Fisher was the first badass princess. I'm a big fan of happily-ever-after flicks as well. What's your favorite romance, Jordan?"

She blew out a small puff of air and raised her hands. "Not sure if I have a favorite. Maybe the romantic comedy *Amélie*. And you?"

"Umm...I'd have to say *Desert Hearts*."

The title shot through Jordan's brain. She wanted to raise a clenched fist in victory and scream yes. Instead, she stared down at her shoes, bit her lip, and at last, looked at Emmy. "No denying, it's a classic. You have finesse like Vivian, but I find it difficult picturing you as shy."

"And you have an adorable smile when you let your guard down."

As they entered the locker room, Jordan had the sensation of floating through air, yet a wave of unease soon struck her. The room was split into equal halves, each side with full amenities. The showers had curtains, but the dressing areas were open. She had no idea which side of the room Emmy had chosen. Jordan was having enough trouble keeping her eyes off her in clothing.

"Take care." Emmy hugged Jordan. I'm going to have to move fast and get out of here. I'm late picking up Betty Jean."

The momentary embrace jolted every nerve in Jordan's body. The softness of Emmy's cheek, the fullness of her breasts, and the smell of lavender in her hair were an undeniable pull. At that moment, Jordan would have licked the glistening sweat off her body if Emmy had asked. She had to calm down, put her crush on hold, and control the heat creeping up her neck.

"That was fun working out. Enjoy the rest of your day and tell Betty Jean I said hi."

"Likewise." Emmy paused. "I'd like to see you soon, but I'm going out of town for a few days. Maybe we could do something this weekend."

Jordan could not hold back on her warm, gushy feelings. "I look forward to seeing you."

"Splendid."

Emmy briskly walked to her locker, and Jordan had to force her eyes away as Emmy stripped off her T-shirt. At least it was the opposite side. Emmy was different, and Jordan wanted to take her sweet time.

She hustled over to the other side of the wall. Within minutes, Jordan's muscles were relaxing under a hot shower. All but the facial ones that were curled up in bliss. She took her time dressing and walked out of the gym in an energetic stride, still in a happy daze.

Her elation was cut short when she saw a suspicious guy leaning against a beat-up truck, blatantly watching her every step under dark sunglasses. The crazy guy was not wearing a coat as if he wanted to show off his bulging muscles. His physique didn't match his long hair, shaggy beard, and sloppy clothes. He looked like a redneck, and she regretted not exiting from the back and taking a long way around. Now she had no choice but to walk past him.

"Nice day we're having. You going back to work?"

The last thing she wanted was to talk to this guy.

"Yep. Busy. Have to run." She could sense his eyes still upon her even after lengthening her stride. At the bottom of the hill, she glanced back up. He hadn't moved. Out of all the men who had ever glared at her like meat, he was the spookiest. Yet, she had a strange feeling that she somehow knew him.

Emmy threw her bag into the car, and slowly drove out of the parking lot, a smile still played on her lips. She laughed to herself. Jordan's demeanor sliding from a poised woman to a shy, playful creature was endearing. *She certainly was not shy when checking me out.* Emmy also wondered if Jordan understood her own beauty. In the short time she had been in town, she had noticed it wasn't only men who fawned over Jordan. Women stole sideways glances, ogling Jordan with either envy or hidden desires.

She liked Jordan's rich dark brown puppy dog eyes and quirky smile. Somehow, her mouth could curl up in the corners in a way that was so freaking cute. Her slim, athletic body had the right amount of curves, and her breasts were the perfect size for hands to explore. Emmy wet her lips thinking again about Jordan's attempts at flirtation. Emmy would bait her and turn up the heat with every adorable attempt. And Jordan's attitude was a big turn-on. She was confident but not cocky. It was refreshing to meet a beautiful woman who was down-to-earth and didn't let success go to her head.

Yes, Jordan spiked her interest from the moment they first met, and desire grew every time she ran into her. There was only one thing in the back of Emmy's mind nagging at her. She had been proudly out for many years, and one of her steadfast rules was not to get involved with a woman hiding her sexuality.

Maybe Jordan was not entirely in the closet. If not, Emmy hoped that would change soon. Besides, it wouldn't be long before others noticed. Whether Jordan realized it or not, her reaction to Emmy was becoming more sassy and bold. Yes, she wanted to know Jordan a lot more.

As Emmy pulled up to the Humane Society, Betty Jean walked out of the office and stood, her hands were firmly planted on her hips.

Emmy had barely exited the car when her aunt said, "Where did you go? You're late."

"Sorry, I was at the gym. Besides, you love this volunteer work."

"Yes, dear, but my replacement has been here for over an hour."

Emmy walked up and wrapped her in a hug. "I'm sorry for losing track of time. I'll be more considerate next time."

"Apology accepted. I know you're a dog person, but I think those kittens took your heart the other day. Maybe you could spend more time here."

"Are you laying a guilt trip on me, Auntie?"

"Yep. Is it working?" A grin replaced Betty Jean's scowl.

In the car, Emmy turned to look over her shoulder to safely back up and saw Betty Jean eyeing her. An inquisitive sparkle in her eye matched the grin.

"As they say around this part of the world, Auntie, what's that look on your face?"

"She's gorgeous, isn't she? I could see the sparkle in your eyes."

"What? The cat?"

"Jordan. I imagine she looks even better in gym shorts."

Emmy was floored. "How the hell do you know I saw Jordan at the gym?"

"Honey, I wasn't born yesterday, and I've got eyes and ears. You do recall us running into Gwyneth the other day, correct?" Betty Jean wiggled her eyebrows. "I saw you perk up when she said Jordan goes to the gym on weekdays around two o'clock. Now isn't it a coincidence that it's a Monday and you happened to go at that same time?"

Emmy put the car back into park. "I have no idea what you're thinking but whatever it is, stop. I'm an adult."

Betty Jean's smile fell, and her tone grew serious. "I know it's been a long time since Heather's death, and it's good to see you come back to life. Think about what you're doing, though. It's a small town."

After Emmy had started to drive, she answered, "I understand your concern—"

"What if you're wrong, and she's not gay?"

Emmy snickered. "Oh, trust me on that one. There is no doubt." She reached over and grabbed Betty Jean's hand. "Stop worrying."

Betty Jean cocked one eyebrow. "Okay. I'll try."

As Emmy drove, she thought about life after Heather. She had rarely dated anyone, and a couple of one-night stands turned out to be flops. She'd felt no intensity until now. And now was only a smile, a glance, flirting, and an immense physical desire. But there was more. Emmy saw strength and charm in Jordan.

She didn't know where things were going, but they were heading in a positive direction, and she wasn't about to let go. In an instant, she felt Heather whisper to her, *Sweetheart, six years is a long time to mourn. It's time to move on. I like her. You deserve some happiness. Live life to the fullest.*

Chapter Five

After tossing and turning most of the night, Jordan woke early and couldn't get back to sleep. She relaxed in her favorite chair, sipping a strong brew, and watched the sunrise. The splendor of the yellow and orange hues seeped through her body.

Despite her effort, she could not stop thinking about yesterday. The physical attraction was off the chart, and Emmy's self-confidence and flirting were a hook that wouldn't let her go. And the *Desert Hearts* comment. "OMG," Jordan shouted to the empty room. "She had me there!"

Her cell rang. The ringtone identified the caller as her mom. "Shit, I forgot," she mumbled, stretching to pick it up. "Morning, Mom."

"Hi, honey. Are you done with my cordless screwdriver? Could you please bring it with you?"

"Yeah, sure, Mom. Um..." Jordan rubbed her forehead.

Gwyneth laughed. "Ten a.m. You have time. See you then. Love you, hon."

"Bye, Mom. Love you."

She had always admired her mother's fortitude and feminism. A widow twice before the age of thirty, Gwyneth Lange-Simón was a striking woman who had raised three kids yet managed to get herself through college. Among her many talents was the knack for bringing out the conversation in people.

Her mother likely suspected she was gay but had never asked, and Jordan had learned a long time ago to steer the discussion to safe topics. Never any details about her intimate life. And life in Spain was a mystery with the conversations only centering on the restaurant and Madrid art galleries.

She didn't think her mother would love her any less, but her brothers' reactions would be sharply divided. Carter was not the concern. Gerry had somehow grown into an extremely religious and political nutcase, and his mouth flapped with judgmental harshness the older he got. She tried to stay away from him as much as possible.

Chugging the last of the coffee, she read some emails before getting ready.

Gwyneth thought of her second husband as her daughter hopped out of the SUV. They shared the same dark Latino features and business sense. Yet, she didn't understand where Jordan had gotten the brooding side with an impermeable and aloof shell. Losing Karen had been a nightmare, but getting into the Madrid International Culinary School after high school had helped, and Jordan finished with top honors. Yet Gwyneth never expected her to live in Europe for fifteen years. As Jordan unzipped her coat, Gwyneth gave her a crooked smile and held out a travel mug.

Jordan grudgingly accepted and shrugged. "I guess since it's warmed up to a balmy thirty degrees."

"Ah, you can't let a little cold bother you." Gwyneth may have looked like a fair maiden, but her morning walks were what made her hardy.

Jordan snapped her fingers. "Oh, the drill's still out in the SUV. Remind me to get it later."

They walked along aptly named Cold Run Valley Road, their hoods pulled up to block out the occasional wind gust. She filled Jordan in on her latest adventure with Carter, Angie, and the kids.

As usual, Jordan remained quiet and moved on to a safe topic. "Are Grammy and Poppa still refusing to discuss assisted living?"

"Unfortunately, yes. You should visit more often. At eighty-nine and ninety-two, we don't know how much time they have. The bout of pneumonia Poppa had last year was a wake-up call. He's acted like he's had something on his mind since then, but I don't know what it is. He won't talk. They'd love to see you, and it would do you some good. Also, I've been worried about you."

"How so?"

She could see Jordan's jaw tightening but was damned tired of her detachment. "You work too much. When was the last time you had a vacation?"

"Well, the restaurant isn't going to run itself."

She stopped walking and made Jordan look her in the face. Jordan's lips were pursed. "The restaurant is well on its way to success. You've pointed out how Robby is a valuable chef and manager. You recently hired Jo, who you say is following in both your footsteps. The other night, you complimented the rest of the staff." She was exasperated with her daughter, and Jordan's stone face didn't help the mood. "You're working yourself to death! You need to take some time off. And I don't mean you taking time off from work to do accounting at home. Even taking two days at the National Culinary Convention and returning immediately to work is not rest!" She put her hand on Jordan's shoulder. "When was the last time you went for the entire convention and spent extra time enjoying the sights? You need to have some fun like your last vacation."

Gwyneth thought she caught the hint of a smile. Jordan shook away from her grasp and replied in a deadpan voice, "I'll take that into consideration," and casually walked away. Before Gwyneth could catch up, her cell phone rang.

With her mom busy on the phone, Jordan recalled her last vacation in Martinique. Yes, there was beauty all around from the gorgeous, white sand beaches to the beautiful blue ocean. Oh, what fun. She had uploaded pictures to her Facebook account, the one she kept public and open to her family. On that page, she raved about the hotel and how she was enjoying scuba diving, relaxing on the beach, and meeting people. A few had teased her about grabbing a handsome, wealthy single guy while she was there. She teased back stating all potential dates wanted her to be barefoot and pregnant in the kitchen, cooking only for them.

Her friends and family never caught the subtlety. Always about meeting people with little reference to gender and tons of neutral pronouns. Yes, plenty of beauty in Martinique. She never mentioned the nightlife. Never talked about the cool gay guys who knew how to party and the many cute lesbians she danced with. There was no mention of the shame Jordan locked away inside over her one-night stands.

Her mom caught up. "I'm serious. You need time off."

Blowing out an exaggerated huff, Jordan turned to her. "I'm looking at taking some time in March before the spring tourist season ramps up."

"Good."

They continued their stroll on the black asphalt road, sipping their coffee, with her mom doing most of the talking. Jordan was cold, and the gray overcast sky matched her mood.

Gwyneth was about ready to scream at Jordan's silent avoidance. She was never one to stick her nose into her adult children's business, but she was concerned. Jordan lived four miles down the road, and they hardly saw one another.

Jordan didn't appear to have any friends outside of the restaurant staff. That could not be healthy. What had happened in Spain? Jordan's Spanish roommate, Luciana was always around when Gwyneth visited. There had not been one word from Jordan about this girl since returning home. Were they lovers? Had she crushed her daughter's heart?

She had tried to wait patiently for Jordan to bring up the subject. *Dammit. She'll soon be forty, and I'm not gettin' any younger. I don't care whether she is a lesbian, bisexual, pansexual, or whatever people identify with nowadays.* All she wanted was her daughter back and not some stranger. Still, Jordan wasn't the only one holding back. Pangs of guilt pierced Gwyneth's heart.

"Perhaps you should see someone. There are some good therapists in Redington near the college. The one you saw after Karen—"

"Mom, I don't need a damn psychologist!" Jordan kicked a rock and picked up the pace before stopping and lacing her hands behind her head and stretching her elbows out. "I'm just busy and tired. That's all."

They walked farther. Gwyneth couldn't let it go. "Maybe the accident—"

Jordan whipped around. "Drop it, Mother! That's in the past. Nothing's wrong! Perhaps I have been working too hard. The restaurant is my dream. You don't understand what it's like to keep a business running in this sleepy little town." Jordan marched away in a royally pissed-off huff.

Gwyneth's phone rang again. She looked at the number. It was Dave. No one had put two and two together that they were a hot item. That was her surprise. She muted the ring and let it go to voicemail. When she looked up, Jordan had stormed ahead a significant distance with her long legs.

"Honey, please, wait up."

Jordan kept her brisk pace while shouting over her shoulder, "I'm fine Mom. I know you mean well. Just stop worrying."

"Err..." Jordan smacked her hand hard on the steering wheel, and the sting spread to her palm and wrist. She had driven to the lookout after the spat with her mom. This was one of her favorite scenic spots no matter what the season. Today, she vacantly stared out the windshield and didn't bother getting out.

She rarely bickered with anyone, but her mother's reference to the one year she had tried desperately to forget irritated her. She hated that psychologist. He was sterile, clueless, and smug. Jordan did what was necessary to get out of high school. She shoved the pain deep inside and told him exactly what he wanted to hear. She never told anyone the truth. It was in the past, and she was determined it would remain in the past.

Resting her head in her hands, she chastised herself. "God, why was I such an asswipe to Mom?" It wasn't her mother's fault. She had only been trying to help. "I need to let it go."

Jordan picked up her phone and did what she had to do. It rang and rang as she nervously tapped on the steering wheel. Finally, her mom picked up. Without giving Jordan a chance, her mom blurted out, "Honey, I'm sorry that I brought up the topic."

The sincerity in her voice made Jordan feel even guiltier. "It's okay, Mom. I'm the one who needs to apologize. I was an obnoxious jerk." She tried to sound more upbeat. "I'm all right. Things have been going great, just hectic. Jo's been goading me to go with her ski club to Pennsylvania. Apparently, about fifty members make this trip every year. And she assures me that alumni and professors attend, so I shouldn't be the only one over thirty."

Gwyneth chuckled. "That sounds like fun. Jo's such an energetic soul. It was a smart move to hire her."

"Yeah," Jordan said, thankful for the diversion. "She's been a tremendous asset to the team. She absorbs everything we teach her. Soon, she'll be more skilled than Robby and me. Come by someday for lunch. I have to go now."

"Thanks for calling. I love you, Jordan."

"Love you too, Mom. Bye."

She gently banged her head on the steering wheel. *Situation resolved, at least for the moment. I need a spa day.*

On the way to work, she pulled through the coffeehouse drive-thru. Her phone buzzed with a text message as she placed her lemon balm herbal tea in the cup holder and tossed her change in the center console. She pulled into an empty parking spot.

Opening the message, her heart warmed seeing a picture of Carter and the kids. They were decked out from head to toe in gear and standing next to the climbing wall at Mega Mountain Outfitters in Redington. They wore the widest grins.

Carter's message: "They love it. I love it. Angie's going to kill you. Thanks for the gift, sis!"

Snickering, she typed, "Happy for you, but I didn't tell you to buy a climbing package with the gift card. That's on you, bro."

He replied, "Ah, what Angie doesn't know won't hurt her. It might hurt you. 'Cause I'm sticking to my story. Keep low for a few days."

Have to admit, I'm pretty lucky with Mom and Carter. After taking another sip, a new quote on the container caught her eye. In colorful letters were the words "Live on the good side, the bright side, the true side of everything!" —Christian D. Larson. She rotated the cup around, and saw "The best is yet to be." —Robert Browning. Flipping on the radio, she caught the tail end of one of her favorite Olivia Newton-John songs, "Learn to Love Yourself."

Her body and breathing stilled as the gentle melody washed

over her. The song's message was simple. Let love into your heart, and it will lead you peacefully home. She hoped it was that easy when her time came.

Chapter Six

The *Desert Hearts* movie revelation kept playing over in Jordan's head along with visions of key scenes. Thoughts of Emmy filled her like tumbling through a kaleidoscope. Nerves popped with excitement resembling alternating vivid colors. The thrill rolled up with hope made her feel giddy and balanced at the same time.

The wet snow that had been falling since late afternoon was hardly the dusting initially predicted. Instead of driving people away, the restaurant was busy all night, and the distraction did little to snap her out of daydreaming. She looked forward to going home and curling up with a book before bed. A nice collection of erotica short stories would do.

"Hey, Jordan. What are you thinking about? That new menu can't be the cause of that sinful smirk on your face."

"Ah..." Although taken off guard, Jordan couldn't drop the smile if she wanted to.

"Just playing with ya." Jo's energy oozed out.

Hiring Jo had been one of the best decisions Jordan had ever made. The twenty-eight-year-old was honest, hardworking, and dependable. Her culinary skills had significantly improved over the year, and she showed a keen grasp of business concepts.

"Wow, Jo. From your attire, I assume you're not going home."

"Like it?" She twirled, displaying exaggerated supermodel poses.

The tight jeans and stylish purple sweater and black jacket were finished off with polished black leather boots, but what really set Jo apart was her punkish hair. Brown and short on the sides with a spiked top and highlighted blond tips. Her appearance and assertiveness silently screamed out, "World, here I come." If Jordan didn't know better, Jo could easily have been mistaken for a cute lesbian.

"Chic. Watch out with those boots—you might fall on your ass in the snow."

"Nah. The bottoms have a decent tread, and if I do fall, it'll give me an excuse to leave Lost Dog early so Ted can massage my ass." Her eyebrows shot up, and she glided over and put her arm around Jordan. "Why don't you join us? There's music, and our friends are in town. I'll buy you a drink."

The typical Lost Dog Saloon crowd was younger, but what Jordan couldn't stand was the guys hitting on her. "I'm not sure with the snow. Tomorrow's an early day."

Jo shook her head. "You have to live a little. It's the first snowfall of the winter! In less than a week, Christmas will bury us. Come out and celebrate."

"I appreciate the offer, but I'm tired."

She took Jordan by the hands. "Do you think that flimsy excuse will work on me? This group is a load of fun. Most are straight. A few are gay or bi. Nobody cares. They're fun people. Come on girl! Besides, your SUV can take the snow."

This wasn't the first time Jo hinted at Jordan's sexuality, but the "love everyone" attitude made Jordan more comfortable.

Maybe a couple of drinks would take her mind off Emmy. "Okay. Just for a short time or I'll be sleepwalking tomorrow."

"Now we're talking." Jo winked and pulled her out the door.

A good three inches was on the ground, and it wasn't supposed to stop until sometime after midnight. The snow fell faster as they walked. The flakes were huge, and up ahead looked like a mini blizzard. As they came closer, they realized the snow flying around the park was more than Mother Nature.

Jo's exuberant personality bubbled to the surface, and she squealed, "Snowball fight!" She took off running then stopped and turned. "Come on, Jordan. You promised."

Oh, what the hell, Jordan thought. Although the public square was filled with dozens of people, they soon found Jo's group. More stood on the saloon's entry patio watching and egging on their friends. Occasionally, someone would call a truce, run up to the patio, and grab their drink. Although illegal, many had plastic cups filled with their favorite beer or toddy on city property.

In the mayhem, someone handed Jo and her a shot glass. From the smell, it was clearly Fireball Whisky. Jo immediately downed the shot.

"Don't be a wimp, Jordan!"

Letting her inhibitions go, Jordan swigged the cinnamon-flavored liquor and joined in the snowball fight. Everyone was having a blast, and the laughter was contagious. Jo and friends kept passing her shots. While she knew better, she didn't turn them down.

Inside, Emmy had joined her cousin's group on the upper level. The difficult drive back from DC had taken longer than planned, and she knew she could use a drink and some laughter. Tomorrow, she would go to lunch and see Jordan.

After introductions, a chair was added at the other end of the overflowing table. Annoyed not to be sitting near her cousin, Emmy made do. The Lost Dog had a vibe, and the view wasn't bad either—the view of the park and the appealing waitress servicing their table. *Although nothing compares to Jordan,* she mused.

The cousin was sweet, but Emmy could do without the husband. He never said anything negative to Emmy's face, but it irritated the piss out of her when he left the room anytime anything remotely gay popped into a conversation. The most annoying thing was when he tried to set Emmy up with guys. Was tonight one of those nights?

The minute she sat down, the man sitting across from her wouldn't leave her alone. He blabbed on and on. She glared at her cousin sitting at the other end, who lifted her glass in a toast and mouthed the word "sorry."

My freaking God. This guy yaks more than any person I've ever known. Even when she interjected about the snowball fight looking like fun, the guy droned on about his job. Needing some fresh air, she excused herself, and he offered to join her. *Shit.*

Emmy walked into the chilly night toward the merriment.

"You're not seriously going to join in, are you?" he scoffed.

"No. Just going to walk the perimeter and stay out of reach."

Occasionally, a snowball would come their way narrowly missing them, and they'd hear "sorry" as the thrower realized they were only out for a stroll. Of course, the walk would be more enjoyable if the dude had not insisted on joining her.

Halfway through, the situation changed when he stepped closer and draped his arm around her shoulders. "Curt," she said, abruptly pushing his arm away, "I think you're a wonderful guy, but I'm not interested."

"I'm sorry. Have I offended you in some way?"

"No. You're not exactly my type." She had been out since university and wasn't about to start lying now. "I'm a lesbian. This"—motioning between the two of them—"is nothing more than two friends going for a stroll."

As the fact registered on his face, his cell phone rang. Relieved, Emmy walked a few steps and let out a long sigh. Whap. A snowball hit her on the side of her face. Shocked, she turned and saw Jordan looking at her in dismay.

"Oh my God. I'm so sorry. I was aiming for Curt. He's a family friend."

Emmy stood glaring at Jordan for what seemed an eternity before breaking into hysterical laughter. She reached into the snow, scooped a handful, and sprinted toward Jordan. She packed the ball as she closed the gap.

Jordan knew Emmy meant business and tried to dash for cover, but the snow and alcohol made her footing unsure. Whap. The wet snowball hit the back of her head and slid down her coat. She twisted to face Emmy, and both reached down to reload. They chased each other in circles while blasting away. Others hit them from all sides.

Without warning, Jordan was tackled, and her arms were pinned over her head. She didn't resist, and Emmy hung over her staring into her eyes with a devilish grin. All Jordan could think about was, *Damn, your mouth looks so kissable.* She breathed in Emmy's scent, and a subtle perfume—jasmine this time—filled her nostrils and jolted her body.

Inching closer and brushing her lips across Jordan's cheek and ear, Emmy murmured, "I could get used to you on the bottom." She lingered, lightly kissing the edge of Jordan's mouth.

Momentarily overtaken by the touch, Jordan's body quivered. Unexpectedly, her trance was broken when Emmy stuffed snow down the front of her jacket then hopped up and ran away laughing.

Jordan yelled out for the others to get Emmy. Running and slipping through the barrage, Emmy managed to cross the street and yell out, "Safe space. No snowballs." She stood snickering with a look that Jordan thought was absolutely adorable.

Jordan threw the snowball to the ground and sauntered over. The Fireball had warmed her, and she let her guard down.

"You throw a mean snowball for a European."

"Well, do you think it only snows in America?" Emmy glanced down at Jordan's clothes. "Looks like you've been out there too long. You're soaked. Why don't you join me inside and warm up?"

"I'd love nothing more."

Jordan followed Emmy upstairs where introductions were made. Curt had also returned and greeted Jordan with a bear hug. She asked how his mother was doing. He told her she was getting better and rattled on more.

The group snagged some chairs and motioned for the women to join them, but the waitress stopped them.

"Sorry folks. You're overcrowded as it is. I've got a small table near the fireplace once the busboy clears it off. From the looks of you ladies"—she eyed Emmy and Jordan up and down—"you are about ready to catch your death. Go!"

Jordan peeled off her wet coat, hat, and gloves, and rubbed her hands vigorously in front of the roaring fire. When she turned around, Emmy sat with an appreciative look on her face.

Without taking her eyes off Jordan, Emmy waved at the waitress then held up her empty beer bottle for another. "What are you having?"

"Oh, I think I've had enough." Jordan sat down. Not sure if her words were slurring or not, she was nervous. Her clothes were soaked, but her body tingled from Emmy's attentive stare.

"One more won't hurt. I could drive you home if you like. Relax a bit while you warm up. The house pale ale is awesome."

Jordan didn't want to overdo it, and neither did she want to mix drinks. As she pondered drink choices, she glanced back and forth between the menu and Emmy.

"Ahem," the waitress said, tapping her pad. "I don't have all night, honey."

"I'll have a Coke with one shot of Fireball Whisky."

"Oh, and please bring us the spinach dip," Emmy shouted as the woman hurried away, again, with her full attention on Jordan. "Wow. You must be cold. Here, take my hoodie."

Jordan admired Emmy's torso while she struggled to strip off the tight hoodie.

"No, I couldn't. I'll get it wet."

A sly grin lit Emmy's face. "Well, I do like the wet T-shirt look, but I don't like to see you shivering. Take it. You can give it back later."

Although the alcohol had slowed her mind, the meaning finally dawned on Jordan, and she could feel erect nipples prominently protruding under the thin fabric of her blouse. "I...ah..." They perked up more as she fumbled with a reply.

"Just a minute." Emmy departed and returned with a Lost Dog T-shirt. "Put this underneath."

"Thanks."

Jordan could barely walk from the intoxication—not from the drink but from Emmy. Thank goodness, no one was in the bathroom. She took off the wet T-shirt and slipped on the tie-dyed one. Before putting on the hoodie, she deeply breathed in Emmy's lingering scent. As much as she had tried, she was falling fast. *God, how am I going to get through the night? She's so hot, and I'm half-plastered.* She mustered up her courage and walked back to the table.

"So, Jordan Simón, there is a rumor about you."

"Oh, and what might that be?" Her eyebrows scrunched a bit even though she was trying to act cool.

"Besides being a fantastic chef, you are apparently an accomplished artist."

"Ah, my stained glass. I'm afraid it's an embellished rumor. I was never good enough to make a living. I do a few presents for birthdays and Christmas."

"Somehow, I doubt the downplay of your work."

"What about you? Any special interests?"

"I enjoy hiking and snowboarding. I stay on a mixture of intermediate and easy trails. But unlike you, I can't cook worth a damn. Any chance for private cooking lessons?"

"Maybe for the right price."

Emmy leaned in. "And what would that be or would you be willing to exchange lessons for another service?" Her voice was bold, seductive, and hit every nerve in Jordan's body.

Jordan was faint from the mere thought of different possibilities, including a vision of Emmy in the kitchen wearing nothing but an apron. It had been a long time since Jordan had flirted with someone she was interested in, and she didn't want this moment to end.

"I love to ski. Maybe you could show me how to snowboard." *Lame answer, Jordan.*

Fortunately, the drinks and appetizer came to the table. The food at Lost Dog was decent compared to most bar food. Yet, Jordan's mouth was watering for other reasons. As their discussion continued in a less provocative tone, they hit on another commonality: music. To Jordan's surprise, Emmy followed a lot of indie artists while Jordan only knew the big names.

With each passing second, Jordan forgot her surroundings and became lost in Emmy's eyes. As their laughter intensified, another round of drinks mysteriously appeared. They both looked up at the waitress.

"Courtesy of a guy named Curt." Turning to Emmy, the waitress said, "He said what a pleasure it was to see you tonight and enjoy the rest of your evening. Also, no hard feelings and he hopes you get lucky."

As the waitress turned and swiftly walked away, the hairs on the back of Jordan's neck pricked up, and her smile disappeared.

Emmy reached out and touched Jordan's hand with her fingertips. "I was chatting with him about some business prospects. He wished me luck. That's all. So, let's enjoy the drinks."

Jordan had a hunch Emmy was telling a little white lie. It didn't matter. She was beginning to let go. Soon, the smiles and laughter returned when the conversation turned to travel adventures.

They had lost track of time when Jordan's cell buzzed. She didn't want to be rude, but the text was from Jo. *Shit, I never said goodbye.*

"Excuse me."

Jordan quickly read: "Saw you with the cutie from the snowball fight ☺ I'm at the bar on the left. Looks like you're having a great evening. What happened to your curfew? It's now after 2 am. Oh…good luck with the beauty rest. Good night."

Three hours. I'm going to hurt tomorrow.

"Anything wrong?"

Jordan tucked the phone back into her pocket and scrunched her shoulders. "No. Just a text from a friend." Then Jo walked by, gave two thumbs up, and mouthed "way to go." This time, there was no panic. Jordan felt good.

As the bartender yelled out "last round," Emmy said, "We should wrap it up and get out of here. Do you want a ride? I've only had three beers tonight."

Jordan knew Emmy was right. "No, I should be okay."

"How many shots of Fireball have you had?"

If the words had come from anyone else, Jordan would have been offended, but Emmy's tone showed concern and caring. Alluring as it might be, she didn't want to rush with her. She already had to fight to keep thoughts of Emmy's naked body out of her head.

"I'm all right. I only had that one shot in the Coke over the past couple of hours."

Emmy raised her eyebrow and Jordan confessed. "Well, two drinks since Curt bought us one. I'm okay, honest."

"Okay. Do you mind walking me to my car?"

Jordan wondered how many more people would think they were a couple. *Screw it.* She could not say no to that gorgeous face. "Not at all."

Outside, the snow had stopped, and a good four inches covered the ground. Emmy was grateful that Jordan had helped brush the snow off the car, but now Jordan stood nervously glancing around, hands stuffed in her pockets and staring at her boots and kicking snow.

It was late and cold, and no one was in sight. Emmy bluntly broached the topic that Jordan had evaded all along. "I'm sure you've kissed women in public before, but I guess you haven't done so in Oakville."

Jordan's head snapped up, and Emmy could see desire smoldering underneath. Jordan stepped forward, leaned down, cupped her face, and kissed her. Emmy was delighted when Jordan's mouth parted, inviting her inside. The passionate kiss set Emmy's senses ablaze. She was already looking forward to the next one.

Jordan stepped back. "It's late. You had better get in your car before you freeze to death, but I want to see you again."

"I'd like to see the brave Jordan again."

Jordan's lopsided grin appeared. "I'm off in a couple of days and planned to hit the spa. Sort of a pre-Christmas present to myself. Meet me there, and I'll treat."

"Hand me your phone." Emmy punched in her number. "Call me tomorrow with the details." She let her fingers mingle over Jordan's when handing it back.

"I look forward to the occasion."

Satisfied that she had melted a little bit of Jordan's hard exterior, Emmy jumped into the car and cautiously moved along the snow-packed road. Glancing in the rearview mirror, she saw Jordan watching her drive away.

Chapter Seven

The spa was a definite need today. Jordan had strained a few muscles the day before helping the crew restock the pantry and refrigerator, and no matter how much she stretched, she ached. Yet, nothing was going to slow her down. She was meeting Emmy. Being a weekday, no other clients would likely disrupt their privacy, but Jordan wanted to make sure. She bought the works, paid a fat tip, and reminded the spa owner of a favor past due.

Entering the room in a soft, fluffy oversized robe, she eyed Emmy lying back, her arms resting on the hot tub rim. When she disrobed, she liked how Emmy's eyes looked over her body. At the same time, Jordan admired Emmy's creamy breasts, scarcely covered by her swimsuit.

"By the way, when you're not in your chef jacket and dress slacks, why do you hide under those baggy gym clothes? You've got a body most women would kill for."

"I like to be comfortable. And it's been a while since I've had a good reason."

Emmy seemed to relish making her squirm, and she liked it. While she had been the pursuer in past relationships, the idea of Emmy chasing after her was simultaneously terrifying and exhilarating.

"So, how long have you worked in the banking business?"

As she slid into the tub, Emmy handed her a water bottle. "Too long and I find talking about work boring. Tell me about your life in Spain."

"It was a desire to learn about my father's heritage and the cuisine."

"And? Certainly being a chef is not your entire life. Tell me about your adventures."

"I loved hiking the Sierra de Guadarrama. So serene and a great variety of terrain for all levels. Madrid's museums and all the little galleries are fun."

Emmy perked up. "Yes, I loved the small local art galleries. What about concerts and the clubs? The nightlife in Madrid is one of the best in Europe."

Taking a swig of water, Jordan tried to sound unruffled. "I'd go dancing sometimes."

"Bailamos was my go-to place when I was in town."

Jordan instantly choked and coughed multiple times. Emmy slid over to make sure she was okay.

"Water just went down the wrong hole." Jordan cleared her throat. "All better." Yet she was flustered because Emmy had mentioned the number one lesbian club in Madrid—a club Jordan frequented for hookups before her relationship with Luciana and after their breakup.

"I don't want to give you the wrong impression like I'm some player," Emmy said. "I love the music, and my wife loved to dance."

Emmy had been married!

Emmy's radiance drifted away, and her tone grew serious. "We were together for twelve years. She was diagnosed with aggressive breast cancer and died six years ago. I didn't want to spoil the mood the other night at Lost Dog since we were having such a good time. Does it upset you that I didn't mention her until now?"

"Of course, not." Jordan could see the hurt in Emmy's eyes and grasped her hand. "I'm sorry. I can't imagine how hard that was for you."

"Thank you for your concern." Emmy's features softened. "Heather wouldn't want me to get bogged down in sorrow, yet dating hasn't been on the forefront of my life. I've put too much time into work and need to change."

"Me too. I need to slow down and enjoy myself more."

"Can I assume there will be more endings like the other evening?" Emmy's fingertips lightly touched the side of Jordan's hand. "I like the outgoing Jordan with the soft lips."

Jordan's gaze lingered, and her heart fluttered as time seemed to stand still. She said at last, "I can arrange that," but the tender moment was interrupted by the attendant.

"Ladies, you don't want to turn into prunes. Would you like to move into the relaxation room?"

"Shall we?" Emmy stood giving Jordan a full view of her body.

"That's...that'd be wonderful," Jordan said.

When Jordan didn't move a muscle, Emmy leaned over, her ample cleavage tantalizingly close to Jordan's face. "I can't carry you," she whispered. "Besides, if you want more, you'll have to participate in the chase." She winked and got out of the hot tub.

Somehow Jordan got her quivering body to move. In the relaxation room, the smell of sandalwood drifted through the air, and a soft flute and waterfall sound played in the background. Attendants placed warm blankets on them and brought them juice of their choice. Jordan selected pineapple and Emmy chose mango.

Jordan had to muster up some courage after Emmy's touching and honest revelation. She sat up and her body tensed. Emmy's expression changed to one of concern. Willing her voice to hold out, Jordan said, "I was in a relationship in Spain.

Unfortunately, I was the only one who was serious. My family never knew that she was more than my roommate. Actually, I've never told them I'm a lesbian." Jordan took a deep breath and gradually blew it out. "I have a shitload of guilt, but every time I thought about coming out, I got scared. Scared about my business being harmed. Scared of my one brother, who would go off the cliff and drag a few other family members with him." Karen's face flashed through her mind. "There was an accident way in the past." Her stomach muscles clenched. *Let it go. Breathe.* "Life goes on. I've wasted too much time beating myself up and worrying about others. My fortieth birthday is in February. I was thinking, might as well break the news to as many as possible in one shot." Her wry laugh probably did nothing to hide her conflicted thoughts.

Emmy wet her lips and reached out for Jordan's hand. "You haven't exactly been waving the rainbow flag. I know it's hard, but trust me, you will feel better living in your own skin. You're charming and fun to be around, but I want to be in a relationship out in the open. No secrets from family and friends." Jordan tightened her jaw at Emmy's words and her stomach fell. Emmy scooted closer and reached up and brushed Jordan's cheek with the back of her hand. "I didn't want the night at the saloon to end. I also enjoy your company, and you're extremely attractive. So, if you're sincere about coming out soon, how about we go on some dates? I know we keep running into one another, but let's call it what it is. See where it goes."

Relief and excitement surged through Jordan, and she reached for Emmy's hand. Their fingers intertwined briefly before they settled back in the loungers. The door opened, and an attendant approached.

"Ladies, are you doing okay? Can I get you anything?"

"We're good." Jordan rushed the words out, and the attendant left.

Emmy chuckled. "You don't like to share your dates with anyone do you?"

"I'll take as much time alone with you as possible. So, new topic. If you don't mind me asking, how did your family handle it when you came out?"

"My father had a little difficulty with the idea at first since our family is Catholic, which I no longer practice. Surprisingly, my stepmother didn't have much of an issue, even though she and I disagreed on many things. Almost two years into our relationship, we joined my family in the Lake District. It was the first time my brother Christian had met Heather. He wrapped his arms around her like she was a long-lost family member and proceeded to tease me about how I had hooked up with such an elegant woman. His attitude opened the door for my father, and from that day forward, he never once voiced his discomfort."

Jordan told her about her brothers, and her frustration with Gerry. "He's always stirring the pot. Carter's always handing him his ass, and Mother's always stepping in." She laughed off the seriousness of the family drama. "How well do you get along with your brother?"

"Unfortunately, our relationship is estranged. I used to look up to Christian. He is a successful architect, typically a fun guy to be with, married, and loves everyone." Her eyes fluttered, and she sighed. "As in, he has multiple affairs. He seems to follow the Old European male chauvinist bullshit when it comes to his wife. I caught him a couple of times and the last time was on his veranda screwing the maid. To cut to the chase, I ended up telling his wife and suggested couples therapy. He denied it, she stuck by him, and they both stopped talking to me." Emmy's face twisted with emotion. "I never cheated on Heather. Christian's selfish carelessness pisses me off because it disrespects our family. His wife is an idiot for staying with him, and she's probably only doing so because of the money. But that's their problem."

Before Emmy could tell her any more, the attendants returned. "Ladies, it's time to move to your massage rooms."

"Oh wow, that felt great. What a generous gift. Thank you for paying." Emmy brushed her hand over Jordan's back as they walked to their cars.

"My pleasure."

Emmy stepped closer. "Now about our date. When can we get together?"

Jordan leaned up against Emmy's car. "I'd like to take you out to dinner, but my schedule's a nightmare until after New Year's. We will have to play it by ear. I do hope you will drop by my restaurant more often."

"I will."

"Do you have specific holiday plans?"

"No, other than shuttling Betty Jean around. I do have a friend coming to visit after New Year's. She is supposed to help me apartment shop. I'll have to bring her by."

Jordan felt a tinge of jealousy and briefly thought of the possibility of Emmy having a friend with benefits. *Stop it. You're jumping to conclusions.*

As if reading her mind, Emmy grinned. "Becca has been one of my closest friends for over twenty years. She is not a love interest." The conversation dangled on a bit of mystery when she added, "I wouldn't be surprised if you already knew a bit about her."

The statement was odd, but Jordan was relieved that the friend would not be a contender for Emmy's affection.

Before Jordan could reply, Emmy's phone rang. "Hi, Auntie. What's up? Uh-huh...I'm leaving town soon...No problem. Milk and fresh green peppers. Got it. Oh, do you mind if I invite a guest for dinner? Okay, bye. Love you." Emmy slipped the phone into her back pocket. "It will be a perfect nightcap to my evening if you are able to join us."

Like the other night, Jordan didn't want their time to end. "Lead the way."

Emmy and Jordan burst into the house laughing. Betty Jean bolted upright. Her reading glasses bounced off her head, and her book landed on the floor.

"Goodness, gracious! Can't you girls be quiet? I think you might have woken up the neighbors down the road."

"Sorry to have scared you, Auntie."

"Sorry for the rudeness, Betty Jean."

Emmy pulled Jordan into the kitchen and stole a quick peck on the lips. Jordan's heart jumped when Betty Jean rounded the corner.

"Pour me an iced tea, please. Still got more than an hour on dinner, but maybe you girls can help me."

"Sure. What can we do?" Jordan said.

Unexpectedly, Emmy thrust the tea into Betty Jean's hands. "Let's go, Jordan. She's head chef." Emmy spun on her heels and walked out.

Betty Jean stood with her hands on her hips. "Oh, I've got it under control. Go on, skedaddle."

Jordan scrunched her eyebrows. "What just happened?"

Betty Jean chuckled. "Emmy was banned from the kitchen a long time ago. A word from the wise—don't let her cook or you'll be in the hospital. Your cookin' is to die for. I suspect Emmy will be visiting your restaurant more often and bringing me home her leftovers. Unfortunately, they'll be cold because she seems to like to spend time fawning over you."

Jordan's mouth dropped. "Okay."

Betty Jean slapped her hand on her thigh and rolled into a cackle. "Lord Almighty, I can see the wheels in your head turning." In a more serious tone, she said, "Darlin', you two are friends. If it becomes more, then no one on this earth is in any position to judge you. Only God has the right. And in case you're wonderin', I don't gossip." Her eyes crinkled in a mischievous smile, and she flicked her wrist. "Go on and get to know one another while I show you how real good ole West Virginian cookin' is done. Besides, child, your family's from the south valley. We do it a little different here in the western part of Sideling Hill. You ain't tasted cookin' until you've tasted my people's cookin'!"

Did Betty Jean just give me her blessing to date Emmy? Stunned and relieved, she breathed deeply and hustled into the living room.

Emmy motioned for Jordan to sit next to her. "Sorry, I'm not very handy in the kitchen. I hope it's not a prerequisite for dating."

"So, I hear. Are you using me for my culinary skills?"

"Yep. You serve up such deliciousness. I can't wait to taste what's next."

Jordan blinked several times, but couldn't think of a comeback line. Her throat went dry as she watched Emmy's mouth turn into a brilliant smile.

Emmy patted the sofa. "Let me show you some of Betty Jean's scrapbooks."

Everyone knew Betty Jean was a major contributor to a recently published book on county history, and Jordan could see why. Every entry was meticulously labeled with beautiful calligraphy, relevant data, and stories about the people in the photos.

"Despite Betty Jean's tough country girl reputation, she's a deep-down softie with a wicked sense of humor."

To illustrate her point, Emmy yelled out to Betty Jean, "Still alive in there?"

"Yes, child. You've got to hold your horses."

"Well, how long? We're about ready to starve to death in here."

"Settle down. Besides, cookin' good ole possum takes time!"

Jordan sat up straight, horrified. "She is kidding, isn't she? I know some people do eat possum around here, but please tell me she's not serious. I'm adventurous, but I'm no Andrew Zimmern."

"Yes, she's joking." Emmy could barely speak from the laughter bubbling out of her.

They went back to their conversation and soon lost track of time. Jordan honestly couldn't remember when she had been so relaxed.

Betty Jean hollered, "Come and get it!"

After the meal, Jordan raved. "That was delicious. You're hired if I open up another restaurant specializing in local cuisine."

Betty Jean waved a hand. "Thanks, dear. A dash of love is what makes the dish." Her rosy cheeks gave away her modesty. "Oops. Forgot the moonshine. It's in the basement cellar. Be right back."

Jordan's eyes widened. "She's joking again, right?"

Emmy took a sip of water and shrugged her shoulders.

"Here we go," Betty Jean said upon her return. "Caramel apple flavored to go with the dessert. Why the look? Don't fret. It's legal, top grade with a smooth kick."

Although they sipped slowly, Betty Jean poured a couple more shots. They finally had to insist no more.

"Oh my, look at the time. I should get my weary bones to bed soon," Betty Jean said.

"We'll clean up, Auntie."

"Alrighty. Jordan, it was a pleasure to have your company. Please stay as long as you like. Good night girls."

After washing dishes, Emmy and Jordan continued their discussion in the living room. Between bouts of laughter, Jordan relished the occasions when Emmy would touch her forearm or knee to make a point. She enjoyed taking in every little facial expression from the curve of Emmy's smile to the scrunching of her nose. It wasn't long before the antique grandfather clock chimed eleven.

"Damn," Jordan said. "I can't believe what time it is. I need to get going."

Emmy slowly reached out and delicately traced the outline of her jaw. The touch and the look of desire made Jordan tremble inside. For the next few minutes, they gently explored exposed skin with their mouths and hands, teasing but not yet going into forbidden territory. Jordan sensed the loss of warmth when their lips parted.

"Let's get you on your way before I do something in this living room I shouldn't." Emmy stood and pulled Jordan up.

Jordan rubbed her thumb on the back of Emmy's hand then lightly kissed her forehead. "See you soon." She relished the feel of Emmy's skin and didn't want to let go. The dazzling smile that spread across Emmy's face, lighting up her hazel eyes, only made it harder to break contact.

As Jordan walked toward her SUV, Emmy shouted, "I won't forget where we left off."

Jordan was unable to wipe away her grin as she waved goodbye one last time. Yes, Emmy was worth the risk. Never before had she fallen so hard and fast. Emmy's impending job in DC briefly popped into her thoughts. A long-distance relationship built on weekend visits would not be easy, but she felt so alive. She also thought of her family. Dating Emmy meant others would soon figure it out, and she would rather be the one to do the telling. She kept visualizing Betty Jean saying, "It's time to put on your big girl pants and get the job done."

Chapter Eight

*J*ordan took a deep breath. She was exhausted. Filling in for her employees to give them time off with their families was one reason. Another was Emmy. They'd had dinner out of town the night after Christmas. Unfortunately, they didn't end the evening in one another's arms and instead had to rush home. Betty Jean had taken a spill and called in a panic. Although it turned out to be only a sprain and bruising, it was anyone's guess when Jordan would see Emmy again.

As she moved into the dining room, the roar of chatter and laughter didn't bother her. It had been a long time since she'd been this content. The warm feelings of happiness were impossible to put into words. Her growing desire was a rush, and the short phone calls and texting added to the thrill.

After exchanging a few pleasantries, she noticed Emmy in the middle of the room. Ecstatic, she ambled over, trying to appear composed. "Mind if I join you, Ms. Russo?"

"Please do."

Emmy's clean, light fragrance drifted up and filled her senses. "Looks like you need some dessert. We have several. I recommend the Turrón ice cream topped with a chocolate layer. It will enliven your tongue and taste buds."

Emmy's lips curled into a playful smile. She leaned back, resting her arm on the back of the chair. "Sounds sinfully rich. Delicious dark chocolate over a light creamy base. That certainly conjures up delight." She licked her upper lip. "How do you handle the base? It must require a balance of slow and continuous stirring. I'm sure you whip the cream into soft peaks and the egg whites into stiff peaks while gently folding everything together at the right time. My guess is you're an expert at timing and getting the right amount of consistency."

Jordan tried damn hard not to lose it, but the double entendre sent tingles through her body. She swallowed, and it was all she could do to get the words out. "Oh, it's easy to work with. Although, mixing in the right amount of hard crunchy almonds and honey can be tricky."

"I'm sure." Emmy lifted the cup to her luscious lips.

"Do you have any plans for New Year's Eve? It's only a couple of days away."

"Possibly," Emmy said, drawing out the word. "There is this one woman I've been dying to spend time with, but her calendar is rather full, and her life is complicated. Still, I'm hoping to be a dear friend and show her exactly how much fun she is missing."

Jordan felt brave. "And what might that be?"

"Let me think." Emmy twisted her mouth. "Hmm. I have meant to show her some excellent exercises for flexibility and stamina. I'm positive she is rather strong, but I wouldn't mind testing her hand and forearm strength. Of course, if she's not ready, a movie could be an alternative. A good movie is always *Better Than Chocolate*."

The look on Jordan's face was priceless. Emmy had never seen such a crimson blush. The restaurant was packed, and they spoke at normal volume, but no one would have gotten the movie reference unless they were gay.

Just as Emmy wondered if she had taken the banter too far, Jordan said, "Well that depends. A film *When Night Is Falling* may be best. It could be *A Perfect Ending*." Jordan cleared her throat. "*A Perfect Ending* with all the good parts and minus the tragic secret."

Now the shy woman had disappeared, and Emmy was surprised and elated. "Hmm. So many possibilities. What about you?"

"What about me?"

Emmy put her elbows on the table and leaned over. "Will you have any stamina left after the New Year's Eve party?"

"Only one way to find out." Jordan's voice dipped to a sultry tone.

A waitress rushed up. "Jordan, there's a phone call for you in the kitchen."

After looking at the retreating woman with an odd expression, Jordan said, "I have no idea who that could be. I'll see you tomorrow."

"I wouldn't miss it for the world."

Emmy watched Jordan's graceful stride. God, how she wanted that woman.

As the staff skillfully moved around the kitchen, Jordan walked up to the phone receiver laying on the table near the back door. This was weird. She had a separate number for the office phone as well as her cell. Who could be calling her on the kitchen phone? Hopefully not a complaining customer.

"Hello, this is Jordan Simón. How can I help you?"

There was no answer. She plugged one ear up to block out the noisy kitchen and repeated herself. Again, no reply. Then she heard a click.

Stepping away, the phone rang once more. She pivoted and stared at the device for a caller ID, but the screen read "unavailable." After hesitating for a couple of rings, she picked it up. Again, her words were met with silence. As she began to think there was a bad connection, she heard a male voice snicker.

She snapped, "Is there something I can do for you, or not? I'm busy." His snicker tapered off. More silence. Not wanting to alarm her employees, she replied in a quiet but strong tone. "Don't call again or I'll alert the authorities." She hung up.

Furrowing her brows, Jordan saw the waitress. "Debbie, do you have any idea who that was?"

"Didn't give his name."

"And you don't recognize the voice?"

"Nope." The waitress hurried out of the room with a basket of fresh bread while others looked her way curiously.

"Probably nothing. Some jerk is likely playing a prank." She turned her attention to helping the staff.

Chapter Nine

"Good evening, Ms. Russo. I'm happy you're able to join us for New Year's Eve."

Emmy ignored Jordan's extended hand. Clutching her purse with one hand, she grabbed Jordan with the other and drew her in for a peck on the cheek. "Thank you for inviting me, Ms. Simón."

"The pleasure is all mine." The light kiss electrified her, and Emmy's simple purple velvet dress with a black silk scarf loosely draped around her neck created a fabulous look. Now aware that others were watching, Jordan took a step back and motioned Emmy into the room. "How is your aunt?"

"She's getting around better." Emmy looked flustered. "Regrettably, Betty Jean's friend was supposed to spend the night but canceled. Besides making me feel guilty for leaving her alone on New Year's Eve, Betty Jean insists that I be home by one a.m. to give her one of her meds. I'm sorry, but I fully intend to catch up another night."

"I hope so. Let me introduce you to a few people."

Jordan took her elbow and led Emmy over to a group of artists. Most were acquaintances or town gallery owners she had bought pieces from over the years. She was comfortable with them and knew Emmy would be as well. Two waiters approached: one with hors d'oeuvres and another to take drink orders.

After a bit of conversation, Jordan said, "If you'll excuse me. I need to say hello to the mayor." She tipped her head. "Boring stuff, but it's gotta' be done. Emmy, you're in good hands."

Jordan couldn't hang on to Emmy all night even though simmering feelings were about to boil over. They had only met a little over a month ago, and she had previously warned Emmy that the New Year's Eve party was a mix of business and pleasure.

She didn't want to leave the group, but there were a lot of people she had to greet, especially the Republican mayor. While she disagreed with many of his views, he was business savvy and was trying to bridge the gap between all sides. That wasn't why she invited him. It was because of the old saying, "Keep your friends close and your enemies closer," and the fact that his wife was Jordan's hairdresser.

Soon after the state same-sex marriage ban had been overturned, Jordan overheard his comment on a state religious freedom bill that the right-wing movement was pushing: "Hell, we've got a seasonal economy. We can't turn away the queers. They flock here in droves for the nature crap. As long as they are civil and don't flaunt the shit, I could care less." After those comments, she wanted to know where he stood, and the need was more urgent as a situation with Jo's friend had occurred over a week ago and was already the hottest gossip in town.

His wife spotted Jordan first. "You haven't been in for a trim."

Jordan accepted the air kiss and friendly hug. "Yes. I'll have to make an appointment. Good thing my style is basic." She shook the mayor's hand. "Jim. Glad Diane was able to drag you out. You work too hard."

"I'm afraid we can't stay long. Got other commitments but couldn't pass up the opportunity to chat."

"Oh, Jim. You know darn well you came for the food." Diane giggled. "But we did promise to meet up with old friends. Only one drink tonight, and we'll have to scoot out the door."

"Let's get you taken care of." Jordan walked them to the bar and personally mixed their drinks while they loaded up on appetizers. "Jim, what's the news with the bypass?"

"God that would kill business."

"Agreed," she responded.

"I think I've talked the council out of pursuing that for now," he said.

Jordan was the perfect host. As they finished their drinks, she brought up the topic that interested her the most. "What happened at the courthouse? I heard something about a fight that got out of hand."

He rolled his eyes and huffed. Jordan didn't know if he would answer. After a big swig, he said, "A young woman in the county clerk's office was fired. A sassy twenty-something." He craned his neck and scanned the room. Apparently worried that they could be overheard, he leaned in and spoke in Jordan's ear. "She's claiming it's because she's a lesbian. I don't care, but they all got in a hullabaloo over this damn same-sex marriage ruling. The supervisor claims she's been egging it on for some time." He scratched his head. "Now someone else has stepped forward saying it's the other way around."

Jordan kept her emotions in check and thought of how to respond. Before she could get any words out, he looked her in the eye. "I called her this afternoon and told her I was overriding the supervisor, and she's got her job back. Thank God, she's not suing. I'm also bringing in a consultant to teach the staff some manners. We don't have to whistle the same tune, but we all need respect, and they need to do their job without shoving their personal views down someone else's throat." He crumbled his napkin. "What really chafes my ass is they were yelling in front of customers."

"Honey, watch your language! You're in front of ladies and in public," Diane berated him.

He turned to his wife. "Yes dear." After taking a swig of his cocktail, he glanced back at Jordan. "Don't worry. It's under control. Besides, most everybody just wants to get along anyway."

Nodding, Jordan was silently relieved. The consultant was a good idea and made Jim seem more reasonable. Only two hours from Washington DC, Oakville had always teetered on the edge, politically and socially. An influx of city dwellers and tourists, as well as a widening generational gap, added to apprehension, and older folks were extremely uncomfortable with confrontation and more worried about appearances. It was not unheard of to have undisclosed family stories and secrets appear generations later.

Most people were naïve and probably scared. The community was changing from traditions people had always known to new ways that locals did not understand. Many had never traveled extensively, and 98 percent of the county population was white. Even though her dark skin resembled her grandmother Simón's Costa Rican side, Jordan had rarely experienced racial prejudice. Locals tended to support their own.

The mayor departed, and the party continued. Jordan milled around, playing the attentive host, making sure to bump into Emmy as often as possible. She would have relished being alone with her, but the party had been planned long before they met.

As the partygoers welcomed in 2015, Emmy casually placed her hand on Jordan's shoulder, and her fingers brushed the side of Jordan's neck. She stretched on her toes and said into Jordan's ear, "Happy New Year. I'm still holding you to a date night. Shall we do a movie or something else?"

Emmy was amused that her words caused an immediate visceral reaction. Maybe it was her imagination, but she detected goose bumps under her fingertips, and Jordan was trying but unable to suppress a grin. She looked so damn adorable, and Emmy fought the urge to kiss her right there. They were brought back to reality when the boisterous guests demanded Jordan make the first toast.

Jordan, yelled out to the crowd, "To all my friends and business associates, I wish you all a blessed and successful year. And despite our differences that seem to be pushing our country apart, please let your heart and compassion be your guide."

The cheering was loud from all corners of the room. Emmy was gently pushed aside as the merrymakers engulfed Jordan. She watched the interaction. Jordan attempted to politely say goodbye to the other guests and make her way back to Emmy. Each time she glanced over, Emmy would make a question mark in the air with her finger. Watching Jordan squirm made the buildup all the more perfect. Perfect to let her words marinate in Jordan's brain until her question was answered. Perfect to ramp up Jordan's desire. She would wait in sweet anticipation.

When things began to calm down, Emmy sashayed over, smug with the thought of another opportunity to tweak Jordan's emotional meter again. "What's my answer?"

Jordan's eyes held a mischievous glint. "I forgot to tell you about a tradition I have on New Year's Day."

Jordan took a drink. Obviously, letting her words dangle on purpose. Emmy's excitement grew.

"And what might that be?"

Jordan's eyes were dark and playful. "Dinner," she said through a smirk. She bit her lip. "After a good hike."

Emmy could not believe her ears. "Did you say hike?"

Jordan only nodded, her smile gleaming.

"Let me get this correct. New Year's Day. You want to go on a hike! First, it's winter. Second, there's still snow on the ground. And third, it's cold as bullocks around here, and there always seems to be a threat of some sort of storm."

Jordan chuckled. "A New Year's Day hike is a tradition I revived when I returned home. A little cold won't hurt you."

Emmy moved her mouth but couldn't seem to make any words come out. *Is she toying with me?*

Jordan straightened up. "The cold front moved out today, and the forecast for tomorrow is partly sunny with temps rising to the mid-forties and light winds. There's really not much snow on the ground. With proper layering, we'd keep plenty warm. You said you have hiking boots."

Emmy twisted her mouth, mulling over the idea. "You're serious?"

"I've got an easy trail we can do and extra outdoor clothing I can loan you." Jordan leaned down. "Afterward, I promise to please your palate."

Emmy grabbed another glass of champagne as a waiter passed by and took a large gulp. "Count me in."

Chapter Ten

*B*y midmorning, the sun was shining, and only patches of snow were here and there. A perfect day for a hike. "Wow, I can't believe the weather here changes so quickly."

Jordan admired Emmy's form even though she was layered up in clothing. "I told you, today is going to be gorgeous. There's a trail up Cacapon Mountain along the ridge that's about four miles round-trip. How does that sound?"

"Let's go for it."

The hike began through the woods then became narrower and rockier as they climbed. They kept a good pace, frequently stopping to check out the lovely surroundings.

"The rock scramble is up ahead. The summit has a three-hundred-sixty-degree view with a flat spot that makes a great picnic location. You don't have any fear of heights do you?"

Emmy laughed. "Now you ask. I can take whatever you throw at me. Just because I happen to be a little older and less in shape, doesn't mean I can't manage."

This was the first time Emmy had ever expressed a lack of confidence or mentioned an age difference.

Jordan glanced down Emmy's body. "Oh, I'd say you're in shape. In fact, a nice curvy appealing shape."

"Okay, Casanova, lead the way."

Jordan handed her a pair of climbing gloves, and they climbed on the side facing the sun. There were numerous handholds and footholds and no less than a twenty-foot drop in the most difficult section. Overall, the activity was invigorating and well worth the view. At the summit, Jordan removed the small backpack and stretched out a thin foam mat, which elicited a sly grin and a bit of teasing from Emmy.

"Are you intending to bed me up here?"

Jordan chuckled. "It's for under a sleeping bag, but it's cushiony, and it'll keep our butts warm."

Passing Emmy a water bottle, she placed lunch in the middle of the mat. They both sat quietly eating pita chips and hummus, apple slices, and peanut butter sandwiches, looking out at the valley for some time before Emmy broke the silence.

"Have you ever wanted to be anything other than a chef? What made you decide to live in Europe?"

Jordan shrugged. "Well, I did love singing as a child, but for the sake of everyone's eardrums, I discovered my real aptitude was cooking. I never dreamed that one day I'd make it as a top chef in Europe and eventually own a restaurant." Jordan drank some water as she thought about how much detail to reveal. "I stayed in Spain rather than return home for a couple of reasons. One, I loved the beautiful city of Madrid and the freedom I felt when I was away from the town and my family. And the other reason"—Jordan stared back out into the valley—"was Luciana."

Emmy placed her hand on Jordan's shoulder. "The woman who ripped apart your heart."

"Yep. I once loved her. Or at least, I thought I did. Anyway, she cheated. The worst part is, I didn't have a clue. She apologized, and I wanted to believe her because we had been together for over eight years. When she begged for forgiveness, I gave her another chance despite the awful feeling in my gut." Jordan gazed out at the valley before continuing. "It's the same old storyline of any serial cheater. Except she was an expert. In the end, I found there had been numerous affairs, including one so-called mutual friend."

"The important thing is you figured it out. We all have our share of hard knocks. Life goes on."

"How about you?" Jordan said, wanting to get off the topic fast. "Have you always wanted to be in finance?"

"I worked my way up to managing one of the most lucrative mutual funds at a private firm in London, but success does not bring happiness." Emmy shook her head. "The hours were long, and some clients were a pain. And the men. Jesus, they'd hit on me when no one was around. About a year after Heather died, I snapped and quit." She bit her lip and drew her knees to her chest. "A big factor in my decision to leave was when my boss grabbed my breasts from behind and told me he could make me straight. I could have sued. Instead, I punched him and walked out the door."

"I'm sorry you had to go through that." Jordan bit her lip. "But your exit must have been a sight to see. I bet you've got a mean right hook."

Emmy casually bumped her shoulder and gave her a side-ways grin. "Yeah, I did enjoy giving him a bloody nose, but I had no idea what to do next. Luckily, my friend Becca and another wealthy client also broke with the firm. They retained my services as a private consultant and kept my financial ass from falling off a cliff."

"How did you get the job at Berkeley International Bank?"

"They offered me a part-time job working on global projects to help impoverished nations. After six months, they moved me into a full-time position, raised my salary, and put me in charge of the India sector. I soon learned that getting sucked into the man-agement vortex was not what it seemed." She shrugged. "I may have been in charge at the office, but the country's overall conservative view of women as mothers and homemakers made it challenging to do business. When the part-time position in Washington DC became available, I nailed the interview."

"You seem extremely comfortable in your skin. When did you come out?"

Emmy arched her eyebrows. "Lots of questions. Is this how you interview for the position of main squeeze?"

"Sorry. Just curious." Jordan wet her lips. "Besides, the position's yours if you want it."

"Oh, really?" Emmy reached over and lightly tickled Jordan.

"Yes," Jordan giggled. "Now answer the question, please. I want to get to know you better."

Emmy grew serious before answering. "I told my family and a few close friends in university and opened up completely at work when I met Heather. I wanted the world to know I loved her. After her death"—Emmy swallowed—"I worked too much trying to bury the pain. Excessive work is not a remedy. It's avoidance."

Emmy's words rang true. Jordan hung her head and whispered, "Yeah, guilty as charged. After the club scene, work became my drug. And continuing to bash my head against the wall is no remedy."

"I take it you're referring to one-night stands and not dancing."

Jordan swallowed hard and nodded.

"You really tensed up when I mentioned the club at the spa. And you did it right now."

Jordan straightened her spine and faced Emmy. "I was stupid. I thought as long as both parties were single and agreed, that it would—" She blew out a long breath. "The momentary thrill never balanced things out. It made me feel worse, and I want you to know that time in my life is over. I don't want a casual relationship."

"Good, because I'd drop your ass if your intentions were only for sex. I want the whole package. The friendship, the caring partner, and yes, I'll take the passion. But! I do not share. I'm into monogamous relationships."

"I want that, too. I have no intention of ever going back to the club scene. Oh and…ah… I've had two physicals since then, and I'm healthy."

"Nice to know. I am too. And thank you for your honesty. It pisses me off to date then find out something is being intentionally concealed. I don't get that with you. I believe your sincerity. You're a little reserved but kindhearted. Have faith and don't give up. Once you let go and forgive yourself, things will get better."

Jordan's gaze slowly moved from Emmy's face to her hands. "Meeting you has given me more of a reason. Your confident personality is a turn-on."

"And what was that eye movement down my torso?"

Jordan looked back out to the valley and twisted her mouth trying to stop a gleeful expression but said nothing.

"Uh-huh. So, you only like me for my personality?"

"Well, you are gorgeous." Jordan tried to look at Emmy out of the corner of her eye.

Emmy's voice was throaty and low. "What's my best physical feature?"

Jordan was sporting a wicked grin as she squirmed. "You don't mince words and get right to the point."

"Honesty, remember? After all, this isn't the first time you've looked me over." She inched closer. "Not that I mind."

"You were at the gym in some rather tight-fitting clothes."

"And?" Emmy's grin was wide.

"You were very sexy."

"And?" As Emmy drew out the word, her fingertips played with Jordan's hair and moved down to her earlobe and cheek.

When Emmy firmly grasped her chin, Jordan said, "You fill out your T-shirt nicely." Emmy cocked one eyebrow forcing Jordan to go on. "And yes, you were in an awesome bathing suit at the spa. I like breasts, okay?"

Emmy chuckled. "Well, thank you. I think you're sexy, and I love everything from your rich brown eyes to your lean legs. But remember, I want the whole package. And I thoroughly enjoy teasing you, but I can stop if it's bothersome."

Normally, anyone playing with her would piss Jordan off. For some reason, it made Emmy more endearing, and it was a huge turn-on.

"No. I like it, and you seem to know when and where you can turn up the heat. By the way, you know I'm turning forty next month, but you've not mentioned your birthday. When's the big day? I'm guessing you're in your late forties?"

"And if I wasn't?"

Jordan shrugged, "No big deal."

"I'll be fifty-two on September the fourth."

Jordan wrapped her hand around Emmy's neck and pulled them together. "Twelve years. I don't care. Life's short. I enjoy being with you, and I want the whole package."

She kissed Emmy with intense hunger. As lips and tongues explored, a few wind gusts reminded them it was still winter. They packed up and headed down. In sections that were broad enough to stroll side by side, they held hands. The stroking of hands and small talk intensified the pent-up desire.

"So, what did you think of the hike?" Jordan asked as she unlocked the SUV.

"Wonderful."

"We've got about an hour before sunset. Let's get back and cook some dinner."

"Only dinner?" Emmy feigned a pout.

Jordan wanted to take Emmy right then and there but suppressed her animal instincts. "Well, I can fix something a lot nicer than peanut butter sandwiches. I baked a moist cake that we can eat with a chocolate drizzle. We could eat it anywhere you like," Jordan said with a devilish "I dare you" look that left plenty of room for innuendo.

"Anywhere in the house? Anywhere with the drizzle? With fingers or without?" Emmy leaned in and spoke in a low, sultry voice. "My tongue wouldn't let any little drop of goodness get away."

Jordan cleared her throat. "Don't worry. I'll make sure of it." She pulled the SUV onto the road.

"No worries." Emmy placed her hand on Jordan's upper thigh and gave a little squeeze. "I can wait."

Removing Emmy's hand, Jordan grinned ear to ear. "I'd be more than happy to skip dinner and go straight to chocolate drizzle. First, you have to keep your hands to yourself. I can't drive if you touch me. Deal?"

"If you insist."

The setting sun painted the sky in a warm orange blaze. They stole glances of one another between bouts of laughter and stories. Lust was building, but this time, Jordan felt much more. She had never been this at ease and happy.

Within a split second, she saw motion out of the corner of her eye, but it was too late. A deer streaked past. The SUV scarcely missed the deer's hindquarter. Relief lasted with a blink of an eye as another deer appeared in front of them. The airbags deployed. Seat belts cut into their shoulders. The vehicle shook as loud crunching sounds and thuds underneath racked their senses. They were jarred to reality—a reality like a carnival ride gone terribly wrong—a mixture of disorientation, adrenaline, and fear that brought a prompt sickness to the stomach and panic to the mind.

Through it all, Jordan maintained control of the SUV and pulled off the road before blurting out, "Son of a bitch! Second time in fifteen months. You okay?"

By the time Emmy said, "I think so," Jordan was looking her over carefully.

Emmy's eyes were wide, and her skin was ashen. Jordan put her hands on Emmy's face. "It's going to be okay. I want you to gently move your head from side to side and up and down. Stop if you feel any pain. Tell me every little thing."

When she was satisfied that Emmy was not injured, Jordan jumped out and put up safety flares, called for help, and inspected the vehicle. The damn thing was probably totaled. Jordan opened the door, and Emmy's head turned at the loud creak. While some of Emmy's color had returned, she still looked distressed. Jordan settled in and reassured her.

"The state police and EMTs are on the way. Standard procedure. Everything's going to be fine."

"You've hit deer before?" Emmy's voice shook.

"Unfortunately, yes. It's common around here. Most people will hit one or two in their lifetime, but lucky me, they seem to like my vehicles."

Emmy peered out over the dented hood. "Is the damage bad?"

"Besides the crumpled front, the bumper's been partially ripped off. If you think that's bad, the underside of the vehicle has taken a beating and fluid is leaking."

"Not drivable?"

Jordan chuckled. "Not a good idea. Look on the bright side. I'll be getting a new SUV."

"I would have preferred you getting one a different way."

"So would I. At least we're okay." She tucked a strand of Emmy's hair behind her ear and embraced her.

The state police and medical arrived followed by Doc Albertson.

"Good evening, Doc."

"Evening, Jordan. Let's get you both in the back of the ambulance for a quick check."

The EMT checked Jordan out in silence while Doc introduced himself to Emmy. She could feel the worry lines intensify on her forehead, but her concern eased as she watched them. Doc was charming Emmy. They chatted like old friends as he took Emmy's vitals and ran down the standard checklist. When he whispered something in her ear, Emmy threw her head back and laughed. Jordan was instantly relieved, and her muscles relaxed some.

"And how's the cantankerous one over here?" he asked, pointing to Jordan.

"I'm not difficult. Really I'm not." Jordan countered.

Emmy snickered. "That's not what I hear."

Doc nodded. "Call me if anything changes, and I expect to see you both by close of business tomorrow." He patted Emmy's hand. "An extra precaution, my dear. The tenacity in the ornery one there can run deep."

"We will," Emmy said as they both eyed Jordan.

Jordan felt like a little kid again. "I'm...well...maybe a little stubborn, but I promise."

"I know you prefer seeing Dr. Beth. She'll be back soon. Now get on outta here and get some rest."

Emmy cocked one eyebrow sharply. Jordan shrugged as her lips slightly curled.

By the time the paperwork was done, they were drained. The state trooper offered them a ride to Jordan's mother's house. Before he got in, Emmy said, "Tell me more about Dr. Beth."

"I like Doc," Jordan calmly answered, "but he's in his seventies, and it's more comfortable with a woman." Her color drained. "That's not how I meant it to sound. She's a top graduate of WVU and"—Jordan hesitated while the trooper slid into the driver's seat then whispered—"we had a long discussion during my spring physical. I was completely honest."

Emmy rubbed the top of her hand, interlaced their fingers, and squeezed before releasing.

Gwyneth had settled down in her favorite recliner after dinner watching an episode of *Downtown Abbey*. She was startled by a creaking noise from the kitchen door. Alarm was soon replaced by joy when she saw her daughter's head poke around the corner. Waving her in, she was happy to see her, and with a friend no less. One, she had never met before.

"Hi, Mom." Jordan hugged her and didn't let go.

"Is everything all right?" Gwyneth could easily see that both were a little upset.

Jordan unwrapped herself and produced a weak smile. "Hit a deer on 522. Mom, I'd like you to meet Betty Jean's niece, Emmy Russo."

"Pleased to meet you, Mrs. Simón."

"Please call me Gwyneth."

Gwyneth turned her attention to Jordan, her voice stern. "You need to check in with Doc."

"He arrived with the medics. Plus, we will pop by tomorrow. I thought I could borrow your old Outback to take Emmy home."

"Absolutely not. You've been through too much tonight. You both look exhausted and shaken. You're spending the night, period. Go rest in the living room. I'll fix some tea." Gwyneth gave her that universal mom look. "Go on."

On the sofa, Jordan leaned over. "She can be just as bull-headed as Betty Jean."

"I heard that," Gwyneth said carrying a tea tray from the kitchen. "My God, have you eaten anything recently?"

"Nope, and I'm starved. We climbed up to Cacapon ridge and did the Old Bear scramble today."

"Please do not go out of your way," Emmy added. "If you happen to have some wine and snacks, I'd be grateful."

Gwyneth laughed. "It's no bother. You girls relax."

Their eyes were getting heavy when Gwyneth returned with hearty beef stew, homemade bread, and a bottle of Cabernet Sauvignon. They perked up at the smell and dove into the hot meal.

Gwyneth and Emmy hit it off, talking about various BBC shows. Her daughter had finally brought a friend home. She smiled to herself.

After they were finished, Gwyneth noticed yawns and droopy eyelids again. "Time to get some rest, ladies. There's too much junk piled in the one bedroom, and I've partially painted the other spare bedroom. Smells to high heaven. You'll have to share the full bed in Jordan's old room. You two don't mind, do you?"

The wine had apparently loosened their inhibitions and revealed a mixture of emotions. Gwyneth was slightly surprised and amused. Jordan, who had never been skilled at hiding her feelings, had a slight blush, even in the living room's dim light. Her smile was forced, and she hesitated. Emmy bit her lip, trying to suppress a grin and not doing a good job of it.

"Yeah sure, Mom," Jordan answered weakly. "We'll manage." Her reaction was almost like when Gwyneth would catch her as a youngster taking cookies without permission.

"I'll make sure she gets a good night's rest," Emmy said.

Gwyneth noticed a hint of mirth in Emmy's eyes.

"Good. There're old T-shirts in the dresser from all you kids. They'll do in a pinch as a nightshirt, and the heat is turned up to keep us toasty."

"Sounds heavenly. I'm sure we will be plenty warm. Thank you for the meal and hospitality, Gwyneth."

Gwyneth walked away pondering the exchange. *I wonder if they are more than friends?*

Once upstairs, Jordan shut the door, rested her forehead against it, and kept her back to Emmy. "This wasn't how I imagined our first night together."

"What? In only a full bed? In a room down the hall from your mum's master suite? Or using old T-shirts for PJs? We could sleep in the nude. After all, your mum did point out the heat is turned up."

Jordan swung around to see a delighted Emmy smirking, sitting on the bed with her legs crossed. Jordan spoke in a loud whisper with a tone of panic. "This isn't funny. I admit I often think about seeing you in the nude and sleeping with you, but my mother is nearby."

Emmy stood and closed the gap. She placed her hands on Jordan's hips and pulled her tight, so the tips of their noses touched. Her sweet scent filled Jordan's nostrils. "Relax. I'm too tired anyway. I am positive though that I will sleep soundly wrapped in your arms." She tenderly kissed Jordan. "So how about it? Promise to keep me warm and safe if I promise not to take it further?"

Jordan finally melted into Emmy's embrace. "I'm exhausted. Let's get to bed. You can have the hall bathroom first. I don't want to see you nude until I can have you—all of you."

Emmy pulled away and purred, "Okay, Miss Prim and Proper."

When they crawled into bed, Jordan worried she would be unable to contain herself, but spooning with Emmy was the most peaceful and comforting thing she had done in a long time. Their embrace was soft and tender as they drifted off to sleep.

Chapter Eleven

Jordan woke to an empty bed. She rushed to dress and almost fell over as she caught her toe in the leg of her jeans. At the top of the stairs, she heard her mother's voice followed by roaring laughter. *What in the world are they talking about?*

Emmy brightened when Jordan rounded the corner. "I've talked your mum into telling me some of your childhood stories. I hear you were quite the adventurous prankster growing up."

Jordan shot her mom a glare. "Mother, what have you said about me?"

Gwyneth laughed heartily, stood, and greeted her daughter with a kiss on the cheek. "Oh, stop worrying. Sit down, and I'll bring you a cup of coffee."

Jordan gave Emmy a look. All she got in return was a devilish smile. Emmy pointed outside at the bird feeder hanging off the deck. "The goldfinches are beautiful. Nice to have a splash of color with the gray, barren winter trees. They've been attacking that seed out there."

Jordan leaned over. "You're changing the topic."

"What topic?"

"So what devious tales has my mother spun?"

"Oh, the usual. Putting a fake mouse and spider around the

house to freak her out. The time you put superglue on the ATV and Carter had to crawl out of his pants to get off. Your speeding incident at seventeen followed by putting extra crushed red peppers in the policeman's lasagna for retaliation. I hear he stopped you frequently after that and issued you warnings."

"How long have you been talking?"

"Oh, a couple of hours." Emmy burst out in laughter. "All right, it's been less than an hour but an immensely entertaining hour." She dragged the last words out in a playful tone.

"Yeah, paybacks can be torture. I'm sure Betty Jean has some great stories about you."

Gwyneth watched the banter between the two. Her daughter had warmed up to Emmy with a bright smile, and it did not go unnoticed when she placed her hand on top of Emmy's while teasing her.

Jordan hadn't socialized much since returning from Spain. Tonight she was basking in the glow of Betty Jean's niece after having known her for only a short time. Seeing the undeniable chemistry between the two, Gwyneth decided that if Jordan hadn't broached the subject of her dating and sexuality before her birthday, she would.

Gwyneth's thoughts were broken when Jordan asked, "Mom, why do you have so much toast and fruit? This is enough for a small army."

She smiled and placed a cup of coffee in front of Jordan when a knock came at the door. "That would be Betty Jean and Elizabeth."

Gwyneth and her older sister Elizabeth were Betty Jean's best friends from all the way back to elementary school. The door opened, and the three women hugged as if they hadn't seen each other for years. Not forgetting their good manners, Jordan and

Emmy rose and greeted everyone. The coffee flowed as they jabbered away. Soon, Jordan tried to excuse herself by saying how they needed her at the restaurant. When she asked for the keys to the Outback, she got an earful.

"Jordan Marie García Simón, sit down and relax, or you'll be walking home."

"It's nearly nine, and I don't want to leave the crew short-handed."

With a look that would make anyone think twice, Gwyneth held up her hand. "I've already called Robby. He's taking care of everything. Please sit down and join us."

"Yes, please," Emmy chimed in. "I'm leaving in a few weeks to house hunt in Washington DC and stop by the new job. I'd like to enjoy your company for as long as possible."

Jordan immediately broke into an impish grin and sat back down. The reaction did not go unnoticed. Gwyneth looked at Betty Jean, who raised one eyebrow and slightly tilted her head as if to confirm her suspicions.

Elizabeth was unfazed and went over to the coffee pot to help herself. All the time, she jabbered about the local gossip, something about the state police office in town. "Well, the new twenty-something trooper is a graduate of the WV State Police Academy. She's pretty with her hair in a bun but in a buff masculine way. She's toned and looks like she means business."

Jordan jumped in. "What are you talking about, Auntie? Did you get a speeding ticket again? Been out drag racing Uncle's F-150?"

"Well, I did get a warning. I was only going ten miles over." Everyone snickered while Elizabeth remained solemn. "Anyway, she's a sharp-dressed woman. The scuttlebutt is she's a lesbian. A butch. Kind of out of place for our small rural town. Not that I think that's bad, but it's sort of uncharacteristic for these parts. That's more a city thing."

Gwyneth immediately chastised her sister. "Elizabeth! I think that's inappropriate to spread rumors about someone. People should not be speculating or revealing someone's private business. Besides, what if you're wrong? Sexual orientation has nothing to do with how she performs her job. I'm just happy we've finally got a woman trooper stationed in the county."

"Hear, hear. I couldn't agree more." Betty Jean held up her mug. "I, for one, am tired of people putting labels on others. People need to get over their obsession with being gay or straight."

Gwyneth watched as Betty Jean discreetly glanced at Emmy and Jordan. Emmy sat undisturbed while Jordan jammed some toast in her mouth followed by a big gulp of coffee.

Elizabeth looked at her good friend. "Why, Betty Jean, it's been ages since we've been together, and I've missed you so much. Do you secretly have a thing for me?"

Betty Jean cocked an eyebrow as if she was about to make one of her famous smart-ass remarks when Elizabeth chuckled.

"Things like that don't bother me. It's just that—" Elizabeth hesitated as she looked uncomfortable. "The rumor came from Gerry. He was over with one of the other fellas from his church. They were helping me move some furniture. I'm afraid their viewpoint and language were rougher than what I've said."

Tension hung in the air. The mere mention of Gerry changed the mood, and Gwyneth sighed. "I'm sorry to hear that. Despite my best efforts, Gerry seems to have chosen the road of intolerance toward those who think differently." She frowned for a moment. "He's even tried to judge some of my behavior. I hope that God one day shows him a lesson and softens his heart. I have little patience with bigoted, narrow-minded people. It breaks my heart that he is bent on following a path of his interpretation on righteousness and imposing it on others."

"I smell cinnamon rolls in the oven," Emmy said abruptly.

"Oh my Lord, I forgot them." Gwyneth jumped up and nearly

knocked over her chair. She retrieved them from the large stove. "Not too bad but a little on the well-done side."

"I'm sure they'll taste wonderful, Mom," Jordan replied while Elizabeth launched into more idle chatter as she helped Gwyneth with the rolls.

Out of nowhere, Jordan felt Emmy's hand on her knee under the table. Emmy leaned over and whispered, "You have a wonderful mum even though I would have liked better circumstances." She squeezed Jordan's knee and left her hand in place causing the rush of warmth and tingling up through Jordan's core.

Oh my God, could this get any more awkward? Jordan swallowed, shoved more food in her mouth, and wiggled her leg to signal Emmy to remove her hand.

"Tell us, girls. What happened yesterday with the deer?" Betty Jean had been paying more attention to them than the others.

Elizabeth stopped her chatter "Deer? You didn't hit another one did you, Jordan?"

Jordan hung her head. "Yes, the deer got me again. My SUV might be totaled." Jordan once again breathed a sigh of relief as the conversation headed away from social issues. That was all it took, and soon the discussion was all over the map from the new car dealership to plans to expand the high school.

After a couple of hours had passed, Jordan was stern about leaving this time. Her mom reluctantly relinquished the Outback keys. As she put on her coat, Emmy volunteered to walk her out.

Outside, Emmy said, "I've had a marvelous time over the last twenty-four hours except for hitting the deer. I would kiss you, but that picture window in the kitchen would give too much of a show for the ladies."

"Yes."

"So when am I going to see you again? You still owe me dinner and a movie. I'm not going to lose you to the new state trooper am I?"

"Well, I do love women in uniform, and you'll be busy in DC soon."

Emmy gave Jordan a punch on the shoulder. "We talked on the hike about long weekend visits. I'm going to hold you to that promise."

Jordan swallowed hard, and her eyes moistened. "I've done some shitty things in the past. Hurt myself the most and only made it worse by pushing everyone away. I thought I'd never care again until I met you. You're too good to lose. Yet it scares the shit out of me with you going away in March."

"It's only part-time. I'm not giving up on us. There is an us, isn't there?"

As Jordan rubbed away the tears that were threatening to fall, a wild grin formed on her face. "Yeah. There sure is."

Emmy's hand trailed down Jordan's jaw but then fell to her side. "Not being able to show affection around others kills me, but I understand what you've been through. I'm willing to wait. Just a tiny bit longer."

Jordan glanced back at the house. Betty Jean and Elizabeth were jabbering away with their backs toward them. Her mother was at the sink looking out. She waved then sat. Jordan didn't feel alarmed even though her mother could have easily seen the interaction between them. *Maybe Mom does know after all.*

Jordan poked at the cold brown winter grass through the snow with the tip of her boot. "Dinner at my house Monday night?" Without waiting for a reply, she ventured out of the closet, grabbing Emmy's face with both hands and planting a long sensual kiss on her lips. Before releasing, she sucked in Emmy's bottom lip.

Emmy's face ignited in happiness, and she gushed, "I think that'd be lovely, Ms. Simón. Your brave side is intoxicating. For now, I'll resist responding. After all"—she winked—"you need to build up your stamina because I intend to see more of that side."

Jordan waggled her eyebrows and climbed into the Outback and started it up. Rolling down the window, she brazenly joked, "And don't forget to wear a costume. Something with a uniform and handcuffs."

"Really?" Emmy rolled her eyes. "And what costume will you be wearing?"

"Umm, haven't made up my mind."

Emmy made her way back to the house, but before she had a chance to take off her coat, Betty Jean was rising.

"We should be going, dear. You've had a rough couple of days, and I have some shopping to do before going home. You're my driver because I'm too tired. Elizabeth, are we dropping you home?"

"If Gwyneth doesn't mind, I'll stay and catch up a bit and have her take me home."

After the customary goodbye hugs and kisses on the cheek, Gwyneth paused with her hands clasped in Emmy's. "I'm delighted my daughter has met an interesting new friend. You'll have to go on more hikes and other events. She works too many long hours. Hopefully, you won't disappear when you start your job."

"Not to worry. I will be visiting Oakville."

"Yes. Visit and visit often. You're always welcome." Gwyneth glanced around at the other women. "That goes for you all too. Let's spend more time together. Life's too short. I was thinking about having family and friends in a couple of weeks for a Sunday supper. Say beginning at three. You're all invited. The more, the merrier. You too, Emmy."

The women enthusiastically agreed. Emmy would cut short her DC house hunting and rearrange her plans if necessary. She liked Gwyneth and sensed her generosity and caring. She saw that same spark in Jordan.

Emmy tried to focus as she drove, but the past twenty-four hours had been a rollercoaster of events. Her body tingled at the mere thought of Jordan's dinner invitation. Monday night could not arrive soon enough.

At the stop sign, she noticed Betty Jean staring at her. "What store do you want to visit? You do realize I haven't taken a shower since yesterday morning and I'm still wearing the same clothes."

Betty Jean smirked. "That's nothing new around here. Besides, I have to pick up a few groceries unless you want to eat in town every day." She reached over and without warning, gently smacked Emmy upside the back of her head.

"Ouch, what's that for?"

"She's younger than you by probably fourteen or fifteen years."

"Twelve to be precise. Besides, age isn't everything. She's intelligent, talented, and a caring soul."

"Not to mention she's one of the most beautiful women for miles around with warm brown eyes, a smile that melts everyone's heart, and a fit, athletic body."

"That too." Emmy gave her aunt a devilish grin.

"Keep your eyes on the road and watch out for deer."

"Yes, ma'am."

"Are you sure she isn't just experimenting?"

Emmy gave her a sideways glare. "I don't tell secrets, but I assure you that she is one hundred percent lesbian."

They drove in silence for a bit before Betty Jean turned serious. "Take it slow. Make sure you both are going in the same direction. If she comes out then, it will likely be because of you.

It isn't easy being gay around here. I don't think her family would have much of an issue except Gerry."

"I believe you once referred to him as Mr. Know-It-All."

"Yes, he's a frequent equal-opportunity offender to a lot of folks. The more he proselytizes, the more folks get tired of his mouth. I know you're not one who hurts and runs, but be extra careful. She's a wonderful person, and you both deserve some long overdue happiness."

"I couldn't agree more. We're adults, and you have to have some faith." Emmy caught her aunt's quick, troubled glance. "Auntie, what else is bothering you?"

"Truth be told, I'm not worried about your age difference so much as the fact that you love Europe, and I believe Jordan is home for good. Do you think you might consider living on this side of the pond? I mean permanently because I don't think Jordan wants to move again."

"I'm serious about Jordan. I'd like to become a couple that does not hide. As long as she's willing to visit Europe, then I don't see a problem living permanently in America. I don't want either of us cut off from friends and family. I enjoy visiting new places and want to visit the Grand Canyon, Seattle, California, lots of places while I'm living here."

"Yes, but you may have to rethink that since Jordan doesn't travel much."

"Traveling for fun is different. We've both talked about it. Don't worry, Auntie."

"It's not you two I'm worried about. There are crazies around here. Be cautious."

Chapter Twelve

"Jordan, someone's out front for you."

Putting up her hand to cover her mouth since it was full of carrots, she muttered, "Who?"

"Just put aside the paperwork and get out there." Robby smacked her back. "And while you're at it, why don't you eat something besides rabbit food."

At three o'clock, there weren't many people eating lunch, and by Robby's tone, she knew whoever was waiting for her. She grinned when she saw Carter in a booth shoving empañadas into his mouth. Her little brother could sure pack it away. She gave him a big hug and kiss on the cheek.

Carter was a sweetheart who owned a handmade furniture shop and ran Poppa and Grammy's apple orchard. A happy guy who cared more about the quality of his work and his relationship with people than money. He was devoted to his wife, Angie, and their two young children with all his heart.

Around a mouthful, he mumbled, "I love the potato and chorizo ones, but this new smoked ribeye and goat cheese one is the bomb."

"What brings you in today, bro? You usually visit with Angie and the kids, and I'm lucky to see you here once a month."

"Ah, you know I miss my big sister."

"Liar. You came here to stuff your face. If you keep eating like that, I'm going to go bankrupt since you get the family discount." She reached over and snatched one off his plate.

"Hey, get your own!" Carter swatted her hand away.

"I'm sure you've got more on the way." As if like magic, the waiter brought out a platter of garlic shrimp, olives, and stuffed mushrooms and left them both iced tea. "You're going to eat all that? No, don't answer but do tell me what's dragged you away from the farm."

When he stopped eating, swigged his iced tea, and looked up at her, she expected the worst. "I have no idea why, but Gerry called the other day. He wants to talk to me. Do you know what's going on?"

"Me? Are you serious? To him, you and I must be lost causes, forever to burn with all the other heathens. Maybe he wants to talk dude stuff."

Carter rolled his eyes. "He called the house instead of the workshop, darn well knowing I wouldn't be in the house. More like mining for information. Angie answered the phone and said he sounded sincere." Carter used air quotes and a sharp tone. "After he asked how the kids were doing, she told him about the after school club today. At which, he asked to come over and see me in private." Aware of his surroundings, Carter leaned over and said in a whispered shout, "Like what the hell, ask my wife, not me? And arrange it while she is out?" He wiped his mouth and threw his napkin down.

Jordan wasn't sure what to say. As she tried to listen, the waiter sat a big guy down in a booth on the opposite side. She glanced over as Carter carried on. An awful chill ran down her spine. The guy from the gym was in the booth perusing the menu with his sunglasses on. His hair and beard were still ragged. From her angle, she could see the knee ripped out in his jeans, but his white T-shirt looked clean today. A camouflage jacket hung on the booth hook. *What's with the fucking sunglasses inside? Who is this guy?* She refocused on Carter.

"Anyway, Angie agreed. She's going to dinner at her parents' house with the kids in case I need extra time with Gerry."

Carter's hand gestures revealed his perturbed mood, but Jordan couldn't concentrate. The creepy guy's presence rattled her hard. She glanced over again. Her breath and heart nearly stopped. He was leaned back partially against the wall at an angle looking directly at her. She finally tore her gaze away. Fear ran from her head down to her toes. As Carter jabbered on, she racked her brain but could not recall ever seeing the stranger until recently. Her heart beat rapidly, and her breathing was shallow. Using her peripheral vision, she looked at him again, careful not to turn her head. The jerk sipped his drink but hadn't changed positions.

"Did you hear me?" Carter nudged her hand.

Jordan had lost track of what he had said. Looking helplessly at her brother, she finally mumbled, "So what do you think he wants?" As the words left her mouth, she knew the question was about the creep as much as it was about Gerry.

"I have no freakin' clue. He's coming by at four. So any, and I mean any, words of wisdom would be helpful. Better yet, you want to take my place?"

As she was about to say something, he blurted out in a hushed voice, "I don't know how Mom puts up with it. For me, it is way more than the older sibling or the religious thing. I think he's got some real mental issues. And these last couple of years—" He pursed his lips and shook his head. "His bull crap and anger are getting worse. I'm worried he's going to lash out at one of us physically. He ruins most family gatherings. Luckily, you've got the restaurant to give you an excuse to leave."

Jordan silently cringed at the statement, knowing she had her own secrets for keeping away. "Carter, I love you, and I do agree with what you're saying. I also know you two always seem to end up in a shouting match. So whatever Gerry has to say, bite your tongue, nod your head, and get him out of the house as fast as possible."

He bobbed his head in a yes gesture and shoved more food in his mouth. Carter always liked to eat no matter what his mood. This time, he pushed the plate between them. "Help me eat this. It may be my last meal before going into the snake pit, so I don't want to be too stuffed."

Food was the last thing Jordan wanted. The tension that gripped her would not let go. She carefully chewed slowly as Carter wolfed down the rest then stood. He probably thought she was also upset by the news on Gerry.

"Well, guess it's time to face the music. Wish me luck."

"You'll be fine."

Carter squeezed Jordan's shoulder as he left. She remained seated until her nerves settled and sipped her iced tea. With every swallow, a chill ran through her body even though the ice was melted. She dreaded walking by the weird dude but had no choice as he was seated near the kitchen door. At least he had food now and wasn't staring her down. *Get a grip. It's probably a coincidence. No big deal.*

She plastered on a smile when she got closer. "Everything okay?" He gave a thumbs up, and she kept on walking. She felt like fainting when she saw a bulge on his hip. *Fuck! The asshole's packing!*

She walked right by the staff into her office, shut the door, closed the blinds, and plopped in the chair, resting her elbows on her knees and her head in her hands. *Jesus Christ. I hate this state's conceal-and-carry law.* As much as she tried to tell herself the guy was probably no threat, her gut told her otherwise. Tonight, she'd tell Robby they needed to post a "No Firearms" sign.

Chapter Thirteen

*B*etty Jean had not spoken of Emmy's new burgeoning relationship since the ride home the other night. Instead, she had inundated Emmy with chores and running errands. Emmy was certain it was intentional. As soon as she would fulfill one of Auntie's requests, another would come in.

Sneaking out to the restaurant between shopping sprees was exciting, but the crazy demands had to end, and last night, Emmy put her foot down. After Auntie's fake pleas of innocence followed by a warning of "You better think twice," Emmy flat-out told her to back off. Betty Jean unwillingly agreed, and when Emmy said, "And don't be surprised if I don't come home Monday night," her aunt was speechless.

Now with the dinner date a few hours away, Emmy was in a dreamy haze as she walked out of the florist with an exquisite bouquet. Her eagerness to unabashedly kiss Jordan's lips and the thrill of more was building. When she reached the car, her cell rang displaying Becca's number.

"Hello, wild mountain woman. I've arrived at Dulles a few days early and just made it out of customs. Hope you don't mind. Thought I'd drive up to your mountain retreat instead of meeting you in DC."

Emmy hoped she didn't mean tonight. "Of course, I don't mind."

"Shall I take a cab?"

"You could if you wanted to spend a fortune. It would be better renting a car."

"Oh, you of all people should know I can't drive on the wrong side of the street."

Emmy laughed, recalling what it was like to be a passenger with Becca. "So why did you fly in early without calling me?"

"We finished the shoot, and they cut my last scene. They're discussing a script for next season where I get back at my husband over the affair by sleeping with a nineteen-year-old student? I don't think I want to play that kind of professor. I do want some spicy scenes, but I don't want to go from everyone's darling to a tart."

Emmy had to laugh again. "Remind me, what exactly was your character in *London at Night*?"

"Ha, ha, aren't you the cheeky one?" she replied as Emmy reminded her of the old show.

Becca's first major television role featured her as a tough detective working the night shift to bring down the underground drug trade. As the ratings slumped, the scripts had progressed to a lot of skin including a simulated sex scene without a thread of clothing on. Emmy had never let her live that one down. Her newest show was going strong, and her fan base was exploding.

"Okay, Becca. So, you are at Dulles, and we both know you can't drive worth shit even back home."

"Smart-arse!"

"There are several good hotels near the airport. I can pick you up around noon tomorrow. How does that sound?"

"Bloody perfect because I've had enough of trains, planes, and automobiles for a while, and an indoor heated pool sounds lovely. I don't suppose you've got that in West Virginia? I believe the lingo might be a cement pond." She cranked the last sentence out in her best *Beverly Hillbillies* imitation.

"Ah, now look who's being a smart-arse. Sorry but you've caught me at a bad time. I need to go. Text me your hotel info, and I'll see you tomorrow. Bye, luv."

Emmy had not been in any serious relationship since Heather's death, and she wondered how Becca would react to the news about Jordan. Still, she had to have faith in her best friend—they'd been through hell and back together.

Over twenty years ago, Emmy had caught her then-girlfriend with Becca, who apologized immediately saying she did not know the woman was in a relationship. Then the damn girlfriend proposed a threesome. Both Becca and Emmy turned her down, and Emmy dumped her. A couple of days later, Becca and Emmy met again when they were called in for questioning at the police station. Unbeknownst to them, the ex-girlfriend had been dealing in stolen credit card information. After the police were satisfied and released them, Becca and Emmy shared a pint at a nearby pub and eventually became best friends.

Later, Becca introduced Emmy to Heather, an old university chum. When Heather was dying, it was Becca by their side, and it was Becca who helped pick Emmy back up after she buried Heather. Their friendship never faltered and grew stronger. Unlike some, neither believed in friends with benefits. They became blood sisters and stayed in touch even when they lived hundreds of miles apart.

Emmy smiled. *I think Becca's going to like Jordan.*

Jordan couldn't believe how nervous and excited she was about Emmy's arrival. She had been prepping since yesterday. Today, she fidgeted about the kitchen trying to make everything flawless. All the dishes were Italian to honor part of Emmy's heritage. As she floated around, her thoughts split between cooking and Emmy. There was more simmering than the braciole in the tomato sauce.

The chemistry was right between them, and Jordan was sure tonight would be the turning point. They had known one another for over six weeks, and while it was hot and heavy at times, they had yet to sleep together. Jordan had never been nervous before, but Emmy wasn't simply any woman. She could feel it in her heart and bones—Emmy was special, and Jordan wanted tonight to be perfect.

She tore herself out of daydreaming. *Wine. I need a nice red.* Rushing to the basement wine cellar, she scanned her stash of exceptional bottles. *Ah, that's the one.* Tonight was time to celebrate a new start.

She bounded back up the steps. Her body tingled in anticipation. On the last step, she heard the soft knock. Swallowing hard, she put the wine down and opened the door.

"I'm sorry for being a tad late."

Jordan's heart fluttered at Emmy's voice, and her loveliness took Jordan's breath away. Emmy wore an azure-blue sweater that made her hazel eyes pop. Her long blond hair fell past her shoulders, and a deep red lipstick accentuated full lips. As Jordan ogled, Emmy's arm swung from behind her back, presenting a bouquet of yellow roses.

"Thank you." Jordan stepped aside. "Please, come in. Oh, love that sweater."

"Yes, it's one of my favorites." Emmy smiled warmly. "Your home is gorgeous. And this kitchen, wow."

Jordan put the flowers in a vase and hung up Emmy's coat. "Part of the privilege of being a chef is to design a well-equipped playroom. Have a seat." Jordan gestured to the comfy barstools at the gigantic island.

"What? I don't see you in private for a couple of days, and you forget how to kiss me?"

Like a switch that was flipped, Jordan stepped toward Emmy and delivered a fiery kiss. As their tongues mingled, Emmy ran her fingers through Jordan's hair and moaned. After a couple of minutes, they broke contact.

Jordan stroked Emmy's face with her fingertips. "Better?"

"Oh my, much. I see the shy woman has been put back in the box and the tiger is out to play. Now I have to sit down because I am flushed."

Jordan grabbed her again and nuzzled her neck. "Your perfume tonight has hints of jasmine and roses," she said after kissing her sweet spot.

"Umm. The way our greeting is going, we're not ever going to get to dinner. Not that I mind."

One more sumptuous kiss later and Jordan released her.

"Wine?"

"Yes, please."

Jordan poured a healthy portion and laid out the appetizers.

"I need to finish the last dish. Feel free to roam around. I'll join you in a sec."

As Jordan moved toward the stove, Emmy picked up the bottle of Rioja and gasped.

"Is there a problem?" Jordan asked. Emmy's eyes were wide open.

"Jordan, this is a Spanish Marques de Riscal Reserva 1945!"

"It's my best red," Jordan replied nonchalantly.

"This is too expensive."

Jordan reached over the bar and intertwined her fingers with Emmy's. "You're worth it." She grinned wickedly. "However, as much as I'd like to impress you by telling you I bought this special wine just for you tonight, that would be bullshit. So let me quickly tell you the bullshit reason that Ms. Dumbass—me—has this wine."

"Wow. Okay."

"The wine was to celebrate my anniversary with Luciana. It was never opened because another round of her infidelity popped up. I thought about pouring it down the sink, but I didn't have the heart to waste a thousand-dollar bottle of the world's finest." Jordan moved in closer. "While I could resell it, I'd rather share it with someone special, like you because you are worth it. And that is no bullshit." She kissed Emmy again.

"Her loss, my gain."

Jordan turned toward the stove to work on dinner. "Please, feel at home. Explore."

Emmy wandered into the living room that flowed off the kitchen while savoring the flavor from the crystal glass. The house was an eclectic mix of style. Her eyes roamed to the high vaulted ceiling, the elegant timbers, the stone fireplace, and the warm furnishings. A unique glass wall with a French door composed of two stained glass panels separated this room from another that had a large bookcase from floor to ceiling on one wall and a baby grand piano. Emmy walked up to examine the multicolored panels. They were composed of various rectangles and other geometric shapes. She ran her fingers over pieces of the panel. Some were smooth while others were rippled. It added the right splash of color to the room.

"You are an excellent stained glass artist. The geometric patterns are simple yet exquisite."

"Thank you."

"How did you ever find this house?"

"I didn't. I designed it and hired a structural architect to make sure it was built soundly."

"Impressive." Emmy pointed to the instruments. "Do you play?"

"Mom plays the piano, and Carter plays guitar. I amuse myself. To be honest, I'm dreadful. Good self-therapy though. You're welcome to check out the other levels."

"I'd rather relax and watch you cook."

As the evening unfolded, they enjoyed the various courses of dinner by candlelight, hands frequently touched, and their conversation grew more personal. Jordan revealed more about the relationship with her family, and Emmy opened up more about Heather and how Becca had been such a close friend.

The romantic mood was heightened when they shared dessert and coffee in front of a blazing fire. As the fire warmed them, Emmy gathered the plates and cups and sat them down on a nearby table. "I never fully repaid you for the earlier greeting." Her hand stroked Jordan's cheek and played with her hair. The kiss that followed sent an explosive charge through Emmy's body.

The caresses intensified, and Jordan lightly brushed Emmy's chest through her clothing while her mouth moved down Emmy's neck. As inhibitions fell away, Jordan's cell rang. With one hand, she unsuccessfully fumbled to shut it off. Grunting, she broke away.

"I'm sorry. That's my mom. I have no idea why she's calling. Be back in a few." Standing, she pointed her finger at Emmy. "Please, don't forget where we left off." She headed to the master bedroom to take the call in private.

Jordan was annoyed at the interruption, but it was a weekday. As far as her mother knew, she was sitting around. She was thankful there was no emergency and ended the call after a few minutes. Before returning, she lit several large candles and turned down the bed. Every fiber of her body told her that Emmy felt the same way.

Returning to the great room, she found Emmy standing still at the picture window gazing into the dark night. Jordan wrapped her arms around her waist and nuzzled against her back. She was gripped with shock as she realized what Emmy was intently looking at. Yep, it was snowing. It wasn't supposed to start until tomorrow afternoon. Not only had the forecasters screwed up again, but the flakes were enormous and falling rapidly. There was at least an inch on the deck already.

"I told you we had bipolar weather around here."

"Becca arrived early. She's at a hotel near Dulles. I'm not sure I can pick her up tomorrow. I hate driving in snow."

"I can help. Besides the snow, we've both had too much wine. You should spend the night."

Emmy turned into Jordan's embrace. "Yes. In fact, I had already warned Betty Jean not to wait up because I was hoping for a long, luxurious, unforgettable night."

Jordan's mouth stretched from ear to ear, and the butterflies fluttered in her stomach. "Ah, Ms. Russo. What are we going to do all night long? We could finally play cards. We never did even though you mentioned it once. Or we could role-play. I know you're not wearing a costume. Did you bring the handcuffs?"

"My, my, you really are a tiger tonight. I do like this bold side."

"Somehow you seem to cast a spell on me. I want to get into as much trouble as possible. Yet I'm not sure where to start."

"Now you try to play innocent. I don't think so."

Jordan guided Emmy to the oversized sofa. The two women feasted on one another's mouths as hands glided through hair. Desire rose, and Jordan flipped Emmy down on her back and laid kisses from her neck down to her exposed cleavage.

"Oh, God." Emmy gasped. Her voice was low, and her breaths came out in quick bursts. "You're such a tease."

Jordan locked her gaze on Emmy's face. Her fingers traced Emmy's lips then delicately moved over her chin, down her neck, and over her chest before stopping at the top button of her blouse. She waited. When Emmy grabbed a handful of her hair and pulled their mouths together, Jordan's nimble fingers took care of the blouse.

Turned on by Emmy's moans, she broke the searing lip-lock and moved down Emmy's body. When she had Emmy breathless, she stood and offered her hand. "The bed's more comfortable. Besides, the room is warmer, and there's more space for thrashing around."

"Oh, I do like the sound of that."

They stole small kisses and hugs while making their way to the bedroom. Once there, Emmy threw Jordan down on the bed then masterfully stripped off Jordan's blouse. With the same loving attention, she tenderly made her way down Jordan's body. At Jordan's chest, Emmy kissed and bit each of Jordan's nipples through the bra. Jordan encouraged her on by placing her hand in her hair and firmly massaging her scalp.

Emmy placed further soft kisses down Jordan's torso then slipped off the bed and dropped her slacks before removing Jordan's. Her hands glided over the thin fabric between Jordan's legs, and she glanced up at Jordan as if to say, "Beg me."

"Oh my God, who's the tease now?" Jordan said through a whimper.

"Uh-uh. Sit up on the side," Emmy commanded.

In a lustful haze, Jordan did as she was told. Emmy stood in front. With her bra straps hanging, Emmy demurely asked, "Do you like what you see?"

"Yes."

Jordan held eye contact as Emmy unhooked the bra and let it drop to the floor. She trembled when Emmy stepped between her legs, her breasts tantalizingly close to her mouth. Yet Emmy maintained control, firmly resting her hands on Jordan's shoulders. Jordan ached to touch the heavy, firm breasts and lick her light rosy pink areolas and flawless lily-white skin.

Emmy stepped back. "Can you finish undressing us?"

Jordan slid off the bed and eased Emmy's panties down to the floor while placing light kisses along the way. When she began to bury her head into Emmy's core, Emmy grabbed her by the hair to stop her.

"Your turn. Slowly please."

Jordan rose and took off her bra and panties. Facing one another, inches apart, they gently explored. The contrast of her dark skin and Emmy's pale creamy breasts drove Jordan to the edge. Throbbing with excitement, she tightly pressed flesh against flesh and kissed Emmy ravenously. Her hands roamed unable to satisfy her urge quickly enough.

Emmy broke it off and shoved Jordan onto the bed. "Lie back and relax," she said, wagging a finger. "I'll be right back."

Jordan was confused. *Damn, she's had me on the brink several times. What now?*

When Emmy returned carrying two silk neck scarves, Jordan was pleased.

"You told me to bring handcuffs. I figured these would do. Lie down and obey me, and I promise you won't be disappointed."

Positioning herself on top, Emmy loosely tied Jordan's wrists to the bed frame. When Jordan stretched out to take a mouthful, Emmy pulled away.

"I'm in charge. You're going to have to tell me how bad you want it."

"Please."

"Please, what?"

"Please, before I explode."

"Ah, now that's better."

Emmy rubbed her pelvis against Jordan and leaned forward. Soon, Jordan slipped out of the scarves.

"Uh-uh. What's the magic word?" Emmy sat up.

"Please, let me touch you!" Jordan pleaded through labored gasps.

Emmy twirled Jordan's hair, and her lust-filled eyes bore into her. Her body began to grind harder. Jordan's hands squeezed the well-endowed breasts and kneaded the taut buds. At the right moment, Emmy would bend farther, allowing Jordan to take a mouthful. Jordan eagerly sucked one while kneading the other.

As the breathing grew heavier, Jordan flipped Emmy on her back. She kissed Emmy's face and neck with an unquenchable thirst as her hand slid down Emmy's body and teased the apex of her desire before entering the wet folds. With long, teasing strokes, she dragged her mouth down Emmy's body until she was positioned over her throbbing core. Taking a firm grip on her hips, she made soft swirls around her clit with her tongue before sucking forcefully.

Emmy clinched Jordan's hair and breathlessly shouted, "Don't stop. Please don't stop."

The plea delighted Jordan. She worked hard to hear Emmy cry out in sheer pleasure. Each gasp and muscle contraction drove her on. When Emmy exploded, Jordan gradually eased off until Emmy's body relaxed and her breathing calmed. Jordan scooted up and lay next to her with her face propped up on one bent arm. Her fingertips delicately drew circles on Emmy's stomach.

"Did I please you?"

Emmy's eyes popped open. "Oh. My. God. Yes. That was bloody amazing, and I thought I was the one in control."

Jordan shot her a look with a mock appearance of sternness. "It's my house. You play by my rules. I let you think you were in control."

"Is that so? Well, I'll have to let you take control more often because I seem to have gotten the better deal."

"Oh, I'm not entirely sure. It was enjoyable to please you, and my body was tingling all the way."

"Well, I didn't hear you cry out. So, I'll have to correct that." Emmy rolled on top of Jordan, and her hand gently glided over Jordan's skin and cupped her sex, gently stroking.

"Harder please." Jordan moaned.

Emmy lavished Jordan's upper body and slipped two fingers into Jordan's core. Jordan whimpered and groaned as Emmy sucked her breasts while applying just the right rhythm and pressure. When Jordan was close to climaxing, Emmy's mouth moved down. While rubbing, she deftly nibbled and sucked Jordan's center.

Jordan moaned louder as the tempo quickened. "Keep going," she begged. "That's perfect. Right there." Her muscles tightened, and her breath hitched. She pleaded with Emmy through gasps. "Harder." When her body began to uncontrollably pulsate, she could not suppress her small screams, and her body jerked with the climax. Soon both women lay on their backs, their energy spent.

Emmy rolled over into the crook of Jordan's arm. "Happy?"

"Absolutely. I like a girlfriend who equally gives and takes pleasure."

Emmy's eyes lit up. "Girlfriend. Is that a passing title or shall I count on that outside of the bedroom?"

Jordan smiled and kissed her forehead. "I don't know. You're more refined than me. Will you have me as your girlfriend?"

"Depends. Can you make more time for me?"

Jordan giggled. "Yes. I don't want to go to sleep, but we're going to have to shovel snow tomorrow and get your friend at the airport."

"I don't need much sleep."

"That suits me."

They cuddled and made love again before falling asleep early in the morning. Jordan reveled in Emmy's warmth. It all felt so right.

Chapter Fourteen

Jordan quietly rolled out of bed and took a minute to watch Emmy peacefully sleep. After Spain, she had avoided emotional attachment and never thought anyone would fully capture her heart. Now here was Emmy. This new beginning was more than sex. A sense of safety, hope, and happiness mixed with friendship and desire filled Jordan, and the emotions were more intense than anything she had previously experienced.

In the bathroom, she stared into the mirror. Relationships were work. Going forward meant honesty and respect, showing gratitude, and putting the needs of others in front of herself. *Honesty.* Now more than ever, Jordan was determined to conquer her fear because she wanted Emmy in her life.

Jordan dressed and quietly slipped out and put on her cold weather gear in the foyer. Outside, she was met with a good five inches of snow. The forecasters had missed the mark again. After the strenuous shoveling, she went back inside to call Robby.

As usual, Robby sounded chipper. "Morning. What's up, boss? My town street has already been plowed, but I imagine I won't see you until later this afternoon."

"Mind if I take today off?"

"Hello. Hello. Who are you and what have you done with Jordan? I don't have much money to pay for ransom."

"Cute wisecrack."

"So, should I call someone to come help plow you out or do you already have someone who's there to help?"

Jordan smiled. "I can take care of it myself, and mind your own business." Emmy had also entered the room in Jordan's oversized plush robe—hair disheveled, no makeup, and looking gorgeous. "Robby, I have to go, but I promise I'll make the best of the day." She winked at Emmy and hung up.

"I felt a warm peace last night." Emmy flashed that beautiful smile and looked at the snow out the window, her arms around Jordan. "How are we going to get out of here?" she asked sheepishly.

"I'll have it plowed in no time with my blade on the SUV."

"Silly, your SUV's totaled. I don't think your plow will fit the Outback."

"Good point. Well, I've got a smaller blade for my ATV. We've got time. Let's have breakfast first, and I'll plow as you get ready. It won't take me long."

Emmy snickered.

Jordan furrowed her brows. "What?"

Emmy's snickering continued a bit before settling into a broad smile. "It shouldn't take me long to freshen up as I slept in the nude. I have no clean clothes or toiletries here. If you forgot, then let me refresh your memory." With a sultry look, she stopped at the door and dropped the robe, beckoning Jordan to follow before disappearing into the bedroom.

All kinds of fireworks lit Jordan's body, and bells and whistles rattled through her head. She hurried into the bedroom as best she could. Last night under candlelight had been amazing; today in the light should be earth-shattering.

They were a bit late picking Becca up, and they planned to blame it on the snow. Stepping into the lobby, Emmy found

Becca and the two women hugged as if they hadn't seen one another for years.

"Damn, it's bloody cold here. I might have to get another coat. Want to have a drink before we go?"

Emmy smiled. "Another time. Jordan's waiting in the Subaru because we couldn't find a parking space."

"Jordan?" Becca cocked one eyebrow.

"Yes. I've met someone here."

"Wow. You've been here a month and already hooked up. So, I assume by your smile that this Jordan and you have become intimate." Becca might be reserved and polite to the public, but she had a habit of losing her inhibitions when speaking to her dearest friend.

"I've been here almost two months, and it's not a hookup. I really like her." Emmy bumped her friend.

Becca abruptly stopped and grabbed Emmy's arm. "I get it. This is what the wild and wonderful West Virginia motto means. I must be careful since I'm taken."

Emmy punched her in the arm. "Come on, silly. Tell me how is Olivia?"

Becca was silent. When Emmy glanced at her old friend, she saw Becca's jaw tighten and feared bad news. Becca and Olivia had tied the knot almost two years ago and always appeared to be the perfect couple.

Becca bit her lip and finally spit out. "It's a little complicated right now. Let's talk about it later. So, where's your new girl?"

The two walked out of the lobby chatting, and introductions were made. "Emmy didn't mention you were the BBC drama actor Rebecca Young," Jordan said as they shook hands. "A friend of mine back in Spain had the hots for you and watched whenever you were on. She was so happy when you came out."

Becca smiled. "Well, Emmy never told me she was dating a cutie who was a master chef at one of Madrid's hottest restaurants."

"You're not a wacko culinary groupie, are you?"

"Ah, I fancy good food. My agent is always getting on me to drop a few. He was cheesed off when I gained one bloody half-stone on holiday, but I love my bangers and bitter, and I have been known to go on the piss." Becca had shifted to a harsh working-class accent, and Jordan clearly had no idea what any of the slang meant by her twisted expression.

Emmy swirled around, arching her eyebrow.

"What?" Becca chuckled. "Sorry, just messing with you. Let me say it in some words a Yankee like yourself might understand." As if on cue, Becca replied in an upscale London accent. "What I said was that I enjoy food. I gained nearly eight pounds during my last vacation, and my agent was extremely upset with me. While I love gourmet food, there's nothing like a sausage with a cold beer. I've also been known to get extremely intoxicated from time to time and outdrink my friends, including the men." The women laughed.

The trip home was entertaining, to say the least. Before arriving in Oakville, a call came in on the vehicle's Bluetooth.

"Hello."

"Hi, Jordan. Is Emmy with you?"

Emmy piped up. "Yes, Auntie. You're on speakerphone."

"Hi, dear. The furnace has quit. I'm going to stay with a friend until it's fixed because that woodstove just doesn't keep me warm upstairs. Jordan, is it possible they can stay with you until it's repaired?"

"No problem, Betty Jean."

"See you girls later. Bye."

From the backseat, Becca leaned forward between the bucket seats. "Awkward. I hope you two don't make too many loud sounds."

Emmy whipped around. "Becca, mind your manners."

"You of all people should know I have none."

Becca had always needled Emmy with jokes whenever possible.

It was a good sign and meant Becca was comfortable around Jordan.

Jordan reached out and squeezed Emmy's hand.

She smiled at Jordan and settled into her seat, relishing the thoughts of them making love the night before and this morning. The clean boy shorts Jordan had given her were stretchy and comfortable, and she was wearing one of Jordan's blouses.

When they reached Jordan's driveway, Becca joked once again. "Do you wild mountain women have running water? Or will I be forced to use an outhouse."

Jordan snipped, "Please stop cracking jokes."

"Sorry, mate. Just having a bit of fun. I don't mean to offend." Becca meekly replied.

"I know you intend no harm, but please stop. There is a social group of women in our county that are called the Wild Mountain Women. They are lovers of the great outdoors, and my mother is one of them."

Becca's impish grin turned to stone-cold horror. "Oh, my Lord, my apologies. I honestly did not mean to offend."

Emmy tried to lighten the mood. "You'll have to forgive Becca. She lives in Brighton on the south shore. Obviously, the elevation of Oakville is high enough to drain the smarts out of her brain."

Jordan remained stoic. "Anyway, I know you had no idea. Many of them, like my mom, watch BBC shows. You don't want to insult someone, especially a fan."

"Absolutely. I won't mention it again. Sorry."

"No harm was done. Let's forget about it."

"I've got fans here?" Becca asked astonished.

Jordan chuckled. "There's another joke folks don't like to hear. I will share it with you but don't repeat it!" She smirked and glanced between Emmy and Becca. "Satellite dishes are the official West Virginia state flower. And yes, they pick up BBC shows. I'm sure you have fans here." The somber mood was broken as all the women laughed.

As they crested the last hill, the mountain house looked like a stylish mix of tradition and modern architecture with stone, timbers, and lots of glass.

Becca let out a whistle as she stepped into the house. "Nice. Warm, inviting, spacious, and modern."

"She did a fantastic job with the design." Emmy threw her arm around Jordan kissing her on the cheek.

"Your room is on the lower level. Plenty of privacy and an entertainment room with a flat screen." Jordan motioned toward the stairs.

Becca cracked up. "Ah, now I know. You're going to put me in the dungeon for being a bad girl."

"Precisely. Emmy can show you to your room. You can get settled while I work on dinner."

Chapter Fifteen

*H*alf-asleep, Jordan slipped on the pajamas that had been hastily thrown to the side the night before. She almost leaned over to kiss the top of Emmy's head but decided to let her sleep. Jordan grinned. Putting Becca in the downstairs basement bedroom gave everyone privacy. They certainly needed it since Jordan and Emmy had made love into the wee hours of the morning.

As she moved into the kitchen, the smell of strong coffee filled her nostrils. *Gee, this could grow hair on my chest.* She sniffed the pot and cringed, then tossed it down the drain.

While the coffee brewed, Jordan slipped on her coat and stepped out onto the deck for some fresh air. The foul smell of cigarette smoke hit her immediately. Becca was sitting on the patio wrapped in a blanket looking out at the mountain. The obnoxious smoke curled upward and ruined a perfectly tranquil morning. Jordan retreated back inside.

By the time Emmy sauntered into the kitchen, Jordan had breakfast on the table. Emmy walked up behind her and gave her a soft hug and kiss on the neck.

"Smells good."

"I hope you like your omelet southwestern style."

"I love anything you cook." Emmy brushed her hand through

Jordan's hair, down her back, and gave her butt a squeeze.

"Heh, no hanky-panky. Did you forget your friend is staying in the house with us?"

"Is she even up?"

"I saw her on the patio outside the guest suite puffing on a cancer stick."

Emmy scrunched her eyebrows. "She hasn't smoked for years except when she gets really upset."

Jordan kissed her softly on the lips and changed the subject. "I'm sorry I work so much. I wish I could go with you and Becca to DC this weekend."

"Me too."

The reality that Emmy would be living part-time in DC bothered Jordan. Would their new relationship fizzle? Was her paranoia based on her own past in DC? Why was this bothering her now? Then it occurred to her: Becca's strong coffee with cigarette smoke reminded her of the wretched smell of pool halls and the dark corners of DC hangouts.

Her sadness must have shown. Emmy leaned in and played with her hair. "Jordan, she's helping me find a place. We are friends and nothing more. Trust between us is essential for our relationship to grow."

"I believe you. I just hate to see you leave Oakville."

"It's a part-time job."

"I know. What I mean is"—Jordan bit the corner of her mouth—"I'm afraid this small town won't hold your interest, and I'll never see you again."

Emmy cocked her eyebrow and wrapped her arms around Jordan. "You'll be seeing me on long weekends, and I expect for you to visit me in DC. And yes, this town is small and quirky but it has its charms, especially one who has chocolate-brown eyes, silky skin, and a captivating personality. Of course, cuddling and mind-blowing sex will have me crawling back."

"What was that about mind-blowing sex?" Becca whizzed around the corner.

Emmy snapped, "Oi, is your mind always in one place?"

"Yes. So, carry on. Don't let me interrupt the entertaining conversation. Speaking of delicious, which one's my plate?" Becca grinned. Emmy picked up a piece of apple and threw it at her.

"Food fight," Becca howled and picked up a slice of banana.

"Ladies, please. Not in my kitchen."

"Oh my, she sounds like a stern nun." Becca's mouth drew up in an exaggerated pout.

"This kitchen is my sanctuary. Keep it clean." Jordan's voice was firm, yet, her half smile gave her away. "Throw that," she said, pointing a finger at Emmy, "and I'll give you a spanking."

Emmy smiled and threw the piece of apple at Becca.

Emmy was looking forward to spending time with her old friend but hated to see Jordan leave for work. While she had not said the words, she was falling hard and suspected Jordan felt the same. She ravaged Jordan's lips and was delighted that Jordan did not protest even though Becca was still standing on the front porch.

"Oi, it's bloody freezing out here, and you two have to come up for air sometime."

Emmy reluctantly parted from Jordan and addressed Becca. "Yes, Mum."

"Come by for dinner tonight, please?" Jordan asked. "Say around seven thirty. I'll cook you something special."

"With sweet anticipation."

Emmy stood in the driveway as Jordan drove away.

"Gee, Em, you've got it bad for that woman. I haven't seen this puppy dog love since—" Becca stopped herself.

Emmy's eyes softened. "Since Heather. You can say it."

"Blimey, you're over the half-century mark. Sure you can handle her?"

Emmy swatted at Becca. They went indoors and refreshed their hot drinks. Emmy was surprised when Becca stood and went to the bar to spike hers with a shot of brandy.

"It's only ten," Emmy scolded.

"Here, but its three p.m. at home."

"By the way, what's up with the cigarettes? You haven't smoked in years."

"Ah, did Jordan rat me out?"

"No. Your clothes still reek. You're lucky we let you sit down to breakfast. What's up? I asked you about Olivia yesterday, and you avoided my question. Are you two having problems?"

Emmy could tell she hit a nerve as Becca sighed then threw another splash of brandy in the cup before sitting on the sofa with a thud.

"I love her."

"Yes. I believe you two should be celebrating your second anniversary soon. Why the long face?"

Becca sat up and took a healthy swig of her spiked coffee. "She wants a baby."

Emmy shrugged. "So? I thought you two had talked about that possibility before and you were receptive to the idea. Or were you holding back your true feelings?"

Becca's face scrunched up, and she bit her lip. "She wants to get pregnant soon. Like right away." Becca's voice rose in volume with a tone of near panic, and her words spilled out faster. "Pregnant, Em! A tiny life-form that cries and shits and eventually talks back when it becomes a teenager. Crikey, we'll be old when the little snot is at university!"

Becca's tone startled Emmy. "I don't think you're going to endear yourself to Olivia by referring to a child as an 'it' or 'little snot.'"

"Dammit, Em. I don't want a child!"

"Okay, but have you told her? As in calmly sit down and talk about the pros and cons. Have you honestly thought about her point of view?"

"Pros? Are you listening?" Becca's face was red. "I don't want a child, let alone a tiny baby."

"Shit, Becca, avoiding a life-changing conversation is not going to solve anything. For Christ's sake, don't throw away your love because you haven't thought it through. Muster up some bravery and talk to her. Olivia deserves the courtesy. And ignoring her and her feelings is downright cruel. You're not an asshole, so stop acting like one." Emmy knew Becca well enough to understand she didn't want to end her marriage. She pushed harder. "Are you sure you don't want a child? You've got enough money to hire a nanny and for Olivia to stay at home."

"Guess you'd know my money situation since you're still my port-folio manager." Becca rubbed her face. "It's not about money, Em. And yes, it scares the crap out of me." She squared her body to face Emmy and raised her eyebrow. "By the way, how old is Jordan?"

Emmy rolled her eyes. "It's not the same thing."

"That wasn't my question. She's younger than you. I can tell. How much younger?"

Emmy sighed. "She turns forty next month."

Becca beamed. "She's got a little cougar crush going."

"Twelve and a half years is not a big deal to me. Sharing the same core values and heading in the same general direction in life are more important than age. Now stop deflecting. We're talking about you and Olivia."

"Yeah, it's easy to dish but hard to take. Think about you and Jordan. She's young enough. Does she want to ever have a child?"

The thought had never crossed Emmy's mind. Yet, she knew it was a good point. "I'm not sure."

"Ah-ha, I got you on that one. See, not so easy, is it?" Becca's eyes were gleaming now.

Emmy rose to refill her tea. "I'm not the one married. You are."

Becca huffed. "Let's move on. Talking about Olivia and the little snot is depressing."

Emmy shot Becca a harsh look. "Stop being an asshole!"

"Fine, I'm joking. I'll think about it...the situation...possibility... whatever, and I'll not call a baby a little snot. Let's move to neutral ground. What about DC? Do you have things lined up for Friday and Saturday?"

Emmy booted up her laptop. "The agent sent me a custom pdf with several properties. We've got a day and a half to tour them. I booked two rooms at the Hotel Palomar for both nights."

"Jordan knows, right?"

"Yes, I've been trying to entice her to take the weekend off, but no luck. Here. Look through this pdf and tell me what you think."

"Em, I hate to point out the obvious. The long-distance thing is seriously going to crimp your new relationship even if you both cut your working hours."

"Jordan is special, and I'm not only talking about her killer body. I want to make it work. The job is only part-time, and I can work on my private financial business anywhere."

"Sorry, mate. Didn't mean to hurt you." Becca patted Emmy's hand. "I've missed you. Before India, you used to drop by the set occasionally, and we'd have a monthly dinner while you would make my eyes cross talking about my financial situation." Becca laughed. There was a bit of silence before she spoke again. Her voice cracked. "I looked forward to you moving back to the UK after the India job. Now you're here." She gave a halfhearted smile. "If the fireworks shooting out from your entire body are any clue, I'd say you might be staying in America for a lot longer than the job requirements."

"That's a distinct possibility, but I never abandon my old chums." She wrapped her arm around Becca's shoulder. They needed to get the apartment hunting out of the way. Yet as the job date came closer, the move was beginning to worry her.

Chapter Sixteen

*R*obby peered over at Jordan and walked to her station. She was not prepping according to the menu. Oblivious to her surroundings, she spread duxelles onto homemade crêpes then transferred two large seared beef tenderloins onto the crêpes and wrapped them.

"Yum. Beef Wellington."

She jumped. "You snuck up on me."

"Sorry. I didn't know you accepted special orders. Do we have British VIPs visiting?"

Jordan shrugged. "Friends who are British. I thought I'd cook them something special since it's slow."

Robby got a kick out of ribbing Jordan. "Well, if you don't mind, please fix some extra. I'd like to have some later."

"Sure thing. Oh, any chance I can take this weekend off? Being short notice, I understand if it's not possible."

"Hmm, let me think." Robby put on a serious face and rubbed his index finger against his lips. He was enjoying purposely making her wait. "Several days off, fixing a special dinner, and contemplating taking the weekend off." He grinned. "Anything I should know?"

"Nope." She scrunched her shoulders and turned toward the spice rack, partially hiding her face.

"Why I think that'd be wonderful. You can use a little R & R."

Robby slapped her on the back and walked away chuckling to himself. He could see a positive change in Jordan. She seemed happier and carefree lately. He was certain of one thing. Whoever was coming to dinner tonight was in for a culinary delight prepared with love and joy.

An hour later, Robby was worried. The maître d' had just announced Robby's wife had arrived for dinner. He was in shock and silently kicked himself for his careless stupidity. He had called Linda earlier, gossiping almost like a teenager. He never thought she would come to the restaurant to spy on Jordan's friends.

"Wow," Jordan said to him after hearing Linda had arrived. "That's good luck. There's plenty of food. You and Linda should join us."

"That's a lovely idea, Jordan, but we wouldn't want to impose on your dinner."

"Please, I insist. There's plenty of food. The staff can handle any orders that come into the kitchen this late at night."

He nodded. "I'll start setting the table." Walking into the dining room, he gave his wife a wicked look and whispered, "This is pretty low, Linda. Jordan has now invited us to eat with her guests. Don't you dare tell her I called you. Look as if you are utterly surprised and in awe." He shuffled about, helping put together the table. They had just sat down when Jordan came out of the kitchen.

"Linda, nice to see you again." The two hugged. "How's your dad doing? Has he fully recovered from his fall?"

"Wonderful. Thanks for asking. Yes, he's hopping around like nothing happened."

As the two friends released their embrace, Emmy and Becca entered and were ushered to the table.

Jordan hadn't planned on this twist for the evening, but she vowed to make it through. After all, if Robby and Linda were her friends, they wouldn't care one way or the other.

"Robby and Linda, I'd like you to meet my friends, Emmy and Becca."

Jordan's mind quickly shifted. How would she handle possible probing questions? The thought didn't linger long as the radiance of Emmy washed over her. After half a glass of wine, she excused herself to the kitchen to finish the meal. She brushed off Robby's insistence to help. Before departing, she absentmindedly squeezed Emmy's shoulder.

Promptly at eight, she brought out the meal. Everyone was laughing and having fun as if they were old friends. Linda had recognized Becca from the BBC soap operas and peppered her with tons of questions. At one point, the two were deep in character and scene discussions. The laughter helped Jordan push aside her worries. These were her friends.

Robby hopped out of his seat when he saw Jordan's hands full. "Sit down and enjoy yourself. I'll carve the meat."

She took him up on his offer and sat along the plush wall bench next to Emmy. Her leg brushed up against Emmy's, and she suppressed a deep intake of air. The touch made her want to drop everything and take her home now.

"I poured you a glass of Rioja. I thought it would be good to aerate for more flavor," Emmy whispered and slipped her hand under the table as Jordan was adjusting her linen napkin. "Although, it's not as satisfying as the other night."

Jordan squeezed Emmy's hand. "Thank you."

Throughout the evening, Emmy and Jordan casually touched from a friendly pat on the hand above the table to Emmy brazenly slipping her hand under the table to caress Jordan's upper thigh. Since the conversation, laughter, and wine flowed, Jordan didn't think anyone caught on. The more it occurred, especially under the tablecloth, the more intense her feelings became. Jordan had never taken risks like this before. It was wildly exciting and maddening all at once. Thank God, Linda and Becca carried most of the conversation.

They lingered past the restaurant closing with everyone having a jolly time. Soon, Jordan went to excuse herself to help clean up the kitchen.

"Oh no, you don't." Jo appeared out of nowhere and gently nudged Jordan to sit. "I've got it covered. By the way, I hope you all left room for the dessert." A waiter placed the almond-and-jam-flavored Bakewell pudding on the table. Another was right behind with fresh coffee and tea.

"Bon appétit."

"Wow, I thought I was coming to a Spanish tapas restaurant. You've gone out of your way to fix a scrumptious traditional British meal, and that's one of my favorite desserts. Thank you for the hospitality." Becca beamed.

Emmy laid her hand on top of Jordan's. "Yes, thank you. I didn't expect such lavish food. Thank you for taking the time."

"You're welcome." Jordan glanced at everyone, but her gaze lingered on Emmy.

It was almost ten thirty when the group rose to depart. Jo assured Jordan that everything was under control. "Skedaddle, you all, before I get the broom and chase you out."

Jordan gently placed her hand on the small of Emmy's back as everyone was saying their goodbyes. She gushed watching the sparkle in Emmy's eyes and how everyone was at ease and jovial. All at once, she noticed a figure looking in through the front picture window. Her blood ran cold. Outside, the creep stood with his face pressed up to the glass, grinning at her in his camouflaged jacket. At least he wasn't wearing the damn sunglasses. She thought his eyes were light colored, but it was impossible to make out details from this distance. Yet, she was not going to give him the satisfaction of returning his glare.

She had to get them out of here. "It's been a pleasure but I'm beat, and Emmy's got some chores tomorrow for her aunt. Becca hasn't gotten used to the time and needs to catch up on sleep." She was pushing Emmy, not too harshly but with a purpose.

Emmy leaned over. "Are you in a hurry to get me into bed?"

"Yep." Jordan chanced another look back at the window. He was gone. All she wanted was to get home. Tomorrow, she'd order security cameras for the house and have maintenance performed on the restaurant's system. She'd also ask around. Maybe somebody had some information about this vagabond. She hoped he wasn't a mental case.

Robby slid into the passenger seat. "Well, that was a fantastic meal and evening. Now we know her special guest is a famous British actress. Although, I would never have known if it wasn't for you watching those BBC shows."

Linda giggled. "You've got to be kidding."

"What?"

"You missed it, silly."

"Missed what?"

"Her special guest wasn't the actress. Her special guest was that blond Emmy that she was flirting with all night."

"Flirting? What are you talking about? I didn't hear any flirting going on?"

Linda roared in laughter. "Darling, it wasn't verbal. The stolen glances and the brushing of hands. Emmy continuously touched Jordan when making a point. She didn't do that with Becca."

"What?" Robby was dumbfounded. Jordan and Emmy knew one another better, but he was sure the special meal was for the famous actress.

"From the look in Jordan's eyes, I'd say she and Emmy are

quite an item." Linda stopped laughing and dropped her voice. "And I think hands were under the table a time or two."

"You're speaking like they are lovers."

"Well, I'm thrilled that Jordan has finally found someone. There's not exactly a large population of gays in our community. Emmy seems so sweet, and they're such a cute couple."

Robby scrunched his face up. "What gives you the idea Jordan's a lesbian? Linda, you've got to be careful."

"Don't tell me you've got a problem with it!"

"No! I think the world of her, but I don't think she's gay."

"I can't believe you're that blind. Yes, Jordan's a knockout and every man, no matter what age, notices. Yet, she pays them no mind other than to be the polite, smiling proprietor."

Robby looked at her in his befuddled innocent way. "What in the world makes you think she's gay? Because she doesn't date much?"

"She doesn't date at all. Plus, I've caught her eyeing a few women a bit longer than normal. She always follows up with a compliment on jewelry or clothing. And don't forget, I had a lesbian friend in college. I've got a little gaydar."

Robby's mouth hung open, and he leaned back in the seat. As Linda drove off, he pondered whether Jordan was gay or if Linda was off her rocker. He valued his friendship and business association with Jordan and only wanted the best for her. And if looks and mannerisms were any measures, then Emmy had a boatload of beauty and style, and her humor dazzled everyone.

Becca was giggling in the passenger seat.

"What are you cracking up about?"

She couldn't stop herself and soon had Emmy joining in. Their uncontrollable laughter went on for several minutes.

"Stop it. I have to drive, you lunatic." Tears rolled down Emmy's face. "What's so funny anyway?"

"Oh my Lord." Becca caught a couple of deep breaths before continuing. "You two were like a teenage couple on a date."

"No, we weren't."

"You flirted with her all night, and she ate it up. I thought the idea was to keep things quiet until next month?"

Emmy knew she had flirted with Jordan but played coy. "It's in your head."

"I'm positive that Linda picked up on some of it. I'm not sure Robby did. Like most guys, it likely went over his head."

"Okay, but don't say anything. She's come a long way in accepting and loving herself. I don't want her to lose that courage, and I don't want to frighten her."

Becca made a gesture of zipping her lips.

"I mean it, Becca. Promise me."

"I promise."

About that time, Jordan pulled up in front of Emmy's car. All Emmy could think about was getting into bed and snuggling. She didn't believe in love at first sight, but that theory was being blown to hell. She was going to miss Jordan this weekend.

Chapter Seventeen

*T*apping on the door interrupted Emmy's sleep. She rolled over and glanced at the clock. *Seven, freaking seven.* After yesterday's exhausting apartment search, she wanted to sleep late Saturday morning.

She closed her eyes and pulled the extra pillow over her head, but the knocking continued. *Maybe, it's not my door.* Even though Becca was helping, Emmy missed Jordan. In truth, she was a little dejected that Jordan didn't take time off and join them. *Sleep. Need more sleep.*

When the tapping grew to an irritating thumping, she snapped out of the warm bed and trudged through the room. "Whoever it is, better have a damn good excuse. If it's Becca, she's toast." Squinting out of the peephole, she saw Jordan and instantly perked up all over. She swung the door open and stood with her hand on her hip.

Jordan thrust red roses toward her. "For the most beautiful woman in the world."

Abruptly, Jordan's mouth dropped, and her gaze traveled down Emmy's body.

"I'm delighted you changed your mind. Are you going to come in and undress me or are you simply going to do it with your eyes?" Jordan continued to gawk. "Enough." Emmy grabbed her by the coat collar, pulled her inside, and shut the door.

"I missed you," Jordan said through a breathless kiss. "You're beautiful."

"Even with my wild morning hair?"

"Even with your hair. Your cute tight white tank top and skimpy black bikini underwear thinly disguise my treat underneath." Jordan brushed her hand down Emmy's front then lifted the shirt to kiss her nipples.

"You're skilled, but I doubt you can hold a bouquet in a vase with one hand and make love to me with the other."

"Umm. Watch me," she said through a mouthful.

"Jordan, the scene in *Imagine Me & You* with bodies sprawled over roses may have looked sexy, but I don't fancy thorns in my bum. And spilling the water from the vase is not what I think of as wet. Although you're doing an excellent job getting me there." Emmy ran her hands through Jordan's hair.

"I'll put them down, and we're going back to bed. I want an early breakfast of you." Jordan put the roses on a table near the window and turned on a lamp. The soft light illuminated the space. "Now I can admire my catch."

Emmy grabbed Jordan's hand to guide her to the bed. "Becca and I have lunch scheduled at eleven with the realtor followed by apartment hunting. So let's make every minute count."

The apartments the realtor showed them were a tad out of Emmy's price range and not in the locations she preferred. She had hoped to live near her job. Things were not turning out as she imagined. DC was much more expensive. Like every city, people around here saved by living farther out and paying the price with a killer commute time and auto expenses. If she wanted to be within Metro or walking distance, she'd have to pay more, a lot more. By the end of the day, she was looking forward to a good meal.

"The valet has the vehicle waiting for us out front. After you." Jordan motioned to the door. She had an extra spring in her step and a wide grin.

"We need to wait for Becca."

"She won't be coming tonight." Jordan stepped closer and whispered, "I've planned a romantic dinner alone with you. Shall we go?"

"Oh, yes." As they stepped out to the curb, Emmy lit up. "You got a new SUV!"

"Yes, a Subaru Forester. It's practical, a great retail value, and handles like a champ in the snow. Do you like it?"

"Love it."

They held hands on the way to the restaurant, and all Emmy could think about was how perfect her hand fit into Jordan's.

The next day, Jordan and Emmy were sleeping soundly in one another's arms when the phone rang.

"Oi, you two coming to breakfast? It's eight thirty, and the place is filling up. Should I get us a table?"

Emmy glanced at the clock. "Shit."

"Pardon?"

"Sorry. We slept in. See you in half an hour."

Emmy ended the call and slapped Jordan on the rear. "Up lazybones. We have to hustle. We forgot to set the alarm." Jordan groaned as Emmy ran to the shower.

Downstairs, breakfast was rather quiet, and Emmy figured that everyone was exhausted. She and Jordan had nearly finished while Becca was pushing her food around on the plate. *Is she thinking about a child with Olivia again?*

Jordan extended a handshake across the table. "Becca, it's been a pleasure to spend more time with you. I wish you and Oliva all the best. You're welcome to visit anytime."

"Thank you for everything, Jordan. Perhaps we will visit in the spring or summer."

Jordan slipped her arm around Emmy and kissed her on the cheek. "See you later. Drive safe and give me a call after you drop Becca at Dulles."

Emmy smiled at Jordan's tender display of public affection and grabbed her shirt, pulling her in for a proper kiss. Emmy loved how she was relaxed in the city and hoped it would continue after she came out at home. "Bye. See you soon."

Watching Jordan walk away, Emmy was infatuated and oblivious to Becca's presence until she cleared her throat. Turning, she found Becca studying her with a weak smile. She expected Becca to break out in a giggle or crack a funny remark at any time, but her friend's smile faded and was replaced by a dark scowl. Her eyes were an odd dark color.

Emmy scrunched her eyebrows. "What's bothering you, Becca?"

Becca sipped her brew. She tapped her fingers on the table before gesturing to the waiter for service. After asking for fresh tea, a sullen Becca leaned back and crossed her arms. Her eyes bore into Emmy.

Emmy was concerned. "This isn't like you to give anyone the silent treatment. Speak your mind."

Becca stiffened, rested her elbows on the table, and leaned in to look Emmy in the eye. "You're my best friend and a sister I never had. I know Jordan makes you happy, and it's good to see you enjoying life again. But please, take it slow. Think about what it would mean if you two became serious. Jordan doesn't strike me as a woman who wants to leave her town, and I can't see you living in Oakville even half the week. How soon would living there in the backwoods of America wear off?"

Emmy's hand flew up. "Stop right there!" A few heads in the restaurant turned.

In a whispered shout, Becca snapped, "Get real, Em! You're a city girl, and you've lived your entire life in Europe."

"No, I haven't."

"Two or three weeks on vacation or visiting your American cousins doesn't count."

"Jesus, Becca. I work in a traditional, male-dominated field. I put up with all kinds of crap. And the last post in India was not exactly a hotbed of thrills. Populated yes but still misogynistic and culturally different from other places I've lived."

"Well, I bet more lesbians were hiding in the clubs and western hotels in Chennai than in Jordan's remote neck of the woods."

Emmy pursed her lips. "Perhaps, but I ran across few because it is a lot more dangerous to come out in India than America. And that's not the point. If I fall in love with Jordan and decide to be with her, I could be very satisfied in her small town. She's amenable to me working in DC three days a week. We'll make it work."

"She's not out yet, and you don't know how that hick town is going to react. She might even change her mind about the two of you and go back into that wee tiny closet."

Emmy's blood pressure was rising, and she stared Becca down. "I won't abandon her. She's taken a brave step, and I'll be there for her. It's no one's business what *we* decide is best for us." Becca started to open her mouth, but Emmy cut her off. "And for your information, we've talked about our differences. She is interested in traveling with me and has promised to take more vacations."

"And what about Jordan? She seems a little more outdoorsy than you. Do you have enough mutual interests to meet her needs?"

This time, Emmy didn't hold back. She pounded her fist on the table and practically shouted loud enough for the whole restaurant to hear. "What the hell? Is this the Medieval Inquisition? You've gone over the line!"

Many more heads turned, and in the commotion, they hadn't noticed the restaurant supervisor had come up to their table.

"Ladies. You two look like bright women to me. Please, control your volume and language, or I'll have to show you the door. Am I clear?" They each nodded their heads like sullen children and went back to silently sipping their tea.

Emmy set her cup down and casually draped her arm across the back of the chair even though she was still hot with anger. The fingers of her other hand aimlessly drummed on the tabletop as she glared at Becca. Never had they fought like this before, and Becca had never been so personal or so cruel. *What gives her the bloody right to talk to me that way? What's stuck up her arse?*

Becca broke the ice after several minutes and reached out for Emmy's hand. Emmy withdrew, slumped back in the chair, and defiantly crossed her arms over her chest.

"I'm sorry, Em. I had no right talking to you in that tone."

"Damn right," Emmy tersely replied. She had calmed down a smidgen but was still fuming.

"You've got to think about these things before—"

Emmy bristled and leaned forward. "Before what?" she replied quietly through gritted teeth.

Becca let out a long breath and bit her lip. "Before you fall in love and move here permanently. It may be too late judging by the interaction between you two. I've never seen you so...so enamored with anyone else before except Heather. And there's nothing wrong with that. It's been such a short time. Again, I'm sorry. I just met Jordan and should not have jumped to a big conclusion in a shitty manner. Please, be careful. Take it slow. Make sure. I don't want to see you hurt."

"I'm a big girl, Becca."

"Yeah. Again, sorry. I care too much for you. Forgive your bestie, please."

"Apology accepted." Emmy's body relaxed some, but her muscles were still tight. She pointed a finger at Becca and said in a loud whisper, "Don't ever again presume to tell me, how I feel or what would make me happy. This isn't a rebound relationship if that's what you think."

Becca raised both hands. "Fair enough."

"No, seriously, Becca. We've been best friends for how many years? Even best friends change and grow over time. It was you and Heather who loved to dance. I could take or leave the clubs and the city. And West Virginia is not Siberia. As far as Jordan, I've made it abundantly clear that I like hiking, but I draw the line when sleeping in a tent. She picks the hikes, and I pick the hotel."

Becca chuckled. "No doubt with a world-class spa," she said through a wide grin.

Emmy finally softened. "Absolutely. A girl has to have her wine, massage, facial, and manicure." Emmy smiled and picked up her napkin, throwing it at Becca who was still chuckling. She didn't dare confirm Becca's suspicion that indeed, she was already crazy in love with Jordan. Instead, she spoke of today's impending tasks. "Let's talk about more pleasant things, or you'll have to find another ride to Dulles." She lowered her voice. "I know. Maybe I'll get you in the car, go to the backroads, dump your arse, and make you walk."

After a few seconds, Becca reached out her hand. Emmy accepted and let her anger go. They had been friends too long to let this come between them.

Chapter Eighteen

Since New Year's Day, Jordan had spent practically every spare minute with Emmy. As each day passed, it was getting harder to hide her glee, and Emmy didn't deserve to be in the shadows. Jordan made a solemn promise to change next month. Today, Emmy had agreed to be introduced as a friend at the family gathering.

It dawned on Jordan that this was the first time she had brought a friend over in years. Of course, she didn't feel the day they hit the deer counted. Overall, Jordan was pleased that she was not freaking.

As Emmy drove past the road to Gwyneth's house, Jordan said, "Where are we going?"

"I promised to pick up the project notes for Betty Jean. Remember? That's why I wanted to leave early."

"Oh, yeah." But when Emmy turned into the state park, Jordan's throat constricted.

"The woman left them at the desk of the lodge. It shouldn't take too long."

Driving slowly up the windy road, one of the park's best scenic points was on the passenger side. Jordan's breathing nearly stopped. It was the spot where some friends took the Polaroid of her and Karen. Other than the high school yearbooks, the Polaroid was the only photo Jordan had left. Jordan touched the pinky ring that Karen had given her as a birthday gift, closed her eyes, and leaned her forehead against the window. She jumped when Emmy touched her thigh.

"Are you still nervous? We could have a drink at the lodge then head over to your mum's house."

"No. It's okay."

Jordan remembered what she had learned from the book *Learning to Fall: The Blessings of An Imperfect Life*. Essentially, Simmons had said that acceptance was the beginning to live fully. The pathway was to let go of fear and embrace love and compassion by opening our hearts and minds to the beauty and gifts that life has to offer. She opened her eyes then reached over and brushed Emmy's cheek with her fingertips. The day would come when she would let go and tell Emmy and others about Karen. Right now, she had to tackle one thing at a time, and today, she was determined they would enjoy themselves. It was a setting where Emmy and the family could start to get to know one another before Jordan dropped the big bomb.

"Jordan. Oh, Jordan." Emmy snapped her fingers to break her trance. "We're here."

"Ah, sorry. You were saying something."

"I was saying that Betty Jean and I saw your mum with Carter's children the other day in the grocery store. They're cute and well behaved."

Jordan smirked. "They are cute but as for well behaved"—she sighed—"they can be a challenge. At Mom's house, they turn wild because she spoils them rotten. I have some earplugs in the glove box if you'd like to bring them along."

"Amusing. I'm sure tonight will be fun."

While Emmy appeared to be looking forward to the evening,

Jordan's thoughts kept running a million miles a minute as she wondered how they would receive Emmy. Her body was beginning to tense up.

Emmy laid her hand on Jordan's leg. "Take a couple of deep breaths. It's only dinner."

Jordan managed a lukewarm smile as they got out. Once inside, Emmy was a social butterfly and fit right in. Everyone was interested to know how Betty Jean was getting along, then Aunt Elizabeth launched into a long-winded story. Taking advantage of the distraction, Jordan walked up to Carter who was shoving a deviled egg into his mouth.

"When did Dave start coming to dinner?"

"This is the first time he's been to a family dinner besides community BBQ. I wonder if he and Mom are dating."

Jordan choked on her drink. "You're joking, right?"

"Why? Doesn't Mom deserve some happiness?"

"She does." Jordan stumbled over her words before finally spitting out, "But we hardly know him."

"Yes, but from the looks of it, Mom seems to know him pretty well." Carter grinned widely as he stressed his last words. "And I'm betting you're a little uncomfortable with the thought of Mom having a physical relationship."

Jordan's face contorted. "Ah...I...okay, you're right. Don't need that visual. New subject." Jordan was about to say something else before they were called to the dinner table.

Everyone was warm and receptive. Gerry and Anne were their usual reserved and standoffish selves. While the kids usually did not eat with the adults, tonight they were sitting nearby at makeshift tables. The young ones were acting as if they had eaten only sugar all day. The noise ground on Jordan's nerves. She guessed Grammy and Poppa had turned down their hearing aids.

Dinner went smoothly, but the kids became excited again with the cutting of the cake. The noise level was out of control.

Gwyneth stood and tried to calm them down but was unable to control the ruckus.

Dave stood. "If you all don't hush up, there'll be no cake and ice cream for any of you. I'll take it all home. Please sit and use your indoor voices." The kids instantly sat at attention.

At six foot four inches with a deep rich voice, Dave was a guy who commanded attention. Jordan had met him on a few occasions when he was working at her mom's house. *Damn, Carter must be right. I wonder how long they've been dating.*

The kids were relatively calm as they stuffed cake into their mouths. Dave smiled and motioned to Gwyneth.

She rose, gazed into Dave's eyes, and was now glowing. "I have an announcement to make."

Oh, shit.

"I want to thank you all for coming tonight. Other than major holidays, it's rare that we are all together. Emmy, welcome to our home." She raised her glass. "A toast to the family and friends, and good health and happiness to all. Cheers."

Everyone raised their glasses or coffee cups. "Cheers."

Gwyneth did not sit down. "I also want you all to know that Dave is much more than my friend. We've been seeing one another for over a year." She brought Dave's hand to her lips. "I'm a lucky woman. This kind man makes me very happy, and I want you to know that we're getting married."

Everyone gushed with good wishes but Jordan. She made no attempt at hiding her slack-jawed expression. Emmy sharply elbowed her to wake up. Jordan mumbled, "Congratulations," trying to sound sincere but could not ignore the thoughts tumbling around her brain. *Christ, Mom's sixty-eight. I don't need a dad.*

After the dessert plates had been taken away, Gerry focused his attention on Jordan. "Well, Jordan. You're the last one. Looks like Mom's going to tie the knot before you even get serious. Why don't you relax a bit and take some time off from that restaurant? You deserve a good man, and I'm sure Mom would enjoy more grandchildren."

Jordan bristled at the comment and said nothing. Carter never stuck his nose in Jordan's business, but Gerry was another matter. He also brought men around the restaurant from time to time to introduce them.

"Cat got your tongue? Why you'll be forty soon. You should date and hook someone. You're almost too old to start a family."

Jordan wanted to reach out and smack her brother. Instead, she glared at him.

Gwyneth stepped in. "Gerry, that's enough, and stay out of her business."

"Mom, it's true. If she doesn't do something soon, she'll be too old to have children. How about you, Emmy? Got a fella back in England?"

Carter rose from his chair. "I think I'll have another piece of cake. Anybody else?" The kids went nuts drowning out Gerry. Anne stepped in, said no, and sent them out of the room.

Thank God. Jordan exhaled. *They don't need to be wound up anymore.* They rushed out, and it was quiet once more.

"Sis, another piece of cake?"

"No, thank you, Carter, but I think Gerry could use a big piece." *Smeared all over his face,* Jordan thought as she glowered in Gerry's direction.

Emmy leaned over and whispered in her ear. "Let it go. It's not worth it, and he hasn't a clue."

Carter continued to divert the conversation. "Mom this dinner was the best, and I am so happy for the two of you. Let's have another toast." He picked up his coffee cup. "Oops, we need more coffee too. Angie, why don't you help me?" He jabbered away about the upcoming basketball season as he poured. Thank God, it worked.

Eventually, things died down, and the night drew to a close. Emmy nudged Jordan and whispered in her ear, "Be nice. Wipe that look of shock off your face. Their bliss is no different than us deserving happiness."

Jordan swallowed. Emmy was right. They were the last to leave. Jordan finally broke into a big smile and hugged them both tight. "I wish you both all the best. You surprised me. Dave, you seem like a great guy, and I know Mom has excellent judgment in people, so welcome to the family." She stuck her hand out for a shake, but he grabbed her and drew her in for a bear hug.

"Your mom will always be your mom, and you kids will always come first." He pulled Jordan away at arm's length with his hand gently on her shoulder. "Don't worry. I'll treat her right. This woman deserves the utmost love and respect."

Outside, Jordan handed Emmy the keys. "Please, drive. My brain is fuzzy, and I'm beat."

Jordan was quiet most of the way home. Emmy occasionally reached out to squeeze her leg.

Finally, Jordan spoke. "I'm happy for her. I am. I had no freaking clue. And...I admit it's my mother. They're both adults, and it's none of my business, but the idea of my mom...you know."

Emmy laughed. "Yes. You know human beings are never too old to enjoy a happy and healthy sex life. They both strike me as private people. I'm sure they wanted to enjoy each other's company without everyone gossiping and judging. Just like we want to explore our relationship in private."

"Yeah, I know." She let out a huff. "And Gerry was his usual ass."

"Yes. When are you planning on getting barefoot and pregnant?"

"Christ, that's all he thinks about. It's like I'm nothing without a man to take care of me."

"He's not going to change. Smile and ignore him. It's your life."

"I try, but it's so uncomfortable around him. I hate it when he's preaching his brand. If it weren't for Grammy and Poppa and Carter, I'd probably have killed him before now. Mom's too soft on him, but that's another story."

They rode in silence a little longer. "You're good with your nieces and nephews. How do you feel about children?" Emmy asked.

Without warning, Emmy slammed on the brakes. They weren't going fast, only about thirty-five mph down the backwoods county road. The headlights shone on three does and two fawns off to the side and dangerously close to the road. The deer stared at them as if to scold Jordan and Emmy for interrupting their evening before moseying across. Finally, their white tails pointed up, and they dashed into the meadow.

"Sorry. I figured you wouldn't want your new SUV to hit another deer. I caught them out of the corner of my eye."

Jordan's pulse was up a few notches. "Yeah. Beautiful creatures. Too damn bad they aim for my vehicle all the time."

Emmy pulled over on the shoulder and put the vehicle in park. Her movements were slow. She unbuckled her seat belt then Jordan's.

"When Becca and I were talking the other day, she asked me about children."

Jordan furrowed her eyebrows. "I don't follow."

"She bluntly pointed out that there might be issues between you and me."

"Now I'm lost."

"I know our relationship is new, but you're young enough to have a child. Have you ever wanted to start a family?"

Jordan's eyes popped. "Whoa! Didn't see that coming. I've had almost one heart attack tonight. Are you pushing me off the edge?"

"It's a question couples discuss. That's all. Jordan, I care for you. Deeply. I want to be your girlfriend. Not in the closet. Out and proud."

"I'm serious. I'm going to do it next month. No more hiding, I promise, but let's get back to this family question thingy because I'm a little confused. Is this a condition for us to become official?"

"No. I've seen what it's done to Becca and Oliva and thought we should talk. Before my heart gets totally overcharged, I want to know if starting a family is important to you. Pushing the topic off until later—"

"So, you think I want to have a baby?"

"Do you? Ever?"

Jordan puffed up her cheeks and blew out the air. "I thought about it once, a long time ago, but I enjoy my freedom too much. Even if I was out, I'm not sure dragging a kid through the bullying from others would be fair. *And* I don't relish the idea of my body going through all the hormonal changes let alone the physical stretching and God knows what." She paused and swallowed. "Yet the more the years roll past, the answer looks like a firmer yes." Jordan looked out the side window, so Emmy could not see her face. When she couldn't take Emmy's silence anymore, she snickered. "Yes, I've thought long and hard about getting a four-legged baby or two." Cracking a smile, she leaned over and cupped Emmy's face. "That's as far as I'd go. Would you agree to a puppy? And only a puppy."

Emmy smacked her leg. "You freaking had me on edge there."

Jordan gave her a toe-tingling kiss. "So, what's your answer?"

"Yes, but let's see how we handle the first puppy before considering a second."

"Agreed. Now let's get home and start a fire. It's freezing."

"Hmm. Like the sound of that. Home."

When they pulled into the driveway, it started snowing again.

"Oh my God, not again. I move to America and all it does is snow."

Jordan glanced at the weather app on her phone as Emmy opened the garage and parked the Forester. She burst out laughing.

"What's so funny?"

"We're supposed to get three to six inches."

Emmy looked stunned. "Bullocks. No way. That's crazy."

Jordan shook her head as her grin grew wicked. "So, doesn't look like you're heading back to Betty Jean's tonight." She waved the phone in the air.

"Let me see that."

When Emmy grabbed for the phone, Jordan held it away and kissed her neck.

"Oh, you know how to drive me crazy. What else do you intend to do to me?" she said in a frisky tone.

"I will be sure to wear you out first, and tomorrow we can make room in the closet for your clothes."

Emmy pulled Jordan's face inches from hers. "Are you asking me to move in?"

"Yes. Well, as many nights that you can spend without Betty Jean complaining." Jordan rubbed their noses together before putting a peck on the tip. "You make me deliriously happy. Please say yes."

"Positively, yes. Let's go inside. I need wine and cuddling. Tomorrow we can rearrange my closet."

It took a second for Jordan to hear the words. "Your closet?"

Emmy chuckled. "Our closet. God, I can't resist teasing you, but I've got an idea."

"What?"

"The one who falls asleep first tonight loses and gets less closet space."

"You're on."

Chapter Nineteen

The morning light crept in through the crack of the drapes as they lay on their sides facing one another under a pile of soft blankets. Emmy's hand drew lazy circles up and down Jordan's arm.

"Open your eyes and snuggle with me."

Jordan opened one eye. "You spent every last drop of my energy last night. And I'm not asleep. I'm relaxing and in deep thought."

"What are you thinking?"

Jordan sat up. "I was thinking about a friend back in Spain. He was out, loud, and proud. A guy who never had an unkind word to say about anyone. He said I would find strength and my voice when the time was right. He also said that if I hesitated out of fear for too long, life would slip by. I'm not going to lose you, Emmy. You mean so much to me." She rolled on top of her and nuzzled her neck. Jordan's hand wandered down Emmy's silky skin.

"That tickles."

Jordan laid kisses from her forehead down her body. "So soft."

"Feels good but this morning breath has to go, and it might be more fun with a little bathing foreplay." Emmy ran her fingers through Jordan's hair. "Come, take a long hot shower with me, and I'll make it worth your effort."

Jordan bolted out of bed. After brushing teeth, they cuddled under the rain can.

"Let's take it nice and slow," Emmy moaned.

With the warm water rushing over them and the steam rising, they bathed one another, kissing and nipping every little spot with soft strokes as they lathered. Emmy inched it up a notch by gradually opening Jordan's legs and soothingly rubbed the delicate folds. The smell of orange, white musk, and vanilla in the shower gel mixed with the scent of sex.

Jordan replied through small gasps, "Don't stop."

The massage drove her close to the brink, and her hands roamed down squeezing Emmy's ass. Her tongue darted in and out of Emmy's mouth.

Unable to take it any longer, Jordan groaned, "More."

Emmy turned off the shower. "I want you in bed, now."

They dripped water on the hardwood floor along the way. Jordan didn't care. Her body's temperature and pulse were escalating, her body tingled, and Emmy's scent filled her. It was more than the smell of mouthwash and shower gel; it was sweet, and she could taste it in her kisses.

"Lie back. Let me pleasure you," Emmy whispered.

Her mouth lavished Jordan's body. Her fingers delicately roamed, unleashing a firestorm within Jordan on every spot she touched.

"Please," Jordan shouted.

There were no more words, only moans as Emmy moved down to her core and took her hard and fast. A couple of fingers adeptly found Jordan's G-spot, lightly applying pressure in small strokes as Emmy's tongue nibbled Jordan's upper body. Her nimble fingers began to move faster and deeper, and Jordan arched to meet every stroke.

Emmy continued to pump Jordan, but the luscious assault of her mouth stopped, and she whispered, "Open your eyes. Look at me. I want to see you when you come."

Jordan's heart thumped more as they locked eyes. She saw a look of desire, contentment, and love on Emmy's face. Emmy's hands thrust deeper, and Jordan quivered, unable to look away even as she cried out moments later when several waves crashed through her. Emmy did not stop as Jordan's muscles tightened around her fingers with each crescendo. Jordan's eyes fluttered for a second.

"Focus on me, sweetie."

Again she concentrated on Emmy's eyes as she writhed about. The look of satisfaction on Emmy's face pushed her over the final peak. When Jordan's body went limp, Emmy slowly withdrew her hand. They maintained eye contact. Finally, Emmy kissed each breast and her mouth before leaning upward on one elbow.

"Did I start your morning okay?"

Swallowing and willing her breath to slow more, Jordan had never loved Emmy's eyes as much as she did right now. They twinkled from the delightful ravage she had completed. "You're welcome to start my morning like that any time you please," Jordan said. She felt the gentle caress as Emmy's fingers moved from her stomach and rested on her chest.

"Your heart's still pounding," Emmy murmured.

"I hope you don't expect me to move anytime soon because you've drained my energy again."

"I thoroughly enjoyed being the source of your happiness, but this time, I'll relax you."

Emmy's fingers worked magic as they moved to massage circles in Jordan's scalp and occasionally to rub her shoulders and back of her neck. Soon Jordan's entire body eased into a slower rhythm. She also relished in the softness of Emmy's body lying partially on top of her.

"What in the world did I ever do to deserve you?"

"You're pretty amazing yourself," Emmy whispered into her ear. "Thank you for opening your eyes during sex. They are the window to the soul and display more than lust." Emmy rubbed the delicate cheekbone below Jordan's eye with the thumb of her free hand. "There are scientific sexuality studies on how humans express themselves through their eyes. Did you know our pupils dilate during climax? At that moment, you gave yourself to me in complete trust. In fact, I believe it was your eyes that first revealed your interest in me."

"Ah-ha. You're after my eyes and body. What about my intellect?"

"Yes. Love the whole package, but it's the eyes that never lie."

They made love again as morning blazed on. Afterward, they spoke of the future. They were happy.

Midmorning, Jordan rose to cook breakfast. Emmy listened to her humming and watched her beat eggs, vanilla, and cinnamon together. As Jordan dipped the bread in the mixture and laid it onto the griddle, Emmy snatched a few berries from the nearby bowl.

"Silly, you're going to eat all the fruit. French toast isn't as good without the berries."

Emmy put one large one between her teeth, leaned in, and Jordan's mouth opened.

"See, I share." Emmy then cradled Jordan from behind.

"I love hugs, but it's hard to cook when you're wrapped around me so tight."

"Umm. I don't want to let you go."

Jordan flipped the toast, and without warning, she stopped and her muscles tensed. After a couple of seconds, Emmy spun her around.

"What's wrong?" She saw a look of terror on Jordan's face. Jordan didn't answer. It was like she was frozen. Emmy heard a low hum and felt a vibration. Then there was a loud scraping noise.

Jordan swallowed, put down the spatula, and looked at the floor. "It's a snow plow."

The roar of the truck and the scraping grew loader. Emmy didn't recognize the woman in front of her. The laughter was gone, her face was ashen, and she wasn't looking her in the eyes.

"Who's plowing your drive?"

"It's got to be my brother Carter. Let's get dressed. I don't want him to see us in robes."

Emmy's body tightened as Jordan grabbed her by the hand and dragged them into the bedroom. Jordan frantically picked up their dispersed clothes off the floor and opened the armoire. She tossed clean clothes at Emmy. "Put these on."

Emmy loved the happy Jordan who accepted herself. The happy Jordan she made plans with. She didn't like who she saw now. The smell of something burning interrupted her thoughts.

Jordan finished pulling a sweater over her head. "What are you waiting for? Get dressed."

"The French toast. Did you forget?"

"Oh, shit! It's burning."

"How perceptive," Emmy said with disdain.

"Please just get dressed," Jordan shouted over her shoulder as she ran to the kitchen.

Jordan heard the honk followed by the thumping of Carter's footsteps on the stairs, and the knock on the door. When she didn't immediately answer, he rang the bell several times. The ear-splitting ding ding ding finally got her to move. God, she wished she had never hung that cast iron bell. Carter was the last one she should be worried about. Still, her pulse pounded, and the rush of blood through her veins seemed like every valve in her heart was going to erupt. She took three deep breaths.

"I'm coming. Hold your horses." She opened the door hoping she didn't look as ghastly as she felt.

"Hi, sis. I was wondering if you could cook up one of your famous omelets for your hungry little brother." At six foot two inches, he towered over his tall sister. "Didn't mean to disturb your peaceful morning."

Forcing an embrace and a smile, she ushered him in.

He wrinkled his nose. "What's the burnt smell?"

"I got preoccupied with something and burnt some French toast. Coffee?" She rarely botched a meal and certainly, never anything easy like French toast.

"That'd be great. Mine went lukewarm a couple of hours ago."

"What drags you out so early?" she muttered.

"I'm plowing for the county for some extra cash. Been out for nearly six hours. Can I have hash browns, bacon, and toast too?" he asked, begging with puppy dog eyes.

"Sure."

Jordan laid out three plates and poured three small glasses of orange juice. It was an awkward moment without an explanation. She didn't know what to say. He picked up his cup and looked a couple of times between the place settings and her. Then his face burst into a bright red.

"Sorry. Looks like I barged in on something."

Jordan's face grew warm. They both tended to blush, but Carter's skin tone was lighter than hers. He resembled the European Spanish side of grandfather Simón while Jordan had the slightly darker Costa Rican side of grandmother Simón. So for him to turn so deep only twisted her gut more.

"Ah...no worries." Jordan stiffly replied.

Emmy entered the kitchen and gave Carter a hug. "Nice to see you again."

"Likewise."

In a stilled voice, Jordan asked, "What do you want in your omelet?" She insisted they sit and enjoy themselves by the fire while she cooked.

Carter took the suggestion. Jordan stole glimpses from the kitchen. Thank God, he relaxed as Emmy chatted and laughed. Everything was normal but Jordan's behavior. Even when she called them for breakfast, she still could not shake the feeling. It was like she had two separate bodies and brains, each contending for the fight-or-flight nerves to take over. She was cooking on autopilot. It wasn't her best but not as bad as the French toast. At least, it didn't look bad. She couldn't remember if she had properly seasoned.

"Looks great, sis."

As they ate, Emmy continued to be composed and engage Carter in pleasant conversation. Jordan didn't budge. From Carter's occasional glances, she could tell he was worried. She had to do something. Her mind raced.

Emmy contained herself. The hurt and angst inside her mixed with rising anger threatened to boil over. After the tender moments they spent together and the dreaming, Jordan was now falling apart. She told herself to calm down and wait. Maybe, Jordan would snap out of it, but as she and Carter carried on a conversation, she became more of a zombie. Emmy had the urge to reach over and slap the shit out of her. If Jordan couldn't face Carter, then how was she going to deal the rest of her family? Emmy silently begged for Jordan to come to her senses.

Abruptly, Jordan broke the silence. "Carter, I don't want to lie to you. At least not anymore." She gripped Emmy's hand.

Jordan's eyes bore into her. There, Emmy saw the love mixed with concern, but most of all, she could see the vulnerable moment when Jordan decided to let down her guard. Jordan was choosing to love and trust herself. Emmy squeezed to nudge her on.

In a voice calmer than Emmy would have thought, Jordan said, "I'm a lesbian, and Emmy is my girlfriend."

Carter finished chewing the mouthful he had bit off and swallowed then broke out into a grin. "Wow. I was wondering what was going on. You've been so damn uptight since opening the door." He stood and tousled Jordan's hair then kissed her forehead. "I love you."

Jordan jumped up and gave him a bear hug. A few tears fell. She started to sniffle.

Carter broke their bond. "Stop looking sad. You're my big sis. If Emmy makes you happy, then it was meant to be. I was just"—he laughed—"worried that I had...you know..." He looked embarrassed. "But I don't blame you. Emmy is extremely attractive."

In an instant, Jordan froze then whacked him hard on the arm. "You're married."

"Yeah, but I still have eyes." Carter winked at Emmy and quickly added, "And I can clearly see you two are right for one another. That's what I meant, Emmy. I didn't offend you, did I?"

"Not one little bit. I know what you meant." She winked. "I'm quite happy with your sister."

Jordan hugged Emmy tightly. "I'm so sorry. You probably didn't expect a big scaredy-cat. I promise to get better."

Emmy felt a little guilty for being mad. Even though Jordan and her brother were close, he was the first relative she had come out to. *Be patient.*

When the emotions finally settled down, Carter said, "I wish you both only the best." He grinned wider. "Now if you don't mind"—he pointed to his plate—"I'm hungrier than a lumberjack. Can you make me some French toast without burning it?"

Jordan jokingly punched him, and he sat back down.

Emmy kissed Jordan's cheek. "You're an amazing person, but

I have to agree with your brother. I'm hungry, and I've never had your French toast."

Jordan laughed and kissed Emmy softly on the lips. "Coming up."

"Gee, sis. Pretty weak kiss. You'd better improve, or Emmy might dump your ass."

Soon, they were back on track with jokes and conversation about everything from sports and Carter's kids' activities, to the upcoming Redbud Spring Festival. While more challenges lay ahead, it was obvious Jordan was finding some peace at last. The transformation was soothing.

After breakfast, Carter stood and stretched. "Gotta go. Angie knows I've stopped off for some good food, but I also promised to plow Mom's driveway before going home to sleep."

They walked him to the door. Emmy was pleased that Jordan held her hand comfortably.

"Sis, Mom always asks me how you're doing when she sees me, and I'm sure Angie has told her I was over here. I will tell her that you're doing well, but you should give her a break. In fact, she's probably already guessed." He winked. "She always knew what we were up to before anyone else. She's got that third eye and mom intuition down pat." He paused. His eyes had a serious look. "Tell her when you're ready. Just don't take too long."

Jordan hugged him. "I promise I won't carry this secret around forever. As for Gerry, I have no idea or if I'll ever be ready to tell him."

"Yeah, he probably will go berserk, but you know he's off the range anyway. Hold true to yourself. Don't let him drag you down. Stand up to him, and I'll be there with you, and I know Mom will be too." Carter kissed Jordan and opened his arms to Emmy. "Emmy, I'm happy my sister finally has met someone as sweet as you. Sorry if I startled you all so early. I promise next time to call ahead."

He wrapped around her tightly and kissed the top of her head. She could easily see why they were so close.

"I thank God you came into my life. You gave me the courage to come out to my brother."

"What you did was courage from within. You needed to do this for yourself and for us. I'm proud you acknowledged your true self and spoke out for our love."

Jordan was ready to burst as Emmy's words "our love" echoed through her head. "I had to take a deep breath and go for it. I was surprised at the relief I felt." Jordan quickly became solemn again. "I want us to grow as individuals and as a couple. This is just the beginning. I'm making the commitment to you. I'll follow through."

Emmy caressed the side of her face. "I believe you. But! You did have me worried there for a bit. I wasn't sure who was standing before me. I was torn between hugging you and kicking your ass."

"In the future, you'll probably have to do both. I'm far from perfect."

"I assure you, it will come easier." Emmy grabbed Jordan's jaw in a tight hold. "And don't sell yourself short."

"I promise I'll try to do my best."

"I know you will."

Chapter Twenty

Emmy groaned when the alarm woke her out of a sound sleep. The space next to her was cold, and she heard sounds coming from the kitchen. It had been several days and Jordan had gone back and forth with anxiety about speaking with her mother. Yawning, Emmy wandered into the kitchen. Jordan was at the table putting jam on toast. Her wrist moved back and forth aimlessly, and she didn't look up when Emmy entered the room.

"I'm sure the jam tastes the same no matter how many times you spread it over the toast."

Jordan stopped but didn't reply.

"It's the crack of dawn. Are you seriously going at this hour?" Emmy stretched to get her favorite mug out of the cupboard. "If you wait, I'll shower and go with you."

"No. I have to do this alone." The icy tone in Jordan's voice was the scared one from the other day.

Judging by Jordan's haggard looks, Emmy suspected she had been up for hours. She grasped Jordan's hand making her drop the knife. Neither Emmy's touch nor the clatter of the silverware snapped Jordan out of her mood.

"Jordan, look at me." The vacant look tore up Emmy's insides. She caressed Jordan's cheek with her hand. "Your mum loves you. You have nothing to worry about."

"I know, but I've been this fake daughter for so long."

"Stop right there!" Emmy clasped her hands around Jordan's face. "You are a hardworking, loving daughter. You're not fake, and no one is perfect. You're scared because you have not sat down to talk—like no bullshit talk—with your mum for a long time."

"Since high school."

"I know you're nervous, but you can do this. Your mum deserves to have her daughter back."

"So many years that have gone by." Her voice cracked. "So much that needs to be said. I don't know how to make it right."

"It all begins with one small step. Have confidence in yourself and speak from the heart. You can't change the past. What was that quote? Something about the present moment is an unfinished house. It's time to remodel and redecorate. Life goes on."

Jordan's muscles tensed and her eyes closed. When she opened them, they were brimming with tears. She nodded. "I have to go."

"Why don't you take an hour and calm down."

"Gerry's coming over around lunch to work on some odds and ends in mom's house. I don't want to risk running into him. I want to get it out of the way." Jordan stood and wrapped Emmy in her arms. "There's simply a lot for me to deal with at one time. Thank you for loving me." She gave Emmy a quick peck on the lips and walked out.

Emmy went back to bed but knew she wouldn't sleep. Today would be difficult for Jordan, and Emmy hoped she would stay strong. She was falling hard for this woman, and their relationship needed all of Jordan.

Gwyneth was surprised when Jordan called and asked to come over to talk for a couple of hours. She couldn't remember the last time they'd had a serious conversation. Jordan rarely shared anymore, and their talks were often lopsided with Gwyneth struggling to fill the gaps. They had to fix this.

At least, Jordan was happy whenever Emmy was around. Gwyneth warmed inside. Maybe Emmy was the one. Gwyneth had heard bits and pieces of positive stories over the years about Betty Jean's niece. She sure seemed like a wonderful person. Hopefully, today was good news.

She dressed and made her way downstairs. As she was swallowing her medicine, she heard the key in the lock and the creaking of the door. It was six thirty.

"Happy to see you, dear. You're extremely early. I'm not even sure my brain is functioning without the first cup of coffee."

Jordan gave a weak smile and hung up her coat. She sat in the breakfast nook with a thud.

"No walk today?"

"Sorry, Mom. I need to talk."

"That serious? Are you moving to Asia or something? You know I won't let you." Gwyneth's tease only resulted in Jordan forcing smile, and she gave no reply. Gwyneth patted Jordan's hand. "I baked chocolate-chip cookies last night. From the look on your face, I'd say we need to have some with our coffee."

Jordan had been a bundle of nerves thinking about how to break the news, but the cookies helped ease the tension. Chocolate-chip cookies were a favorite childhood dessert and were only served after dinner and no more than two apiece. The only other times her mom had allowed them was when serious conversations happened. Now was one of those times. After setting the table with two dessert plates and arranging the cookies and coffee, her mom put a box of tissues between them. *Mom always knows when something is up. How does she do that?*

"Love the new coffee pot. Brews fast and lets me pour midcycle," Gwyneth said.

Jordan didn't reply or look up from the table. They both fixed their coffee with cream and sugar in silence and chewed their first cookie. Although Jordan had rehearsed her words, the order was jumbled in her head, and her mouth was dry.

"This conversation isn't going to go far if you don't talk. I'm here for you, honey. I always have been." Gwyneth tenderly cupped Jordan's face.

Jordan slouched in the chair but dared not look at her mother for fear of losing control. "I'm not sure where to start," she mumbled.

"I do." She gave Jordan's hand a tight squeeze and didn't let go. "I love you, Jordan. You're the sweetest daughter any mother could ask for. Start anywhere."

There were a few more minutes of silence before Jordan faced her. "You know how everyone was upset that Carter and Angie lived together a year before they were married? It's kind of like that."

When Jordan remained silent, Gwyneth prodded. "It wasn't how my parents raised me, but Carter and Angie loved one another. Grammy and Poppa took some time to adjust. I think they did a pretty good job in the end. I liked Angie, and Carter was crazy in love. All I want for you kids and for my grandkids is happiness."

She hadn't expected anything different, yet these were the words Jordan desperately needed to hear. She nibbled her cookie again in silence.

"Who is the lucky person that has stolen your heart?"

Jordan had always used gender-neutral terms. She had become so used to it that she had forgotten when she started doing it. Now her mother had done the same thing. Come to think of it, Jordan had noticed Mom tended to do it in most conversations with her. *Maybe she does know.*

It was now or never. Jordan leaned forward and looked into her eyes. "Emmy." She swallowed hard and looked for any condemnation. "We've seen each other since the holidays, almost daily, even if it's a short visit at the restaurant."

Gwyneth's eyes twinkled. "Good. She's a sweet girl. So why the sadness?"

Jordan ran her hand through her hair. "I've always been a lesbian." A stab of guilt and pain ran through her and the nightmare from years past flashed through her head. She pushed it away. "I didn't know how you'd take it." She couldn't hold back the tears any longer.

Gwyneth scooted her chair closer, leaned over, and hugged Jordan. Through a choked-up voice, she spoke. "As I said before, I love you, Jordan, and you are a most wonderful daughter. I don't give a damn if you're purple with yellow polka dots."

Gwyneth rocked Jordan in silence for a while, kissing her cheek and smoothing her hair like when she was a little girl. Tears flowed on both sides.

Jordan managed to sit up and mumble, "You knew?"

Gwyneth looked deep into her eyes with her hand clasped around Jordan's. "Well, you don't date much or talk about men. I respected your privacy and hoped you would confide in me one day. Working yourself to death is not a solution. Every time I made a suggestion, you pushed me away. That hurt deeply. I was about ready to stop playing the silent supportive mother and force you to talk. In fact, that's why I baked these damn chocolate-chip cookies. I'd already decided that you and I were going to have a heart-to-heart talk even if I had to drag it out of you."

Jordan wiped away the tears and blew her nose. "Carter said you likely knew."

"You've already talked to Carter?"

"I had to. He...um...he came by and plowed out my driveway yesterday morning and had breakfast with us. Ah...Emmy had

spent the night. It was kind of awkward with no explanation."
She glanced at her mother who was grinning.

"Kind of like getting caught with Dave."

Jordan blinked. *Did she really say that?* "This is awkward."

"Yes, a little but we're all human. By the way, you're not the only one in the woodshed." Jordan put her hand up to her mouth as her mom laughed. "Why are so shocked, honey? Do you think I should be chaste for the rest of my life? Life and sex do not end at sixty."

Jordan grabbed another cookie. "Okay. Got it, but TMI."

"Well, does Gerry know about Emmy?"

"Not yet. I don't want to tell him."

"Then don't." Her mom was dead serious. "You tell those you want to tell and when you feel the time is right."

"He will eventually find out. Emmy's not in the closet, and I'm sure people in town will gossip if they haven't already."

"Why should you care?" Her mom sighed deeply. "Whatever happens, you're going to have to ignore Gerry's reaction. Hopefully, he will wake up one day. In the meantime, you can't allow him or anyone else to dictate your happiness. You have to live your life for you. No one else. Don't bow to others' expectations. You don't need his or anyone else's approval."

Jordan was amazed at her mother's wisdom. She sat and stared into her face. She was a gorgeous woman—beautiful inside and out. Dave was one lucky person.

"I love you, Mom. I'm so sorry I didn't come to you sooner."

Gwyneth cocked her head and pinched Jordan's cheek. "You always were the most precocious and independent child. Nothing wrong with that but I'm so happy this is out in the open. I want to see more of you and Emmy. Now how about you hop up and get us some more coffee? There are some hard-boiled eggs in the fridge too."

The conversation had indeed gone well, and the burden was lifted from Jordan's shoulders. "Madrid was pretty liberal, at least where I lived. I had a lot of freedom. I would like to fully be out here." She breathed a heavy sigh. "I know that's not the best idea in this part of the country, but I'm so damn tired of hiding. What I'm saying is that I've decided to come out to more people in the next month. It means the world to me that you'll be there for me."

"I'll always be there, and I'll always give anyone a piece of my mind if they bad-mouth you or Emmy."

"How do you think Grammy and Poppa will take the news? What about your brothers and sisters?"

Her mom reached out and tucked loose hair around her ear. "I suspect the only problem will be Gerry. Be brave. Tell them when you're ready. They love you too, Jordan. Make no mistake about it. You're our flesh and blood. You may get some awkward questions, but I seriously doubt anyone is going to turn their back on you, especially Grammy and Poppa. You know, it's not like homosexuality was magically invented yesterday."

Jordan wrapped her in a big bear hug, and the two sat like that for some time before finishing their eggs. They also had to have one more chocolate-chip cookie. She felt at peace on the drive home.

Gwyneth waved goodbye. She still wondered what had happened in Spain. Hopefully, Jordan would tell her someday. For now, Jordan was happy with Emmy. Gwyneth hadn't been around Emmy much, but she liked the girl. She had a pleasant demeanor and looked a person straight in the eyes when talking.

Jordan coming to terms with herself and wanting to mend their relationship meant so much to her. She needed her daughter. Yet, along with the happiness came the painful reality that Jordan wasn't the only one who had held back. Gwyneth had her own little white lies. As every day went by, her conviction that her actions were for Jordan's good crumbled and guilt ate at her.

Chapter Twenty-One

*R*obby rounded the corner. Jordan was moving about the kitchen and interacting with staff as if she was floating on a continuous happy cloud without a care in the world. He leaned against the counter watching her and silently thought about his wife's comment about Jordan being a lesbian. Since that night, he had noticed Emmy came by more frequently, and Jordan paid her more attention to her than others. But over the past month, it was their smiles, their eyes, and their casual touching that convinced him that his wife was correct. Jordan and Emmy must be a couple. Robby grinned. It warmed his heart to see Jordan shine.

"Hey, Robby. Can we talk a minute?"

"Sure, Jordan."

"I know you have expressed concern about me not taking enough time off to relax." She wet her lips and swallowed. "I talked to Jo about filling in for me this weekend. She has been doing an excellent job under your leadership. Let's give her a crack at taking charge of the staff."

He nodded and smiled broadly. "Yes, I believe Jo's ready too. She has my number if anything goes wrong. Any fun plans?"

"Oh, I plan on visiting DC. It's been a long time since I've seen the museums and been out to the restaurants."

He went for the jugular. "Isn't this Emmy's first weekend in her new apartment?" Jordan's mouth hung open, her eyes widened, and she swallowed again. He swooped in to fill the gap. "It's fantastic that you're helping her. She's wonderful."

Jordan shifted on her feet. "Yeah, she's subleasing a partially furnished apartment from another bank employee. I promised to show her around. Of course, I'll check out one of the trendy restaurants and come back with some culinary secrets."

"Well, sounds like a fun weekend. The temperature's dropping again, so bundle up tight." He winked and saw the crimson creep up her neck. For a woman with a gorgeous dark complexion, Jordan sure did blush easily. Robby felt some guilt for teasing her, but the big brother in him enjoyed watching her squirm.

Emmy ran her fingers through her hair as she nursed her tea in a Washington DC coffeehouse. DC apartments were expensive, and Emmy had been looking for some time. She was lucky to snag a one bedroom with a parking space for $3,000 a month. The location was perfect—near the Foggy Bottom Metro and within walking distance of the Berkeley International Bank. The deal required the rent be paid up front for the remaining nine months. She had just moved essentials into the apartment. Now she had serious job complications.

The meeting with the new supervisor had crushed her hopes. She was told they were short on staff, part-time was impossible, and he wanted her to begin several weeks early. She argued that was not the agreement she'd reached with the hiring officials. The overzealous, thirty-something executive smoothed his tie and added, "You're welcome to resign if you don't like the new terms."

The nasty meeting was under her skin and no amount of tea, or alcohol for that matter, could solve the problem. She rubbed her forehead as the details of the meeting rolled through her mind again.

She had agreed to think it over and was halfway out the door when the executive hurled one last jab to enforce his dominance. "We expect you to quit your private financial advisor role. That is a conflict of interest."

"There is no conflict of interest. All the bank projects I work on are in Southeast Asia. The two private portfolios I manage, which are for friends by the way, have nothing to do with Southeast Asia. There are no connections to companies signing deals with the bank. The legal department has been provided with the necessary disclosure paperwork. The bank has never objected."

"Until now."

"Why now?"

"We have an urgent need for a manager for two regional teams. With your experience, you are highly qualified to handle both. There is also a lot of required extra hours and travel to the satellite offices every other month. That raises the issue of conflict. We need you to be flexible."

Her head was spinning. This was insane. She would not let her new relationship suffer. "This is not what I was promised."

"Yes, but again, that was a verbal agreement."

She wanted to leap over the desk and strangle the arrogant son of a bitch. So much for her loyalty in London and running the Chennai, India office. She could try to go over his head, but it was unlikely to change anything.

"I'll get back to you," she replied tersely. "As far as starting early, sorry, no can do." She slammed the door and walked out, ignoring his last dribbled objections. From that moment on, she knew she was screwed.

She sat pondering her bleak options. Nibbling on her scone, she watched people move in and out of the coffeehouse like ants.

The time with Jordan had been so relaxing. Did she really want to jump back into the hectic world of big banking again? *I should quit and take the full-time plunge into financial consulting.* No matter what she decided, her savings was going to take a pounding.

The bad choices tumbled around in her mind, but at least she was looking forward to Jordan's visit. Emmy's mind floated back to the first night she laid eyes on Jordan. Her crisp white chef jacket contrasted sharply with her light mocha skin. She marveled at the tender, funny, and generous Jordan and that damn grin. Jordan's best smile was the one where her lips were closed and slightly turned up mischievously at the corners, one side more crooked than the other. Emmy had seen that smile a lot lately since Jordan had come out to her mom and Carter.

Now if the damn logistics were not such a hellish challenge. Emmy would have to talk to Jordan about the new complications and consequences. It was only fair to get her opinion since they were a couple. She smiled. Yes, they were a couple. Although Jordan had faltered at times, Emmy was crazy about her.

Jordan cursed herself for departing after lunch. The awful Friday traffic was made worse by the drizzling rain with a snowflake here and there. By the time she arrived, it was nearly four thirty. Against her better judgment, she double-parked on the street with blinkers flashing and called Emmy.

Her cares melted away as Emmy strolled toward her. Before Emmy had settled in the vehicle, Jordan grabbed and kissed her like it had been months since they were together. "I missed you."

"It's only been a couple of days."

Looking into Emmy's eyes, Jordan moved in for another kiss. Sensuous and long, their tongues mingled. A siren and blue lights cut short their celebration.

"Shit." Jordan glanced in the mirrors.

The police were getting out of the patrol car. The one on the driver side was a cute female cop with a tight uniform accentuating her muscular figure. Same-sex marriage was legal in DC, and the city was pretty gay-friendly. The odds of getting a ticket usually depended on whether the police had to make their quota for the month.

When the female officer got to the window, she gave them a stern look. A wave of anxiety rushed through Jordan. *Double shit.* The beautiful face of a black woman with high cheekbones and dark green eyes stared her down. Several years ago, Jordan had gone to Freddie's Beach Bar in Alexandria, Virginia and left with a gorgeous DC cop. There weren't many lesbians in the bar, and the two had hooked up. After the show and several drinks, Jordan had taken her to a hotel in Crystal City where they had a long night of heavy sex. The woman woke as Jordan was sneaking out in the morning. Giving a flimsy excuse, Jordan had promised to call and never did. *This can't be the same woman. Yet how many black female cops have those dazzling green eyes?*

The female officer shined her light in Jordan's face. "Driver's license and registration, please."

Jordan's hand shook as she handed over the paperwork. She heard the radio chatter as the male officer ran her plates.

After several long excruciating minutes, the policewoman spoke without a hint of emotion. "Ma'am, sounds like you've been free and clear of the law. No speeding or parking tickets but you've been careless tonight. Parking here not only unfairly blocks others but is a safety hazard. I could give you a ticket. Given your spotless record, I'll let you off this time."

"Thank you."

Before Jordan could start the vehicle, the policewoman said, "Are you and your girlfriend or wife going out tonight?"

Out of the corner of her eye, Jordan saw Emmy's head snap at the question. She looked at Emmy whose eyebrows were scrunched. *Play it cool.*

Turning back to the officer, Jordan cleared her throat. "Yes."

"Well, be safe and remember to drink and drive responsibly. Take a cab if you party too much."

"Yes, officer. Thank you."

"If you'd like a good recommendation, there's karaoke at Freddie's Beach Bar across the river. I personally think the Saturday drag show is one of the best."

Jordan's mouth sprang open, and only then, did the cop crack a smile. She winked shortly after seeing Jordan's reaction.

"Okay, ma'am. I'm sure you'll have fun and find delicious things to devour on your night of eating out." The female officer titled her head and glanced over at Emmy and winked. "Have a safe evening."

Jordan started the SUV and put it into drive. "Where to?" she whispered.

"The garage entrance is on the side street. I paid for guest parking. That was odd back there. I never met anyone, let alone a police officer, that so crudely implied—"

"I'm sure she didn't mean it that way." Jordan hastily changed the subject. She had already confessed her old Romeo ways to Emmy. She was not going to rub it in her face that the cute cop was a former conquest. "How was the meeting yesterday? Are you going to like or love your job?" Jordan asked casually.

Emmy sighed. "Not as well as I hoped. We'll talk later. I made a dinner reservation at Rasika for seven. Let's get showered and dressed." She pointed up ahead. "Park on the right next to the Lexus RC coupe."

"Do you want to leave early?"

With the vehicle parked, Emmy leaned over and kissed Jordan. "I arranged for a limo to come at six. After dinner, we're being driven around the monuments at night. I've always wanted to do that with someone I care about. And that someone is you."

"Why, Ms. Russo, I didn't know you could be so romantic. And later tonight, I'll bathe you in hugs and kisses. I give the best medicine."

Brightness returned to Emmy's face. "Absolutely, cuddling with you is the best."

The limo driver called from the curb at precisely six as they were putting on their last-minute items. They had cut it close. Walking out the door, Jordan remarked with a smirk, "I can't wait until I see what else you're going to do to me tonight."

"Let's go, you lovesick puppy, or we'll be late. Dessert is later and only if you behave."

Despite the traffic, the limo got them to the restaurant fifteen minutes early. The strong, spicy curry aroma hit them as they walked through the doors. They were seated just far enough away from the musicians, so their conversation was not drowned out.

"I forgot to ask if you liked Indian food."

Jordan beamed. "Love it. And the music is relaxing. The sitar fascinates me."

The entire meal was fabulous, but Emmy's slump showed. She missed parts of the conversation, and Jordan had to repeat herself a couple of times. Emmy knocked her wine over, and now her smile had disappeared.

"Emmy, what's going on? You're a million miles away, and you've barely touched your food."

Emmy rested her head in her hands hiding her face. Jordan reached over and rubbed her forearm.

When Emmy looked up, her eyes were moist. "The senior executive seems to be a pompous jackass. He told me to devote full-time to the bank and that my private financial advising won't be tolerated."

"But the interview committee told you—"

"Unfortunately, I have no recourse because the father of my new supervisor is on the board of directors. So, I'm stuck with the twit unless I resign." Emmy delicately wiped tears from the corner of her eyes with the dinner napkin.

Jordan was at a loss for words. "What are your options?" She had to ask but was afraid what the answer might be.

"They've backed me into a corner. Severance pay is out the window if I resign. Managing Becca and Calvin's portfolios is lucrative but not enough to pay all my bills. I don't have a US license, and it would take several months to set things up unless I went through London." Emmy sighed.

Jordan took a drink of water. She hated to see Emmy in turmoil. Suddenly, Jordan realized Emmy's words. *God, I hope she's not thinking about moving back to the UK.* Jordan took a deep breath, another gulp of water, and wet her lips. It was Emmy's life, and Jordan couldn't make the decision for her.

In a weak voice, Jordan said, "I'm sure you'll figure something out."

Emmy looked at her, eyes rimmed in red. "I have no choice. I'm going to quit the bank. I don't want my job coming between us. I can control my own schedule with my private consulting and split my time between DC and Oakville. With luck, I hope to keep travel to a minimum."

Jordan nodded and kissed Emmy's hand. "I want you to have a fulfilling life and career. We'll find a balance together." Jordan was silently doing the happy dance in her head. "Let's get going before it's too late."

As they approached the limo, the driver exited. Instead of the customary opening of the door, he held roses in one hand. "Ladies, I hope you don't mind, but I took the liberty of purchasing these for you." He gave each a small bouquet before opening the door.

They thanked the driver and settled back in their seats and held hands. Emmy leaned over. "I did not expect that," she whispered.

"Yes. A pleasant surprise."

Before buckling in, the driver double-checked all the sites they wanted to visit. "It's perfectly safe to walk around as long as you stick near the crowds and the well-lit walkways." He started to roll up the inside tinted window then stopped.

"May I tell you a personal story?" His smile was timid. "My daughter came out as a lesbian in college. My wife and I struggled with accepting her. In fact, we didn't speak for several years. We missed her wedding because of my bullheadedness. That's time we will never get back." He stopped and wiped his eyes. "She was diagnosed with cancer shortly after. I swallowed my damn stupid pride and finally opened my eyes and heart. Only then was I able to see what a beautiful couple they were."

Through a choked voice, he said, "We buried our only child three years ago at the age of thirty-two." He blew his nose. "Her wife was more on the butch side. At first, I didn't know what our Katie saw in her." Tears spilled onto his cheeks. "Looks can be deceiving. She may have looked tough, but I never saw a more caring, attentive person. She was there by my daughter's side all the way. We now spend our holidays together, and she's as much a daughter to us as our Katie." He wiped his face again.

Emmy patted his arm. "We are so sorry for your loss. Thank you for sharing your story." Jordan couldn't speak. She sniffled, nodded, and wiped away her own tears.

"Okay, ladies. Enough of the sadness. Tonight, enjoy." He rolled up the inside privacy window.

They rode past the city landmarks in the limo with Jordan's arm wrapped around Emmy and Emmy's head nestled on her shoulder.

"Oh, I don't want to forget." Jordan removed her arm, winked, and laid out dessert and poured chilled champagne. "A toast to the most gorgeous woman in my life. Cheers."

"Cheers!"

Emmy kissed Jordan's nose. "Excellent vintage. But, there's something wrong." She scrunched her face and narrowed her eyes, peering at Jordan. "Hold still." She looked farther, slightly moving her head back and forth. A deep crease between her brows and a frown developed.

Jordan thought the behavior was odd, but she remained still. Without warning, Emmy smeared the sweet basil cream of the Maharani cupcakes on the side Jordan's neck and slowly licked it off.

"Now that's much better."

"Hmm. Well, you seem to also have a problem." Jordan dipped her finger and generously spread the cream on Emmy's lips. She sucked in Emmy's lower lip before kissing her deeply. By the time they broke off, they both were breathless. They finished the dessert and drank half of the bottle when the driver pulled up to the Lincoln Memorial.

While a few people gave them quizzical looks, more nodded and smiled as they strolled holding hands. At the top, they admired the marble statue of Lincoln and took in the breathtaking view of the reflecting pond and Washington Monument.

At the bottom of the steps, Jordan kissed Emmy's hand. "This night's been magical. You've made me so relaxed. I never thought it would be possible to show my feelings in public. And the driver. Wow. People's kindness is what's going to change our country for the better."

Emmy kissed her softly on the lips. "We do make a terrific couple, don't we?"

"We do, and I've made a decision."

"What's that?" Emmy stroked the side of Jordan's neck.

"I'm coming out to the rest of the family on my birthday. I don't want to hide anymore. Are you okay with that?"

Emmy smoothed the hair out of Jordan's face and traced her

fingers down her jawbone. "Nothing would give me more pride than being by your side."

Jordan's eyes moistened, but she wore the biggest smile. She grabbed Emmy, lifted her off the ground, and twirled them around. Emmy let out a squeal of delight.

They laughed and twirled until Emmy shouted, "Stop, silly. I'm dizzy." Jordan gently put her down, and they both stumbled a bit. "Goofball, you're even dizzy. Luckily, we didn't end up on our arse."

Jordan smirked. "Oh, I think I can make that happen. I'm quite talented in that department."

Emmy swatted her arm. "Good thing I like how you think. Let's get out of here."

Chapter Twenty-Two

*A*fter returning from Washington DC, Emmy spent time with her aunt. She missed waking up next to Jordan, but Betty Jean kept her busy. They cleaned the house top to bottom, including the attic, and Betty Jean told old family stories along with showing Emmy photos she had not previously seen. Tonight, Jordan was invited for dinner.

Emmy shivered with delight when the doorbell rang. She opened the door and grabbed Jordan, laying a big kiss on her.

Betty Jean cleared her throat. "Oh, for heaven's sake, Emmy, let her in and close the damn door before we all catch our death."

Jordan handed over a bag. "Dessert. You might want to put it in the fridge to chill." She hung up her own coat while Emmy went off to the kitchen.

"Thank you for inviting me." She leaned over and hugged Betty Jean who patted her cheek with a devious smirk.

"Good to see you. I was worried. You two spend so much time together, I figured you'd been hijacked by aliens. Now sit your weary bones down. It's Wednesday movie night."

As Emmy correctly predicted, Betty Jean's favorite, Casablanca, started to play. Popcorn bowls and water were already on the table in front of them.

Shortly after the movie began, Betty Jean hit the pause button and looked over at them with a frown. "Are you two going to sit like bumps on a log when this is the most romantic movie of all times? You're making me uptight. At least scoot closer together and hold hands. Relax and enjoy."

Betty Jean was never one for mincing words. Emmy snickered and cuddled into Jordan's neck and laced their fingers together. Jordan wrapped her arms around Emmy and kissed the top of her head.

Betty Jean smiled. "That's better."

When the movie ended, Betty Jean's eyes were moist.

Emmy rushed to her side. "What's wrong, Auntie?"

"It's been nice to have you around, and I promise not to be demanding after tonight." She patted Emmy's hand. "To tell the truth, I hope you don't move to DC. You should live here. I'm sure Jordan would agree with me."

"Actually, the DC job is not going to work out. For better or worse, it looks like this you and this town are stuck with me for the time being."

Betty Jean blew her nose. "Are you spending the night?"

"Of course—"

"Yes, dear. I was talking about Jordan. What time should I wake you two for breakfast?" She cracked a grin.

Jordan tried to make an excuse and pointed out she had no change of clothes or pajamas. Emmy's heart fluttered as she watched Jordan's shy side. Although Jordan was tripping over her tongue, Betty Jean wasn't buying any of it.

Betty Jean stood and put her hands on her hips and cocked one eyebrow. "You're spending the night. And don't worry, I sleep like a rock, and Emmy's room is down the hall. So, you two won't bother me if you're the rowdy type. Now what time should I wake you up for breakfast? I've been looking forward to having company."

Jordan was speechless, and Emmy managed to sneak out the

words between giggles. "Auntie, dear. We can wake ourselves up. I promise we will be down by seven thirty."

"Very well." She kissed them good night. Climbing the stairs with a slight limp, she murmured, "God damn arthritis." Midway up, she stopped. "You don't need any pajamas. You two are a lovely, wonderful couple. And as many nights as Emmy has slept at your house, I'm sure you've gone through the lesbian Kama Sutra several times." She continued up the stairs as if it was any other typical statement.

Emmy burst out laughing. Jordan stood in shock, her face a deep crimson. "Oh my God, she's got a set of balls on her."

Emmy hugged Jordan, and her deep laughter became small little snickers. "Let's get to bed." She pulled Jordan up the stairs.

They took turns in the hallway bathroom. When Emmy came out, Jordan was dressed in a nightshirt and sitting on the bed.

"Don't tell me you're shy because I know better. Take off that damn shirt and crawl under the covers and keep me warm. We've come a long way since the night when we hit the deer."

"Yes, but we slept in old T-shirts, and we didn't do anything," Jordan said.

"But we did caress and cuddle."

"Yeah but that's not the same as your aunt pointing out the Kama Sutra!" Jordan said in a whispered yell.

She dropped her robe, and Jordan swallowed. The excitement built as Jordan's eyes caressed every inch of her body. Sliding under the sheets, she patted the bed, and Jordan relented, slipping off the shirt. When Jordan started to say something else, she put her index finger up to Jordan's lips to shush her and began caressing and kissing her face and neck.

"I can take a little more without being too loud." Jordan practically moaned the words.

Emmy licked Jordan's lower lip and sucked it in. "Oh, I promise you'll get more, and we'll see how much you can control your volume." Her hand slipped between Jordan's legs. She kissed her and intensified the rhythm but stopped. "You do like to moan rather loudly."

"I know. This is a bad idea."

"Uh-huh. Can't fool me, bad girl." Emmy threw back the bed coverings and adjusted her body atop Jordan in the opposite direction and took her in with slow circles.

"Oh my God. Are you crazy?"

Moans soon replaced Jordan's words, and Emmy picked up the pace. She loved pleasing her girlfriend, and when Jordan nestled into her, the mixture of tender strokes and nips combined with flicking the tip of each other's engorged clit drove them both on. With each quiver, mouths and tongues moved faster and harder. Now it was Emmy who moaned, and she pressed her pelvis down to meet Jordan's mouth. Control shifted when Jordan squeezed and kneaded her ass while taking her fully. Although lightheadedness from blood flowing to Emmy's core overtook her, she didn't stop lavishing Jordan. The uncontrollable pleasure of muscles tingling and contracting gave way to the explosions that rolled through their bodies.

Intoxicated with love and in utter bliss, they lay still for several seconds before Emmy repositioned and pulled the sheet and blanket over their bodies. She rested her head on Jordan's chest, closing her eyes. She loved the feel and sound of Jordan's heart thumping as her own beat wildly. Their labored breathing took time to taper down. Delicately, Jordan ran her fingertips over her shoulder.

"So, was that an excellent way to muffle the sound?" Emmy asked.

"Yes. You surprised me. I..." Jordan struggled for words.

"You seemed to enjoy yourself. Was there something I could have done to make you feel better?"

"It was awesome. I've never done that before."

Emmy sprang up on one elbow. "Seriously?"

"Yeah, seriously. Jesus, that was intense. Thank you." Jordan kissed her forehead.

Emmy kissed Jordan's chest above the heart. "You're wearing my favorite Jordan lopsided mischievous grin right now."

"You've got a favorite grin, huh?"

"Yes." Emmy took her lips long and hard.

"You make me happy, Em. I've slept more soundly since we've been together and have never been more at peace than I am now."

"Me too. By the way, this is the first time you've called me Em. I love it, sweetheart."

"Just don't call me honey. My mom does that all the time, and it drives me nuts."

Emmy laughed. "Just don't call me babe or baby or I'll likely smack you."

The next day, Emmy shopped for Jordan's birthday present in between chores for Betty Jean. She had found the perfect birthday gift, a leather-bound journal that would go perfectly with the necklace she already had wrapped at the house. The journal would be given at the party. The necklace would be in private. It was a simple white gold design with a fine teardrop-shaped amethyst surrounded by small diamonds. She had personally picked high-quality diamonds. Smiling, she imagined the design highlighting Jordan's luscious mocha-colored skin.

Her cell phone rang. Thinking it was Jordan calling after the lunch service, she enthusiastically answered. "Hey there, gorgeous. What's up?"

"Well, hello to you too, pretty one. I see that the American lingo has already firmly snatched you."

"Calvin?"

"Yes, Lassie."

"What's wrong?"

"Nothing."

"Calvin. You never call without a reason. Your detailed review was completed not long ago. The daily checks done by the computer software haven't caused any alerts. Your positions remain good. So why are you calling?"

"Ah, you got me. I've run across some opportunities, and I'd like to consider some major trades."

Emmy rolled her eyes. "What do you mean by major? Your portfolio is stable and is averaging slightly above the indices. Besides, you agreed to long-term growth without impulsive adjustments. What's going on?"

"I'd prefer not to tell you over the phone. So, how about flying to Scotland this weekend?"

She stopped all of a sudden, and a man who was walking behind her bumped into her. They each mumbled sorry.

"What's that, Lassie?"

Emmy crisply replied, "No."

"Excuse me?"

She swallowed hard. Calvin Thornton was her number one client. Few people had the clout to tell him no. She could not afford to lose him after quitting the bank.

"I'm sorry, Calvin. I've got plans that I cannot break. Can we please schedule another time?"

"What possibly could keep you in West Virginia? It better be great sex because I pay you well, my dear."

She smiled. "I could fly out in a couple of weeks, but I cannot stay long, four days max. Will that work?"

"Must be sex. Sure, my Lassie. I'll make arrangements. In the meantime, don't do anything I won't do. Oh, and I expect to hear all about your new love interest." Laughing, he hung up without waiting for her reply.

When she had departed the London investment firm for the bank, she'd planned to manage only Becca's account. Calvin surprised her by insisting she should continue as his personal financial advisor and trader. He was ridiculously wealthy and could open doors for her. She needed him now more than ever. His influence could help her expand her client base. Now she had to tell Jordan about this Scotland trip.

It was a couple of hours before the dinner crowd when one of the waitresses grabbed Jordan's arm. The girl was pale, her eyes were wide, and her grip was tight.

"There's a guy out front with a gun on his hip. He looks creepy and scares the shit out of me."

Jordan's stomach dropped. She had a good guess who the man was.

"How many customers and where are they sitting?"

"Two tables on the right. He's alone on the left. A few at the bar."

Jordan rubbed the girl's arm. She was only right out of high school. "I'll take care of it. Don't worry. Stay in the kitchen."

Jo was nearby and overheard their conversation. "I'll call the sheriff."

"It's not illegal unless he refuses to leave."

Jo said, "It's still a good idea."

Jordan shook her head. "Just give me a few minutes to talk to him." It was the last thing she wanted to do. Yet, she couldn't jump to conclusions.

From the minute she stepped into the dining room, she recognized him from the long shaggy hair. Her strides were slow and measured. She didn't want to alarm anyone nor did she want him to see her apprehension even though her heart was about to jump out of her chest. As she approached, he turned, wearing the same goddamn sunglasses. *What's with this jerk?*

Today, he wore a sleeveless drab olive-green shirt showing off his well-defined biceps.

She stopped and met his gaze with a firm face. At least his hands were in view on the table. In a low voice, she said, "Excuse me, sir. I'm sorry, but I'm going to have to ask you to leave."

"Why?"

"You're carrying a weapon."

"It's perfectly within my legal right."

There was something about him, yet Jordan couldn't figure it out. "Yes, except when a sign is posted. That makes it my legal right to ask you to leave. If you refuse, then it's against the law. I don't want any trouble. You're welcome to come back when you're not carrying."

"Guess I didn't see it."

"It's new but in plain sight of the front door."

He didn't budge and instead hung his head and removed the sunglasses. Her stomach lurched when he spat on the lenses and used the corner of his shirt to wipe them off. Without looking up, he said, "Okay. Can we talk for a few minutes?"

What the fuck is this guy's problem? "Sir—"

Jordan's mouth dropped when he raised his head. His gray-blue eyes bore into her, and he didn't blink. That's when she saw it: the right eye, the one with the iris that was partially brown. She was dizzy and nauseated.

"It's been a long time, Jordan."

His presence sucked the air out of her lungs, and her body trembled. She hoped it didn't show. "Please leave now, Darrell."

She didn't flinch despite his eyes piercing through her. She didn't want to appear weak.

"I believe the lady asked you to leave." Sheriff Johnson put his hand on Jordan's shoulder. "I'll take it from here."

Jordan never heard the sheriff come in. Swallowing, she willed her body to move out of the way.

"Come on, son. If you don't leave now, I'll have to arrest you."

"No problem, sir." Darrell stood.

Out of the corner of her eye, Jordan could see him casually take a long swig of his drink before moving toward the door.

"See you around, Jordan. We've got a lot to catch up on," he shouted on his way out, making all heads turn.

After he had left, the sheriff came over and softly whispered, "Looks like there might be a problem after all. Maybe we ought to go back to your office."

Jordan wet her lips. She couldn't look him in the eye. Her breathing was shallow, and she thought she might faint any minute. "No, sir. We just didn't get along very well in high school. I'm sure what he wanted to talk about was nothing." She tried to smile and turned and walked away.

She practically knocked Jo over when she walked into the kitchen.

"Damn, Jordan. That was intense."

She trudged toward her office. "Jo take over. I don't want to be disturbed."

Closing and locking the door, she collapsed in the chair with her hand over her mouth to muffle the sobs. It didn't help much, and she flipped on the radio. *No one has seen him for years. Why couldn't he just stay away?*

Her thoughts turned to Emmy. Things were going fantastic. She even suspected she was falling in love. *God, what am I going to tell her?*

She moved over to the futon, curled up tight with a pillow, and grabbed a handful of tissues. Her body shook, and she was helpless to fight off the memories.

She became enamored with her friend Karen in their junior year of high school and would never forget the day things changed. The rain pelted the windows like pebbles, the wind howled, and the lights were out. They were huddled under a blanket in the basement of Karen's house, studying by candlelight and eating mac and cheese.

No one was expected home until later in the evening. With a mischievous smile, Karen grabbed a flashlight, disappeared into the dark corner, and brought back wine. Soon they were mildly inebriated.

As they giggled, hands mingled, and with each sip, inhibitions slipped away. She didn't hear half of what Karen said then perked up when the topic of kissing was mentioned. Karen described her encounters as harsh and gross, especially with her ex-boyfriend, Tommy—a jerk Jordan couldn't stand and who Karen had fortunately dumped.

"Instead of nice, warm, and gentle, they're like pigs at the trough. For once, I'd like a soft kiss. How about you? Have you ever kissed anyone?"

Jordan's smile faded as Karen looked deep into her eyes. She wanted to kiss Karen so badly, yet the haze of booze also brought fear and hesitation.

"You look sad right now. Are you okay?"

Jordan sat there taking in the beauty of Karen's face as her pulse raced and her body tingled. Caught up in the moment, she kissed Karen. Pulling away slightly, Jordan looked for a reaction. She saw a mixture of surprise and bewilderment, though Karen didn't push Jordan away nor did she avert her gaze. After several long seconds, Jordan kissed her again, and to her amazement, Karen returned her kiss. Jordan's emotions roared as their tongues explored and arms tightened around each other. The sensation was amazing, like no other she had experienced. Her heart pounded, and she was light-headed. When Karen moaned, Jordan deepened the kiss with intense hunger.

"You girls down in the basement?" Karen's mom yelled from the top of the stairs.

Bungling in panic, they jumped up and hid the evidence of booze. They popped some gum into their mouths before Karen's mom rounded the corner with a large bright lantern.

"Goodness gracious, I'm relieved to be home and out of that weather." She hugged them both. Smiling, she looked down at the empty bowls of mac and cheese and the candles. "Looks like you two made out okay."

Oh, you have no idea, Jordan thought. Out of the corner of her eye, Karen was grinning.

Jordan wiped away the last tears. Her nasal passages were swollen, and she couldn't breathe well. That glorious year together with Karen had changed her life in many ways, but the hole of losing Karen had never healed. *It wasn't my fault.* No matter the logic and facts, Jordan felt responsible. The guilt that she had tucked away in every crack and crevice came roaring forward.

She spent over an hour in the office beating herself up. It was now close to four o'clock. Soon the dinner crowd would be showing up. Thank God there was a sink in the office. She didn't want anyone to see her like this, but she had to trust someone and called Jo in.

"You look like shit. How can I help?"

"I need you to run the restaurant tonight and play down my absence. Don't mention the incident to anyone. I'm going to crash here and maybe come out later. You haven't called Robby, have you?"

"No, but this concerns me. Are we at risk?"

Even though she trusted Jo, she had to defuse the situation. "Turns out the scrawny bully from high school has shown up all buff and full of bluster. I'm sure he's only carrying to display his redneck manhood. You know, a progun zealot with an attitude."

She could tell Jo wasn't buying the entire story, and so she lied. "He spouted off that it was his second-amendment rights. Then he tried to tell me it was folks like him that prevented crime and protected businesses." She faked a laugh. "His last-ditch effort was an offer of a date at the shooting range. Anyway, no need to worry, Jo. The sheriff's aware, and I'll check in with him tomorrow."

Jo's shoulders loosened, and Jordan was relieved. After shutting the door, she rummaged in her backpack and found a bottle of Ambien. She popped two, lay back down, and put the radio by her head. Exhaustion finally overtook her.

Boom, boom, boom. "Jordan. Unlock the door."

The pills had knocked her out, and it was late in the evening. She sat up in a daze and shouted, "I'm coming." After unlatching the door, Jo bounced in. *Damn, she's always full of energy. Where does it come from?*

"Sorry I pounded, but you weren't responding. Quick, freshen up and take care of your bad hair. Emmy's at the bar. You sure you're okay?"

"Yeah, just a little tired." Jordan yawned. "Keep her occupied. I need a few minutes."

After cleaning up, she stared at her face in the mirror above the sink. *Push Darrell out of your mind. Take care of it another day. Get through tonight.*

She sauntered toward Emmy who was playing with the olive of her martini. As Emmy slid the olive off the skewer into her mouth, Jordan wished she could scoop her up and kiss her right there.

"Mind if I join you, Ms. Russo?"

"Is something wrong? You've got an odd look in your eyes."

Jordan shrugged. "Rough day and my muscles ache. What's up?"

Emmy bit her lip. "One of my clients called. Calvin Thornton, my number one client. He wants me to drop everything and fly to Scotland. I've managed to put it off." Emmy reached out and put her hand atop Jordan's. "There's no way I'm going to miss your birthday."

"Better not miss my birthday, or you'll sorely regret it."

A devious grin replaced Emmy's frown. She leaned over and whispered, "How sorely?"

Jorden whispered, "You always bait and hook me. I don't know how I fall into your trap, but I adore your flirts. Now tell me about this trip."

Emmy took over the conversation and launched into details about Calvin. Jordan was relieved for the diversion but was having trouble concentrating because the Ambien was still in her system. Jordan fought off the drowsiness by nursing a Diet Coke but popped to attention when Emmy said, "It's only four days at the end of the month. Please come with me?"

The plea was hard to resist, but Jordan had a real excuse. "I'd love to, but I'm afraid my passport expires around that time. I've been so busy that the time snuck up on me. I'll miss you." She didn't know what else to say.

Emmy looked heartbroken. She slid off the barstool to leave. "It's late, and I have to help Betty Jean early tomorrow." As she fluffed her hair out from underneath the coat's collar, she whispered, "I hope we can be more open after your birthday. This playing your best friend role is grinding on my nerves."

She turned and left without saying goodbye. And Jordan silently let her go. She felt like shit now, yet she needed some time alone. Time to think. It was all moving too fast.

Two days passed since Darrell had made himself known. She still hadn't heard a word from him. After brushing her hair and smoothing her clothes, she stared in the mirror. The impeccable dress couldn't hide the look of exhaustion on her face. Sleep had eluded her. *Forget it. It was an accident. He's scum anyway.* She tiptoed out of the master bathroom, and Emmy rolled over with her eyes wide open.

"God, it's early. Where are you going?"

"Thought I'd run into town and get us fresh pastries before I head out to work."

"Jordan, what's wrong? We didn't make love last night. We had sex. Have I upset you?"

Jordan rushed to the bedside. "No, Em. I haven't been sleeping well."

"I know you're worried about coming out to your family tomorrow." Emmy rubbed Jordan's hand. "Don't do it because I want you to. It was shitty of me to say I was tired of playing the role of best friend. I'd like nothing more than to shout to the world you're my girlfriend. I simply want you to be ready."

"Em, a part of me may never be ready, but I'll deal with it."

"You tossed and turned last night. Is everything okay at the restaurant? I heard the waitresses saying some guy was disruptive, and the sheriff kicked him out."

She didn't want to worry Emmy. "He's a loony guy from way back. There's no need to worry." She kissed Emmy. "The coffeehouse has the best pastries. I'll be back in a jiffy."

In the SUV, she squeezed her eyes tight. *Calm down. Take care of family matters, then worry about Darrell.*

Chapter Twenty-Three

Jordan pulled into the driveway and saw Gerry's vehicle. "Dammit," she grunted and whipped her head back on the headrest. "He must have gone to the early Sunday service. I was hoping he would be late, not early. The less I see him, the better I feel."

"Who owns that car?" Emmy pointed to a blue sedan.

"I don't know." Jordan had wanted to speak with her mother alone, but the presence of Gerry and others would make that near impossible.

Emmy put her hand on Jordan's shoulder. "Look at me." Their eyes locked. "I understand if you want to wait. Either way, I'm here for you."

Jordan gave her a weak smile. "I'm scared, but I'm tired of being a chickenshit. We both know I have to do this." Her smile widened and she leaned over and lightly kissed Emmy. Stopping momentarily with a mix of emotions, she joked, "Get ready for mayhem. I'll quiz you on names later."

As they walked in, Jordan heard a familiar voice. "Ah, there's the birthday girl. Still the prettiest girl in all of West Virginia."

"Sam?" Jordan couldn't believe her eyes as he wrapped her in a huge bear hug and lifted her off the ground. Gwyneth's youngest brother lived in Alaska, and he hadn't been home for ages. Despite being a bit of a rough outdoorsman, Sam was always the most down-to-earth uncle.

"Are you still working maintenance in the oil fields?"

"Yep, and still hunt and fish in my spare time." Turning to a petite woman with long salt-and-pepper hair, Sam glowed. "You remember my wife, Gina."

"Yes, I do. So nice to see you again." The women hugged.

Sam turned to Jordan. "Who is your lovely guest?"

"I'm sorry. Everyone, this is Betty Jean's niece, Emmy Russo." Warm greetings were extended, and Jordan was relieved that Emmy fit right in. "Where's Grammy and Poppa and Aunt Elizabeth?"

"They're running late." Gwyneth whizzed up placing a hot cider drink in their hands.

"Joe and Vivian can't make it. Several of your cousins are outside by the fire pit."

Mom's brother Joe and his wife were conservative, not as bad as Gerry, but she wasn't close to them or her cousins. Luckily her mom didn't pick up on her feelings.

Gwyneth turned to Emmy. "Where's Betty Jean?"

"Not feeling well. She sends her love."

"Sounds like Elizabeth and I ought to deliver some chicken soup."

"I'm sure she'd be thrilled to see you."

Gwyneth kissed Emmy's forehead before returning to the kitchen. She called over her shoulder, "Go introduce Emmy around. Have fun."

As they walked up to Carter, his son grabbed Jordan's hand. "Auntie, come see the house we built out of this great new kit we got for Christmas. I used some lumber pieces to build a road around it, and I've got some new Hot Wheels. You gotta see it."

"Go on. Angie's upstairs yakking about wedding plans." Carter swung his arm around Emmy. "Don't worry. I'll keep her company with my dazzling charm."

"You wish," Jordan said before being tugged to the basement of munchkin chaos. She trusted her little brother but shook her finger. "Behave."

Carter whispered into Emmy's ear, "It's good to see you. I'm happy for you both."

"Thank you. I feel like I've known you for ages."

In all the hubbub, Emmy had not yet taken a drink of the cider. When she did, the smell of apples, ginger, cinnamon, orange, and something spicy filled her nose. It burned slightly going down. With bulging eyes, she held out the glass. "There's alcohol in here."

Carter looked down at her with the same big puppy dog eyes and wicked grin as his sister. "A little spike in the adult container to get the juices flowing."

"Does your mum know it's spiked?"

"If you recall, she gave you the drink. Although, her version isn't as potent as mine." His grin was ear to ear.

"What about Gerry?"

"He doesn't approve, but it's not his house. You'll notice he and Anne will only drink water. As you can tell, the cider has the right amount of rye whiskey to give it that nice spicy slow burn."

"Mine has extra."

He chuckled. "Well, sometimes we get a little carried away with the proportions. It's Grammy and Poppa's favorite. It keeps them young. Oh, Angie is the designated driver. So, feel free to drink up."

Emmy had a drink or two in early afternoons on special occasions but never would have suspected this in rural West Virginia, especially on a Sunday.

"Come on, let's mingle. I'll introduce you to our cousins. If there is one thing the Lange family is never in short supply of, it's conversation and speaking their minds. Some spiked apple cider and you've got a good rolling party."

That's what worried Emmy. No matter how the family reacted, she would support Jordan and hope for the best.

It was a whirlwind at the fire pit with people coming and going, but it was warmer when Jordan joined them. While Carter chatted with everyone, Jordan drew Emmy off to the side and away from the others. "You look dazed."

Emmy shrugged. "You said there would be a lot of people. Goodness, you didn't mention your family was half of the county population."

"Yeah, and only half are here. Still my girlfriend?"

"Yep. By the way, your hand is still lingering on my shoulder and sending chills down my spine. You're also grinning like a schoolgirl gazing into my eyes within kissing distance. If you don't step back, I'm sure you won't have to tell anyone. But I will expect a rain check later tonight."

As their conversation was finishing, Robby and Linda walked up.

"I hope you don't mind. Your mom invited us."

"Are you kidding, you and Linda are like family."

They talked for several minutes, then Emmy noticed Jordan's Aunt Elizabeth joining others at the fire pit. She bumped Jordan's shoulder. "Looks like more family has arrived."

"If you'll please excuse us. I'd like Emmy to meet my grandparents before things got too crazy."

Jordan had a gut feeling Grammy and Poppa would like Emmy. They found them sitting with Carter and Angie in the living room corner. After greetings, Carter and Angie excused themselves to mingle with others. Jordan was amazed when Carter winked and Angie gave a knowing smile.

Poppa quickly struck up an animated conversation with Emmy. Enthusiastically, he waved his hands telling her all about the apple orchard. Within no time, the two were laughing. Jordan sat next to Grammy and stole glances at Emmy. Seeing her and Poppa having a good time warmed her heart.

Grammy patted her knee. "My family's been here since mid-eighteen hundred, but your Poppa's family... Well, they never did like to talk about the war or the family being split, especially about your great-uncle Hans."

Jordan half listened as she had heard the story before about Poppa's only brother who died in the fifties. "Yep, he immigrated in 1948."

"No. That's the year he became an American citizen. Not the real year he came over."

Jordan furrowed her brow. "What do you mean?"

"He wasn't a farmer like the rest of 'em. He was a scientist. The American military grabbed him and others in early 1945."

Jordan's mouth hung open. *Is Grammy confused?* "The war ended September the second."

"Yes, but the US government took them someplace in the southwest for a secret project. Anyway, they were ten years apart in age, and the war separation didn't help. Still, your Poppa loved Hans."

"He must have been a good guy if the military brought him here for secret work."

"He was. Your Poppa loved him, but their arguments have bothered him to this day."

"No one has ever talked much about Poppa's family. Why weren't Hans and Poppa close? What were the arguments about?"

"Oh, they were close in several ways. Just stuck on one matter that they both stubbornly never settled. Then Hans died, and your Poppa felt guilty."

Jordan saw the sadness in Grammy's eyes, but before she could ask another question, they were being called to dinner.

When she glanced over, Emmy was helping Poppa out of the chair. Jordan helped Grammy. The mystery nagged at her. *What was she trying to tell me?*

As they stood, Grammy clasped her hands around Jordan's face. "He won't make that same mistake with you. Just look at him glowing over Emmy. He likes her. I like her." She grabbed her cane and joined Poppa, and they walked arm and arm slowly to the table.

Did she just say what I thought she did?

Dinner went by with little fanfare, and it was quiet until Angie brought out a huge black forest cake. Immediately, all the kids, including the teenagers, came out of the woodwork and wound everyone up. After singing "Happy Birthday," the young kids grabbed their cake and headed to the basement, and the teens headed out to the fire pit. Only adults were around the table. Jordan grew more nervous as coffee cups were refilled. Now would be a good time but the words she had rehearsed escaped her.

Unexpectedly, Sam stood. "Finally, it's calm. I think we should stand and take a turn to talk about what we're grateful for. I'll start. I'm grateful for having a loving family that is caring and has damn good cooks. Happy birthday, Jordan. Here's to you and the rest of you scraggly bunch!"

Jordan could see Gerry cringe at the curse word. He was in a much darker mood if that was possible. A solemn, brooding mood, which scared Jordan even more.

Each family member stood wishing Jordan a happy birthday and pronouncing what they were grateful for. It was close to Gerry's turn when, unexpectedly, he excused himself to check on the kids. As the positive comments flowed, it was soon Jordan's turn. She felt ready but paused, and her brain spun again when Gerry arrived back at the table.

"We missed you, nephew. How about you tell us what you're grateful for." Sam innocently piped up.

All eyes were on Gerry as he stood, staring down at the untouched piece of cake. When he raised his head, Jordan's stomach did an immediate flop. Gerry's demeanor and his lashing out at family members to tell them how to live their lives had become more and more frequent. Sam and other relatives who lived farther away had been fortunate enough not to see this side of him. Jordan could tell that was about to change.

"We have a wonderful family, but I'll tell you what I'm not grateful for. While we sit around and enjoy our meal and freedom, our values and religious liberties are threatened."

"Gerry, this is not the occasion to discuss politics. Concentrating on what makes you sad instead of happy brings only pain. This is a celebration today. Please stop," Gwyneth said across a hushed room.

Gerry huffed, tightened his hands into fists, and leaned on the table. "Now is precisely the time, Mother. We've been through so much as a country with the economy, nine eleven, and ISIS, but the biggest threat is at home."

As Jordan's eyes met Carter's across the table, his face had that "Oh, shit, here we go again" look.

"Gerry, please stop," Gwyneth pleaded.

"No, Mother. Evil will triumph when good men do nothing and do not stand up for the rights of their families. We are threatened by all the liberalism shoving this same-sex marriage down our throats. Homosexuals threaten the divine sanctity of marriage and what God plans for us as a family. We should all be thankful for Alabama Supreme Court Chief Justice Roy Moore who is standing up for our rights and speaking out. Judge Moore is a man of integrity. Because of people like him, we will make 2015 the year that stops the sickening homosexual agenda, but everyone needs to do their part. I'm organizing a march in a couple of weeks to stand up for our religious freedom. Everyone at this table should join us."

Carter's chair flew back and slammed into the wall as he jumped to his feet pointing his finger at his brother. "You, as always, are out of line! This is your sister's birthday and should be a happy occasion, but you have turned this into a spectacle. And for the record, I'll be at your march holding a big sign about what a bigoted, homophobic asshole you are. Gay people aren't ruining this country, people like you are!"

"Carter! Gerry! Sit down and be still!" Gwyneth gave them that mom look that silently signaled they had better respect her or else. "I will not tolerate outbursts in my house," she said after staring them down. "People can calmly talk or not talk at all. Understood?"

Carter shook his head and sat back down. Gerry crossed his arms and remained standing.

"Gerry, please sit down. Not everyone agrees with you. Trying to force your views on others in a threatening tone accomplishes nothing. And there is no room in my house for bashing other people."

He reluctantly did so. The room was quiet except for the forks clanking as everyone went back to eating cake. Jordan saw Grammy pat Poppa's hand. He stood and walked away. Sam looked stunned. The outburst didn't seem to bother her cousins. The room was silent only for a minute before a wife of one cousin spoke up.

"I don't dislike gays, but I don't understand why they have to flaunt their lifestyle in people's faces. There are TV commercials that normalize their behavior. Like that graham cracker one. Why can't they just keep their life private?"

Gerry didn't miss the opportunity. He rose and banged his fist on the table. "It's because they're sick. Most are fornicators, pedophiles, and just plain vile people." Shaking his finger at everyone, he continued. "Mark my word, it won't be long before bestiality and incest are legalized next. We've got to do something about this."

Dave sprang out of his chair and bellowed in an irritated voice, "Hold on, son. Your mother just told you to stop. This conversation is disrespectful and disruptive. I won't allow this behavior."

"It's my God-given right to speak the truth and protect my family!" Gerry glared at Dave.

"Enough, son! Sit down and shut up!"

Gerry was on an ugly roll. "I love my family, but we lose if we do nothing. Our country loses. Jordan, I know you're busy, and you never get involved in anything political, but I'm pleading for your help. It would mean so much if your restaurant sponsored our march. Just this time, please. It's a critical moment for our country."

Jordan looked at her mother. Her face was filled with anguish as she gripped Dave's hand. Jordan turned back to Gerry, and out of the corner of her eye, Jordan caught a glance from Grammy who looked straight at her and nodded. Despite their support, Jordan's chest constricted. Breathing was hard, and her stomach lurched. She thought she might pass out but knew this had to happen. All eyes were on her. She swallowed hard and hoped that Gerry would not see and hear the fear that still hid within her.

"I can't do that, Gerry. I don't believe in the ugly hatred you spew. Everyone deserves freedom and the right to love whomever they choose. Civil rights should be for every citizen of this country." Weakness was creeping into her body with every second. She fought back the tears and hoped no one caught her voice trembling. "Besides, I don't think your church would be overjoyed taking support from me." Her muscles tensed, and her tight shoulders ached. "I am a lesbian and always have been."

The wife of her cousin dropped her fork. Her hand flew to her mouth. "Oh, dear God." Another cousin said, "Wow. Don't hear that every day."

"Love is love. I am not a horrible person, and neither is any other queer person I know. People who are ignorant or who spread fear and lies are the ones doing a disservice to our country. Turning to hate instead of love is what dishonors God." She swallowed. She could hear her heart pounding in her chest. "And speaking of love," she glanced around the room before her eyes rested on Emmy, "you all should know that Emmy is my girlfriend."

Gerry's jaw tightened, and his face grew redder. "Your lesbian lifestyle is sick."

Dave pointed his finger. "Son—"

Poppa entered the room and shouted, "You're opening a Lebanese restaurant? Isn't one enough to keep you runnin' like a chicken with its head chopped off? And why is everyone hollerin'? I could hear you all sittin' on the commode. Good thing I got my hearin' aid turned down."

Gerry had a self-satisfying smirk on his face as Poppa sat down. He loudly spoke in Poppa's good ear. "She's a lesbian, and she's carryin' on with that woman." He pointed at Emmy with a scowl on his face.

Poppa looked twisted in thought, and Jordan's stomach dropped. Then he turned to Gerry. "What's it any business of yours? Seems like Emmy's a fine young woman." He sipped his coffee and Jordan wasn't sure if the shaking of his hand meant he was having a bad day with his tremors or if Gerry had gotten under his skin.

"She's a homosexual, Poppa!"

"Gerry, shut your trap and sit down! I heard you the first time." The room stilled. Poppa Lange rarely spoke in an angry voice. He leaned back and rested his arm on Grammy's shoulder. "I said sit. I've got more to say." This time, Gerry plopped into the chair.

Everyone waited for Poppa, who looked sad. "I haven't spoken about this for years. In fact, I've never told you, kids." He took time to nod at Gwyneth, Elizabeth, and Sam. "My brother was a homosexual. I didn't like it, but I loved him. Years after he died, I realized I wasted so much time trying to convince him to change. Had myself convinced I was frettin' over his soul. But the truth be told, I was selfish and stupid because I was worryin' about what others would think of me." Poppa waved his hand at Jordan and Emmy. "Go about your business. God only gives you one life to live. Don't waste it letting others control you. Now what about the presents? Gotta have presents at a birthday."

Before anyone could recuperate from Poppa's bold announcement, Gerry jerked Anne out of the chair by her arm. "Get the kids. We're leaving."

Anne grimaced. "That hurts. Don't touch me like that." Her eyes softened when she focused on Jordan. "The Lord says to love the sinner and loathe the sin. I don't understand why people are gay, but I don't hate them. I don't hate you. Gerry chose poor words, and screaming and name-calling never solves anything." Gerry hissed at her and looked like he was going to explode. She didn't back down. "I'll get the children while you apologize for harshly expressing your views."

As Anne headed to get the kids, Gerry's face contorted.

Poppa glared at him. "Open that pie hole only to apologize."

Gerry stared at Poppa before facing their mother. His facial muscles twitched, and his eyes were dark pools of nothingness. When he spoke, the words sounded mechanical, insincere, and bitter. "I'm sorry for banging my fist on the table and shouting, but I'm not sorry for my beliefs." He gave Jordan and Emmy a look. "You disgust me." Grabbing his coat, he stormed over to the door and mumbled over his shoulder, "Tell Anne I'll be in the car." He slammed the kitchen door rattling the windows to make his final point.

Gwyneth, who was clearly stunned, didn't move for several seconds. She finally came around the table and kissed the top of

Jordan's head. "I love you. I'm going to help with coats, and I'll be right back."

"Mom, I'm sorry it came out like this," Jordan whispered.

"There's nothing to be sorry about, honey." She let out a laugh. "And Poppa, you amaze me every day." He nodded.

Everyone was silent as Gwyneth walked Anne and the kids to the car, but Dave winked, and Carter gave her a thumbs up. The cousins and their spouses sat like bumps on a log before one got up. He was Aunt Elizabeth's son. "We should be going too."

Elizabeth shot him a sour look. "What are you in such a hurry for? Your cousin hasn't opened her presents. Sit down." He reluctantly retook his seat.

Jordan was relieved that a burden had been lifted from her soul. She would deal with her relatives' mixed reactions later. Hopefully, they would be respectful enough to allow her to tell others her story on her terms. Yet she was certain Gerry's big mouth would hit the town in no time.

"More coffee or tea?" Carter's wife, Angie, had picked up the pot and was refilling everyone's cup. "By the way, Emmy, I think that is the loveliest sweater and jacket combo. And your shoes, so stylish. Jordan prefers simple, but I hope you can spice up her wardrobe now that you're dating."

The words shook Jordan out of her shock and calmed her nerves. Angie sat back down and continued as if nothing had happened. "Emmy, you should come shopping with us. The kids are a handful, even when Jordan is helping me."

"We've got more excitement in Alaska than shopping. You two should visit us. Emmy, Jordan and I can teach you to fish. Nothing like fresh sockeye salmon over the fire."

Gwyneth stepped back into the house to a lighter mood. "I believe we were talking about presents before I left. Shall we?" She smiled at them but was clearly fighting back the tears.

With fingers intertwined, Jordan and Emmy walked quietly to the SUV.

"I'm proud of you, sweetie."

"Overall, it went better than I expected. I'm still in a daze about Poppa's brother and no one knowing."

"Families are full of surprises."

"I'll ask again. Do you still want to be my girlfriend?"

Emmy wrapped her arms around Jordan. "Yep. I don't scare that easy. I know it was hard, but you handled it well. Besides, I love your grandparents and mum. And Carter's so sweet. Forget about Gerry. Right now, I'm freezing my bloody arse off. Let's go."

At home, Jordan was rolling her neck and rubbing the back of it with one hand. Emmy had come to know that was one of Jordan's habits when things bothered her.

"Start us a fire. I'm going to change and get this makeup off. Be right back."

When Emmy returned, Jordan was leaning against the mantel staring down at the shimmering flames and deep in thought with a half-empty glass of merlot in her hand. She'd lit some candles, and the scent of vanilla wafted through the room. Emmy sat on the sofa and sipped from the glass Jordan had poured for her. Jordan didn't move or notice Emmy was present.

"The fire's going now. Come here and lay back. I'll give you a short massage."

Jordan obeyed, and Emmy lightly rubbed her temples then moved to her shoulders. She could sense Jordan beginning to relax.

"Oh, that's amazing."

"Relax. Give yourself and the wine some time to breathe."

After vigorously kneading Jordan's shoulders, she lightened her touch along Jordan's neck and scalp with gentle circles.

Soon, she heard the sound of Jordan deep in slumber. Emmy smoothed her hair. Jordan had been through a lot, and Emmy loved the strong woman who was beginning to show through more often.

As Jordan slept, Emmy recalled a discussion with her aunt. Betty Jean mentioned Jordan's family had once been more reserved. She also revealed that Gwyneth had expressed regret for letting Jordan move to Spain and blamed herself for the distant relationship. Then Betty Jean said something Emmy didn't understand. She said, "...the timing was odd...maybe that's also part of the reason she moved." When Emmy asked what she meant, Betty Jean cut off the conversation by saying, "That's something for you and Jordan to discuss at some point."

Jordan needed a good rest tonight and some time to process the events. There was no rush. Emmy delicately brushed Jordan's hair and whispered, "We have so much to talk about because I'm crazy in love with you." Jordan's eyelashes fluttered, but she didn't wake. She looked peaceful.

Chapter Twenty-Four

*T*oday was Wednesday and Jordan's actual birthday. She walked into the restaurant as if it was any other day of the year. No one mentioned the occasion, and Jordan wasn't going to point it out. Other than talking to her mom on the phone, she had not seen any other family members since the Sunday party. Perhaps she'd leave after dinner and drop by her mom's house.

The lunch hour was busy, but things went crazy in the late afternoon when a delayed food shipment arrived. Since she had bought ingredients elsewhere, they had to hustle to find room in the walk-in refrigerator and freezer, and fast. It was half an hour before the main dinner rush. As they finished, the crowd came pouring in, almost at the same time. Nearly every table was full.

Jordan breathed a sigh of relief as they caught up with preparing the meals, then Jo was standing before her with a concerned look. "We've got a problem with a large, rowdy group. I think you'd better check it out."

Robby shrugged his shoulders, and they both followed Jordan. She calmly walking into the dining room. In the middle sat her mom and Dave, Elizabeth, Sam and Gina, Carter and his wife and kids, and Betty Jean and Emmy. Sam stood with a big cake as Carter motioned around the room for the entire crowd to sing. To Jordan's amazement, everyone did. She was over-whelmed with joy.

After Robby and Jo's insistence, she sat with everyone for nearly an hour. They couldn't talk her into leaving with them, but she promised not to stay late. "Just a couple of bills to pay, and I'm outta here," she mumbled as she snuck away to her office.

"Jordan! What are you doing hiding in here? It's your birthday." Jo flicked her wrist several times. "Go home and relax. Watch a movie or snuggle with someone." She wiggled her eyebrows.

"I promise to leave after I finish with these bills."

"If you're not gone in five minutes, we're going to drag your butt out the door."

"Deal."

After many years of grappling with her inner turmoil, the feelings of relief and freedom washed over Jordan. She felt blessed, yet the journey was not over. There was one more secret left to be told. She had come so far and wasn't going to let her past, or Darrell, hold her down. She smiled knowing she was going home to a beautiful woman she loved. Tonight, she'd get it all out in the open.

Leaving early, she stepped out into a crisp cold night. Halfway to her SUV, she stopped, breathed in the air, and looked up at the stars. So many shined, even with the dim lighting from the buildings.

"Good evening."

She jumped as Darrell stood at the end of her SUV. Her muscles stiffened. *What is he doing here?*

"I mean you no harm. I'm disappointed we couldn't talk last week."

His gun was on his hip in plain sight. *I don't want to die like this.* Jordan stood ready to make a run for it when he laughed. A chill came over her. A heavy wave of sickness and remorse rolled through her as she recalled the last time she heard his maniacal laugh. The night Karen died.

When he finally stopped, the muscle in his jaw tightened. Even several feet away, she could see the change in his demeanor. Words wanted to come out, but her mouth was instantly dry. The thumping noise of her heart drowned out the sounds around her. She grabbed hold of a nearby parking sign to steady herself. Her brain was screaming at her, but her legs were leaden.

He took a couple of steps toward her. "I'm sorry to have startled you, Jordan. It's haunted me all these years. I'd change it if I could."

She knew this time would come, but she didn't want to remember the graphic details. And she sure as hell didn't want to discuss it in the back parking lot.

His voice changed to more sympathetic. "We were kids. Stupid kids. None of it was our fault. It was an accident."

While that was the truth, she could never think about that day without guilt and pain ripping through her. Like her sexuality, she had tried to bury the trauma, but it lurked within the deepest confines of her mind. She did get help in Spain. It had taken many sessions and several years to accept that she had done all she could under the circumstances. Yet, she had never fully forgiven herself.

"It was so hard to take. It almost destroyed my life. I was lucky to have made it out of high school." Jordan's voice was barely above a whisper.

Darrell scowled at her and wasted little time in blurting out, "You? I ran away. If those cops caught me boozed and doped up, they would have blamed me. I would have gone to prison. I wasn't from a privileged family like you. Do you even have a clue what it was like trying to live on my own at seventeen?"

The feeling of wanting to throw up subsided as she looked at Darrell and felt empathy. Years ago, she had wanted to blame him, but like the guilt she held, nothing was going to bring Karen or Tommy back. It was a pain that refused to leave her heart. The best she could do was go on because Karen would never have wanted her to give up.

"I'm sorry, Darrell. I never thought of how it affected you."

His mood darkened and his face contorted in a hateful look. He had tightened his hands into fists and clenched his jaw again.

"From what I can see, you pulled yourself through and seem to be living it up. Your restaurant is raking in the dough." She recoiled at his threatening tone. He moved closer. "Oh, don't worry. I'm not going to physically hurt you, but you owe me for moving out of town and becoming a ghost. A little money thrown my way would even the score. After all, it spared you from having to reveal your little secret lesbo romantic rendezvous."

The sinister sneer on his face, like that day years ago, revealed his true intentions. Her body shook. Her blood pulsated through her veins.

"You're blackmailing me?" she mumbled.

His body relaxed, and the intimidating laugh was back until broken by his eerie voice.

"Let's see. Everyone thought Tommy and Karen had made up, and the awful tragedy happened because the rejoined lovebirds were drinking." His hand gestures made a sickening theatrical display, painting the horrific day as humorous. "I hear Tommy boy had twice the legal alcohol blood level. And let's not forget the weed. Just two underage kids getting a little over their heads. Pardon, the pun."

His laughter was wild as he now stood in her face with a sardonic expression. *He's crazy.* She had come close to passing out before. Now she slumped on the ground. He appeared pleased with the results and didn't let up.

"Sure convenient for you that everyone thought it was Tommy's fault. I wonder what Karen's parents would have done if they knew you were fucking their daughter." His angry words spilled through his gritted teeth. "How long had you two been getting it on anyway? You both looked pretty cozy that day. By the way, does anyone in this town know you're a lesbo?"

He looked triumphant as he watched the terror his threats evoked. "A good ten thousand dollars ought to keep your secrets safe."

"Darrell," she mouthed by sheer determination, "this is insane. I'm not going to pay you any money. It was an accident."

He closed the gap between them and leaned down, inches from her face. He put his cold, muscular hand on her shoulder and squeezed as his angry eyes stared through her. She was helpless.

"Yes. You will pay. We both left the scene of an accident and never told anyone." His chilling words ripped her apart. "Only, you've got the little lesbo secret going on. How many people are going to visit your lovely establishment when they find out the details of your sinful intimate life?" He let the words sink in as he continued to glare. His final words punctured her heart. "And let's face it, it's your fault. The accident would never have happened if you hadn't taken her out there to fuck her. Think about it. I'll be in touch."

He walked away, whistling to the tune of "Chattahoochee." His steps were in time to the beat as he shouted over his shoulder. "Brings back such memories."

The playful, upbeat song was on the local station's classic country playlist, and she remembered the video. Now that song would only bring sorrow to her. She lay on the ground, curled up, and could no longer hold back the tears. Darrell's threats brought it all vividly rolling back. Her stomach heaved, and she did not have the strength to raise her head. The contents splattered on her clothes and dribbled down her face.

Emmy. Oh, God. I was going to tell her. Mother, why did I never tell you? It was an accident. It was no one's fault. Control. Got to breathe and calm down. I can do this.

Time was elusive, yet she did not pass out. As she lay in the putrid smell of her vomit, the back door opened. She didn't want to face anyone right now, but she needed help.

"Oh my God. Jordan! What happened?"

At least it was Robby. She would have hated for one of the younger employees to see her in such wretched disarray.

"I'm fine. My blood sugar dropped. I need a snack."

"I'll call an ambulance."

"No! I'll be fine Robby."

She shook herself from Robby's grasp, rose on wobbly legs, then fumbled around in her backpack.

"SweeTARTS. I'll pop some of these and be fine."

"Let me help you inside. You can rest and wash up."

"*No!* I've been through this before."

"You look like shit, there's an enormous pool of vomit on the ground, and you think candy is going to snap you back?"

"It's like a glucose tab. It helps stabilize me." Jordan mustered all her strength to control her voice. "Look, you can get me some crackers and water. That helps as well, but I'm not going back in the kitchen. I'll sit in my SUV."

"I'll do it under one condition. You let me call Emmy to pick you up. You're in no condition to drive!"

He didn't wait for her reply as he pulled out his cell.

Jordan reclined in the passenger seat. Her eyes were closed, and she shivered despite having a blanket wrapped around her.

Emmy drove carefully. It was pitch black and sharp ditches lined each side of the narrow, winding country road. She was overwhelmed with concern, which was now mixed with rising anger. First, Jordan had stubbornly refused to be taken to a medical facility and would not tell her or Robby what was going on. Now she was giving her the silent treatment. *Dammit*, Emmy thought. *Who is this dark stranger?*

"Jordan, you have to talk." The words sounded harsher than Emmy intended, but when Jordan's only reply was rustling in her seat, Emmy lost it. "Goddammit, don't do this to me! You're scaring me. Please talk to me."

"I don't know. There's so much. Just don't know where to begin," Jordan stammered.

Emmy didn't know what to make of the dazed woman at her side. She had to do something. Seeing an entrance to a farm field, she pulled over and slammed on the brakes. The car jerked to a stop, nearly missing fence posts. In desperation, she released their safety belts and firmly grabbed Jordan's face with both hands. She pulled her in close. "You've made such progress. Don't shut down on me now!" Tears formed and threatened to fall. She pleaded, "Please talk to me."

In her hands, Jordan felt like a stiff, lifeless form. Without warning, she wrapped her arms around Emmy and buried her face in the crook of her neck and began to sob. Emmy's heart broke seeing her in utter despair.

Long minutes passed, and Jordan choked out some words at last. "Em, I'm so sorry." She shook, and Emmy didn't know what was coming next. Had someone done something to her? Was she sick? She feared the worst.

"Something terrible happened in high school," Jordan mumbled. "My... my girlfriend. It was an accident." Her voice quavered.

Emmy whispered, "I want to help. Trust me. Calm down and open up to me. Breathe."

Through sobs, Jordan sputtered out words that were scarcely coherent. "I never told anyone the real story, but there was one person who knew the truth. He disappeared after the accident. Tonight, he came to blackmail me by playing on my guilt."

Emmy had never seen Jordan this vulnerable and broken. "Breathe, sweetheart."

"I'm sorry, Em. It was an accident. I was going to tell you tonight."

For a tragedy that occurred twenty-plus years ago to have such an impact on Jordan, it could be no typical accident.

Jordan's next words startled Emmy. "Don't leave me, Em."

"I'm not going anywhere. Just don't push me out."

"I promise to tell you everything at home."

Emmy kissed the clean side of Jordan's face and rocked her. "Okay. Let's get you home, showered, and into bed. At the moment, you're not looking too attractive with puke caked on the side of your face. And you stink. Cleaning you up will be better for both our stomachs."

Jordan gave her a weak smile and slumped back into the seat.

Emmy would wait for the full story, but her mind was spinning fast. What was the accident? What happened to her girlfriend? Did Jordan somehow cause the accident? They had shared so much love over the past couple of months, and she had to put her faith in Jordan. Reaching over, she gave her forearm a squeeze and held her hand.

Chapter Twenty-Five

The hot water cascaded over her body and loosened the knots in her muscles. After dressing in her favorite pajamas, Jordan lay in the crook of Emmy's arm and nuzzled her neck. She was welcomed with more kisses, and Emmy's hand caressed her shoulder and arm.

"Please, open up to me, Jordan. Tell me about the accident." Emmy's voice cracked, and her eyes pleaded. "When you wouldn't talk to me earlier, I was hurt and concerned."

Wrapped in Emmy's arms, Jordan felt loved and safe. Her fears began to recede. True love required trust and honesty. *No more secrets,* Jordan told herself. *You promised. You can do this. Tell her. Tell her everything.*

"Life is like a house. Always unfinished, always changing, and never perfect. I know the best balance is to live in the present and not get stuck in the past. Yet sometimes, I'm tearing down the walls at the same time I'm building new ones. I spin in a circle, inside. When I'm like that, it's hard to break out."

"You have to give yourself some credit." Emmy reached out and interlaced her fingers with Jordan's. She rubbed and kissed the palm of her hand.

A tear trickled down Jordan's face. "I fell in love in high school. Her name was Karen." Jordan stopped. More tears streamed down her face.

"Take your time." Emmy kissed the top of her head and stroked her cheek.

Jordan sat up and drew her knees to her chest. She sniffled and wiped away the tears before describing the worst day of her life.

"It was a gorgeous day in May for a picnic along the Potomac. We skipped school to celebrate our one-year anniversary. The area was too dangerous to swim because of the strong undercurrents and sharp drop-offs near the shore. Karen had brought a bottle of wine, which we drank over several hours. We were buzzed, not drunk, and never had—" She sniffled and wiped away the tears. "We had never been intimate in the outdoors. Always private, behind closed doors. But the alcohol made us brave. We must have gone to that exact same spot over a dozen times in the past and were never interrupted." She spoke through clenched teeth. "And wouldn't you know Karen's ex-boyfriend shows up."

Emmy cradled Jordan against her chest and stroked her hair. "Let it out, sweetie. It's okay to cry. I've got you."

"I was in my underwear. Karen had just removed her shirt and was unhooking her bra. Tommy came out of nowhere. I remember his exact words: 'You fucking little sick dykes!' He shoved Karen away and kicked me several times before assaulting Karen. I was going to help, but his minion showed up and stopped me. If I hadn't hit my head, I could have taken Darrell's skinny ass. The jerk-off was only popular because he supplied weed to the upper crust including Tommy's football team. The pain in my ribs and stomach weren't the problem. One of the kicks snapped my head back on a rock." The tears flowed down Jordan's cheeks. "Darrell continued to taunt me. The fighting grew louder. Then I heard Karen cry out as she slipped. I managed to get up and take a few steps before stumbling and falling down at the shore, but they were gone. Darrell was running away, and then there was silence. I blacked out, probably more from shock than anything. By the time consciousness returned, hours had passed, and my head was throbbing. I don't know how I made it to the car."

Jordan's body heaved with heavy sobs, and she lay limp in Emmy's arms. Now they were both crying.

"Oh, sweetie," Emmy said, kissing the top of Jordan's head again. "I can't imagine how difficult this has been for you." She rocked her for several minutes.

"My mom had a long meeting after work and didn't think anything about me being in bed when she came home. I told her I had been feeling ill all day. As for my distraught behavior, she assumed I had heard the news about Karen and Tommy's drowning on the radio. I never told her the truth. Never. She made me go to a shrink for the summer because I barely finished school. Everyone suspected that Tommy and Karen had gotten back together and it was all a horrible accident brought on by teenage drinking and horseplay. No one knew about our relationship, and candy-ass Darrell left town. No one heard from him for years, and I never saw the bastard again until the other night."

"Forget that creep. He sounds like a megalomaniac," Emmy snapped. "Believe in yourself."

"I'm so tired, Em. I had been surviving for years, mentally beating myself up. Spain was an escape as much as it was an adventure. When my relationship started falling apart, I finally sought help. It wasn't easy, especially after my experience with the condescending asshole therapist after high school. He may have sounded professional to my mom, but he was a misogynist behind closed doors. I was never comfortable with him. The therapist in Madrid was the exact opposite. She helped me."

"Good. I'm happy you trusted again." Emmy rubbed her hand. "You're strong."

"At first, I had my doubts even though my gay friend recommended her. The therapist was straight, and her office was an extension of the apartment she shared with her teenage daughter. For weeks, she tried to make me feel comfortable and coax out information. I was petrified when I eventually spoke about my sexuality and Karen's death. Instantly, she showed compassion and understanding. From that day forward, I began to heal. Never completely, but at least I began to love myself. Months before I left Spain, she gave me a copy of Simmons's book. We discussed it in a few sessions, but it took me a couple of years to absorb the words. By then, I had the other problem which I confessed to you on the hike."

"The hookups?"

"Yeah."

"Jordan, that's part of your past, and we've all made mistakes. Right now, you've got me in your corner, and your family has accepted you." Emmy shrugged. "Well, almost all of your family."

"Remember the day in the coffeehouse and the quote from the book?"

"Something about letting go."

"Yes. I knew that I had to let go and forgive myself to achieve peace and freedom, but despite good intentions, I kept teetering back and forth between faking it and coming clean. When I got to the point where I couldn't take it anymore, I felt myself slowly letting go and like Simmons said, 'Fall with grace, to grace.' Meeting you was the incentive. Despite my fear of Darrell, he was the impetus that pushed me over the edge. I can't turn back. I don't want to turn back. I have to move forward."

Emmy gently lifted her face and looked into her eyes. "Push this Darrell creep out of your mind. He can go to hell, and anyone who doesn't appreciate you for who you are can follow right behind him. So, what if he outs you to the town. It won't be easy, but I'm right here. Your mum and Carter are behind you."

"You're right. I am not going to let him have any more power over me, and I'm not going to pay him. It was such a shock, and the asshole picked my birthday of all days. More important, I promise no more secrets, but this weight on my heart won't release until I completely tell my story to those affected."

"You should speak with your mother."

"Yes, but I have to do more." Tears formed again. "I have to talk to Karen's parents."

"Jordan, that won't bring her back, and it's going to open up old wounds."

"I have an obligation. I want them to know we loved one another. They need to understand that I would have saved her if I could."

"And what if their reaction is negative or angry?"

"No matter the consequences—good or bad—this is something I have to face. They deserve to hear the truth and not some twisted version through Darrell or town gossip."

"When?"

"They moved away shortly after the accident. Somehow, I'll find them. I'll never forgive myself if I don't try."

"And what about Darrell? He's not going away easily. What will you do?"

"I don't have a choice. I need to trust the sheriff. The sooner, the better."

With Emmy by her side, she went to Sheriff Johnson's office the next day. Waiting for his answer was agonizing. Now they were back Saturday morning. What a way to start the weekend.

"Good morning, ladies." Sheriff Johnson sat back in the big oak chair eyeing Jordan. "I've researched the case and consulted the judge. He agrees with me. You're one of the victims. There would be no grounds to charge you with any crime." He leaned his elbows on the desk and peered at the old paper file then looked over the top of his bifocals and smiled. "Well, there was the underage drinking, but it's a little late to charge you with that."

His joke did nothing. Jordan kept her mouth shut because she didn't trust her stomach from emptying its contents. Not that she'd eaten much over the past three days.

"Jordan. Look at me." His dark green eyes conveyed concern. "I can't guarantee I can keep Darrell from hollerin' up and down the valley, but I will stop him from extortion. The question is, do you want to press formal charges?"

Jordan wiped a tear from the corner of her eye. "I don't know. It might make him spill his guts sooner. What's your opinion?"

"Hard to say. You might wait on formal charges if you continue to have problems. I do think we ought to slap a restraining order on him." Jordan nodded. "I'll have my clerk help you fill out the forms after we're done here. But I intend to pay the boy a visit." The sheriff picked up another file and tossed it across the desk. "Darrell was livin' way down in McDowell County and has a long record. A DUI, a couple of breaking and entering, possession of marijuana, and a charge of raping a minor. He got out of the latter. The girl was months away from eighteen, and she and the parents eventually dropped the charges." He leaned back. "Point being, I don't need the son of a bitch causing trouble here. While I'll serve the restraining order, I fully intend to run his ass out of town as quickly as possible."

"Yes, sir."

"It's none of my business but what about your family?"

The question was like a dagger through her throat. She eventually choked out the words. "My birthday turned out better than expected. Some of the family's still in a little shock. Nothing I can't handle."

"Does your mama know about Darrell?"

Jordan gripped Emmy's hand. "No, sir. I was hoping you'd be able to help, and I could give her some good news instead of worrying her."

"Well, I'll corner Darrell as fast as possible. He's bad news and messin' with you honestly pisses me off. I'll shut him up the best I can."

Jordan smiled at that one. "Thank you, sir."

"Hang in there. I'll be in touch. And good luck with your mama."

Jordan was thankful she didn't lose it and break down. They walked to the car in silence. When Emmy put the key in the ignition, Jordan reached over to stop her.

"Em. I'd rather face judgment from the town and get it over with." Jordan cupped Emmy's face and saw tears. "I know this is hard on you. I'm sorry. You don't deserve to be dragged through all this drama and bullshit. The thing I'm scared of the most right now is losing you. Please, stay with me."

After wiping her eyes, Emmy tucked a strand of Jordan's hair behind her ear and softly rubbed Jordan's face with the back of her hand. "It hasn't been easy, but I think you're stuck with me. Sure, I've had moments where I've been pissed with you"—Emmy pulled her into a tight embrace—"but somewhere along the line, I fell madly in love with you."

They lingered in each other's arms for several moments. Jordan pushed back slightly and caressed Emmy's face then gave her a long, searing kiss. They were parked in the main lot for the sheriff's department and the courthouse near the donut shop. Jordan didn't care if anyone saw. She deepened the kiss then rested her forehead against Emmy's. They were so close she could feel the fluttering of her eyelashes.

"I love you, Em."

Speaking those three words brought her peace, but as they drove away, she prayed her love would be enough for Emmy.

Farther down the road, Emmy turned on the radio and Jordan couldn't believe her ears. "Learn to Love Yourself" was playing, and once again, the line about love leading home resonated in her heart and mind. It had to be a good omen. How she got so lucky was a mystery, but she was determined to conquer her fears, live truthfully, and make this relationship last. She leaned over and kissed Emmy's cheek.

Chapter Twenty-Six

ordan peered out the large picture window. In the dawn of day, a thick fog painted the sky gray and fuzzy, wrapping its tentacles around the forest on the windward slope as the clouds swept over the ridge. Jordan loved the woods and never found the fog menacing like most people. Instead, she took comfort as it enshrouded the house in a tight sheath. Soon, the sun shone brightly, lifting the fog, but the wind, moisture, and freezing temperatures worked magic creating rime ice. The brilliant white tiny crystals formed along every branch and twig. The beauty and solitude of nature gave her time to think and regroup her inner strength and focus.

Five days had slipped by since she'd told Emmy the heart-wrenching story about Karen. Efforts to reach Karen's parents ended in sorrow. Both were deceased. Guilt still lingered and twisted inside Jordan. Today, she was heading to her mom's house. Her mother had called, upset, requesting they speak, and frankly, Jordan was ready to get it all out. She didn't know how her mom would react, but she couldn't control that. Just like other things, she needed to let go.

Like the lifting fog leaving behind a crystalline world, the consequences of clearing her conscience and speaking her truth were entirely in the eyes of the beholder. That was a risk she had taken on her birthday, and now she needed to heal their relationship. Mom had always told her it was not the fall others would remember but how one stood back up with conviction.

She left the house, oddly at peace. As she pulled into the driveway, her mom stepped outside and motioned for her to come in. *You can do this.* As Jordan came closer, it was obvious her mom's eyes were red, but she smiled and gave Jordan a strong, heartfelt hug. Jordan gingerly stepped inside, almost feeling like a little girl again. Her mother immediately motioned toward the living room.

"No coffee today, Mom?"

"Afraid not. Instead, I've got water and tissues."

Jordan had a bad feeling in the pit of her stomach. *Had Darrell already contacted her?*

Gwyneth was happy to sit. Her roiling stomach and anxiety were about to get the best of her. No matter what, she had to do this. She had to make it right.

"Honey, we haven't been close over the years, and I'm sorry." Tears brimmed in her eyes. "I'm also to blame for pushing us apart."

"No, Mom. It's not your fault."

Gwyneth put up her hand. "Hear me out. It's going to be a long story. First, I need to tell you I love you and ask for your forgiveness."

"Mom—"

"You're not the only one who's held back. There are things I never said to you the day you came out to me. It's my turn to be truthful because I haven't been for the longest time. I've made a lot of mistakes, and I am so sorry." She sniffled. "Yes, I only wanted the best for you, but I took a rigid approach that in the end made things worse. Your grades throughout school were always so high. You could have had any career, yet you were determined to be a chef." She brushed Jordan's cheek and gave a little smile, but her lips quivered. "When Karen died, I came down hard on you. You were falling off the deep end, and nothing was working with the psychologist. In fact, I was downright angry with you. The Culinary Institute of America was within your reach, and I didn't understand how you could not get over Karen and go on with life."

Jordan's eyes widened, giving Gwyneth pause, but she had to go on. "Yes, even back then, I suspected. My heart broke too, but I didn't want to see you hurt. I knew there wouldn't be much of a life for you in Oakville. When you faltered, your dream of becoming a chef and snagging a job in New York City became my dream, and I pushed you hard. I'm sorry. It was wrong, and I made a mistake."

Jordan started to say something when Gwyneth gently put her fingers up to her mouth. "So, I pushed because I also wanted you to go somewhere that you'd be able to live your life and I'd see you often. A place where you had space and time to grow comfortable with who you are." Tears filled Gwyneth's eyes. "And a time for me to grow comfortable with you." She wiped her eyes, and her voice shook. "That year when you failed at The Culinary Institute of America and came home, I just about lost it. I never shared my feelings with anyone, which only drove a wedge further between us."

Jordan sighed. "I guess that's something we share in common. A stubborn will to do things alone without help."

Gwyneth smiled weakly before she broke down. Her entire body shook. Jordan tried to console her, but she sobbed hard. The roles were now reversed as Jordan carefully smoothed her hair and whispered that everything would be all right.

When Gwyneth calmed, she pushed back from Jordan's shoulder. "I have to finish this."

Jordan gave her a kiss and nodded.

"I was a basket case by the time you brought the idea of transferring to Spain. Part of me was worried I'd lose you, but by that point, you seemed better. You had a plan and laid it out perfectly. And there was no way I could stop you since you were over eighteen." She sniffled and patted Jordan's hand. "I was happy when your performance and grades were stellar, but I never thought you would stay in Spain for fifteen years." Jordan felt her mom's hand trembling. "I missed you terribly."

"I'm sorry I only came home a couple of times. And I wasn't exactly the doting daughter when you visited. I didn't want you to know about my real life. Scheduling work to get out of being with you was something I did in part out of fear and in part subconsciously. I guess I've always used work as an excuse."

Tears threatened to roll down Gwyneth's cheek again. "Well, I have a shameful confession. Several actually. I never wanted to see you hurt. At the same time, I also lacked the courage to face the opinions of others. But that's not the most shameful part of what I've done." Her voice broke, and she pulled completely away from Jordan. "I hope you can forgive me for this."

"Of course, Mom. We've both made mistakes."

Gwyneth bit her lip, and the tears released. "As you became more successful, I didn't want anything to spoil your moment to shine. I could tell things weren't perfect, but you were happier in Spain than here. So, when Susan first brought it to me. I just didn't want to follow through. I—"

"Mom, I'm confused. Who is Susan and what did she bring you?"

Gwyneth took a deep breath and looked at Jordan. She knew the fear in her eyes showed, but she had to face her demons. "Susan Browne, Karen's mom."

Jordan's mouth dropped, and Gwyneth saw a mixture of anxiety, surprise, and indignation in her eyes.

Gwyneth wet her lips and moved on. "When Susan was sick, she asked me to visit her. She was in home hospice care and didn't have long. She gave me Karen's diary and a letter."

A million feelings washed over Jordan instantaneously, and she became dizzy. The secret was like a knife plunged into her heart. When she finally got a grip, the waves had diminished, but a tinge of anger remained. After realizing she was holding her breath, she took in a gulp of air and let it out. She had to let the anger go. After all, she had done far worse. She owed it to her mother to listen and forgive.

"What was in them? Do you still have them?"

With a shaky hand, Gwyneth held out the letter. Jordan wiped tears away with a tissue and squinted at the neat but tiny handwriting.

Dear Jordan,

This is a long time coming but time is not on my side. I never really caught on that you were more to my daughter than her best friend. I'm sorry. I was blind.

Moving away never did completely heal our hearts over Karen's drowning. After my husband's death, I found some unpacked moving boxes. They contained Karen's things. Something was calling to me to open those boxes, and when I did, I found Karen's diary.

As I read her detailed account of her love for you and the future plans and dreams you both shared, I was overcome with many emotions. None of which was anger at you or her.

It's hard to lose your only child, and I can't imagine how you felt. My love for her would never have wavered regardless of who she was or who she loved. And my feelings toward you would not have changed. She was such a precious daughter and so full of life whenever she was around you. And now I know why. She wrote about your physical relationship, but none of it was dirty. It was woven with an emotional warmth that you were the only person for her, and how you made her happy.

This diary isn't one of sadness. It's one of joy. Take it and read it. I hope it will give you some closure to this tragedy as it did with me.

With much love,
Susan Browne

Jordan's nose and eyes were dripping. She wouldn't look at her mother when Gwyneth passed her the diary.

"Why did you keep this from me?"

"Honey, I'm so sorry. It was ten years ago. I agonized over giving you the diary because you were doing so well. You'd just been named Executive Chef in Madrid. I didn't want to open old wounds. And the woman, Luciana, I didn't want to upset your relationship, and—"

"Well, that wasn't a perfect relationship." Jordan let out a bitter huff. "She turned out to be a little cheating bitch." Jordan wanted to snap her mom's head off and chew her out good, but the logical side of her brain was screaming at her. *Relax. You've lied too. Give her a break.*

"Honey, I worried your senior year of high school that you would commit suicide." Jordan's head pivoted. Her mom squeezed her hand. "I didn't want to throw you back into that chaos. When you came home to open the restaurant, I thought you had everything together. Well, except you were glued to work."

"Yep, I always did use school or work as a drug to ease my pain." *And you always read me better than I thought.*

"I meant it when I wished you and Emmy happiness. She's good for you. There is a light that shines in your eyes that hasn't been there since back when you were young. And there's playful mischief in your smile that I haven't seen since your time with Karen. As for my selfishness of worrying about others' opinions, I let that go several years back, but I was too scared and didn't know what to say. That's my sin. Not coming to you and speaking the truth. I was on the verge of telling you when you decided to"—Gwyneth chuckled, her tone playful—"shock everyone into reality at your birthday." She clasped Jordan's hand. "You're my only daughter. Please forgive me."

Jordan squeezed her eyes closed and pinched the bridge of her nose. She took in deep breaths. As she released each one, she shook slightly, trying to keep her emotions from exploding.

"Honey, say something. Yell at me if you want, but please say something."

Jordan clenched her jaw. She willed herself to continue. "I forgive you, and I forgive myself." She swallowed hard and opened her eyes. "Today seems a big day for bearing our souls." Her heart pounded, and tears welled up. "There's more to the accident than you know. I saw Karen die, but I couldn't help her." She turned away and placed her hand over her eyes and nose to stifle the cries, but nothing could stop the awful heart-wrenching sound.

"Oh, honey."

Jordan rested in her mother's arms and finally told the story of the terrible day on the river. They clung to each other. The physical comfort relayed the love they had so many times not vocalized.

Instead of going home right away, Jordan drove to the mountain lookout. She sat on the hood of her SUV. There was little wind, the fog was gone, and the sun beat down warming the cold terrain.

She had always been fearful of bigoted people harming her and her business. Now she realized her worst fear had been worry about losing the love of her family and friends. With her greatest fear behind her, she could move on.

Tomorrow, Emmy would leave for Scotland. She trusted and loved her but wished the timing was better. Jumping down, she picked up a stick and threw it out over the cliff. She'd come here to reflect and enjoy the beauty, and she hoped with all her heart that Emmy would stay with her and share the magic of these mountains.

Chapter Twenty-Seven

They were both exhausted from the events. What a week. While Emmy was in the shower, Jordan left a short note before setting out to the grocery store. She wanted to fix Emmy a special breakfast before driving her to Dulles International Airport. She also needed some time alone to clear her head.

Strolling down the aisles, Jordan selected fresh vegetables for her favorite quiche recipe. While debating on buying ingredients for cinnamon rolls, she had an odd feeling and turned around. An older woman cradling a baby and a young woman were scrutinizing her with deep frowns.

The older woman spoke first. "You should be ashamed of yourself bringing sin down on your family. Poor Gerry. I don't care if that English woman influenced you or not. You should have the backbone and the faith in God to do the right thing. You didn't, and I have no sympathy for you. You're a disgusting lesbian, and you'll never amount to anything. Repent, or you'll never get out of Hades."

The young woman spat more venomous words. "You're not a Christian. You're an abomination. Have you even read the Holy Bible?"

The words stunned Jordan. As hurt and fear surged through her, somehow she replied with steadiness. "Ladies, you should reexamine your faith. God and Jesus taught love. Religious freedom guarantees you the right to practice your faith. It does not give you the right to impose your beliefs on me or anyone else. If you'll excuse me, I'm going to check out."

The women blocked Jordan's moves and spat out more hatred. Another woman pushing a cart filled to the brim arrived with two young teenage girls. This woman said, "Excuse me, but isn't your granddaughter born out of wedlock?"

Jordan noticed the irate woman with the baby flinch. "That has nothing to do with this. Josh was in the army. They were going to get married, but he's in Afghanistan now. They're normal people. She is—"

"You're a hypocrite. You should go home and think about ways to improve your life instead of knocking down others. You have no right to judge someone else."

"I am a Christian who cares about values—"

The woman with the two teenagers cut her off in a loud, clear voice. "I want my family to be around people who are decent, honest, and fair. Who they choose to love does not define them nor does it make them evil. You, on the other hand, are a narrow-minded, self-righteous, blow horn!"

The irate woman's shrill response bordered on screaming. "I can't believe you are setting such a poor example in front of your children. She"—the woman pointed at Jordan while clenching the baby—"is not decent. Her sinful fornication—"

The woman abandoned the cart and stepped into the hateful woman's face. Her voice remained loud and clear. "What two consenting adults do in their bedroom is none of anyone's business. Jordan is an amazing person who doesn't deserve your hate. Hate is a sin. I suggest you go home and pray for God to put love back into your heart."

The woman gasped. "What in sweet Jesus is this world coming to?"

"Their senses," the kind woman replied. The two surly women huffed and stormed off.

Jordan smiled at the woman's snappy retort. "Thank you for the support. It's not every day that a stranger comes to the aid of others."

She smiled. "It's been a long time, Jordan. I'm Allison from high school days. These are my daughters Kate and Suzie."

The girls politely stepped forward and shook Jordan's hand. "Pleased to meet you."

"Allison from library club?"

"Yep. You haven't changed much. I've lost a lot of weight and changed my hair color."

"You look great."

Allison grinned. "Thanks. I got married after college, and we moved to upstate New York for my husband's job. We've been back about a month."

Jordan's grin broadened. "You helped me with English, and I helped you with chemistry and math."

"That's right. You also came to my defense a lot when I was bullied because of my weight. Thank you. You made a big difference in my life, and I do think you are an amazing person. And speaking of amazing, the reviews of your restaurant say the food is spectacular. We are planning on going soon." She patted her stomach. "It's going to screw up my exercise routine, but life's short. I think I can handle some cheating with an occasional dessert every now and then."

"Join us anytime. Your first family meal will be on me."

"Oh my, that's gracious of you, but my son and husband could likely eat enough to cost you a small fortune."

"Please, I insist." Jordan pulled out a card and scribbled a note with her cell and her signature on the back. "This will take care of the bill if I'm not around."

After exchanging phone numbers, they parted, and Jordan

made her way to the busy checkout. The cashier began ringing up the groceries but made a mistake. As they stood still waiting for a manager to arrive and fix the problem, Jordan saw the tattoo down her right forearm. In bold black letters, it said, "Let us not love with words or speech but with actions and in truth" ending with "1 John 3:18" in smaller print.

Jordan's attention broke when an elderly woman came up. The white-haired woman wore a necklace with a large crucifix. Jordan said a silent prayer. *Lord, please let me get out of this store without any more drama.*

When Jordan looked back, the cashier said, "Don't let those bible-thumping hypocrites get under your skin. There are lots of good people around here. Lots of good Christians. Not everyone may understand or agree, but there's no need for those ugly words. Sorry, I'm not smiling. My husband just left me for a nineteen-year-old."

Jordan's mouth dropped, and she mumbled, "I'm so sorry."

The cashier began ringing up the groceries again after the register problem was fixed. But she continued to talk. "I'm sure he was screwing around with her long before then. She was our babysitter. That's sick. A married man twice her age using her for his own selfish gain. He messed up everyone's lives because he lacks courage, dignity, and common sense to do the right thing."

Jordan couldn't believe how long the loud woman rattled on without seeming to care who heard. People from other lanes were looking in their direction. When the cashier was about to finish ringing up the last of Jordan's groceries, she began again. "The congregation hardly said anything about him. A few were involved in a rumor that I ignored my husband and deserved it. Can you imagine if that had been me cheating? They would have strung me up on the nearest tree. So, I'm going to a new church." As the transaction was completed, the cashier slammed her cash drawer and grabbed Jordan's hand while giving her the receipt. Her eyes were a mixture of anger and sadness. "I love God, but people who pretend they are the judge and jury need to shut their mouths and fix their own damn lives. So, brush it off." She pointed her finger to stress the next statement. "If you love her and she's worth it, hold your ground and don't let them drag you into their game."

The tiny old woman behind Jordan finally spoke. "Sounds like good advice to me." Jordan nodded and fortunately there were no more comments.

Walking through the parking lot, she tried to process the various sensations and emotions that flooded her body. The roller coaster from tense to cautious and then to happy had looped a couple of times, but one thought stuck with her: *Wow, it may be rough, but things are changing for the better.*

While putting the groceries into the back of the SUV, the sheriff parked next to her. She always parked near the end to get exercise. Thank goodness, it meant no one else was around. She couldn't handle any more surprises today.

"Gorgeous day." He tipped his hat.

"Yep. I take it, you've got news."

"Yep. Sure do." He grinned. "Darrell has left. Gone back south. You shouldn't worry about him anymore. But if anything happens, and I mean anything, I want you to come to me right away."

"It's only been a few days. How did you do it?"

Sheriff Johnson stretched tall and put his hands on his hips. "I scared the livin' shit out of him. He knows he doesn't have two nickels to rub together, and I reminded him that extortion is a felony punishable by one to five years' imprisonment. Plus, I pointed out he's like a one-legged man in a butt-kickin' competition up against me. I can have the town gossiping about his criminal record faster than his dimwitted brain can think." They both laughed.

"Thank you, Sheriff."

When she put her hand out for a shake, he grabbed it with both hands. "We all have a little trouble, and we all make mistakes from time to time. You all were kids years ago. You moved on to make something of your life. Darrell chose a darker path. Forget him and forgive yourself." She nodded. His green eyes twinkled in the sun. "I'm a good lawman, but if you happen to start a discount program for our fine young deputies, then I'd be much appreciative."

"Consider it done."

He tipped his hat again and left.

Jordan bounded up the steps two at a time, her arms full of groceries.

Emmy sauntered into the kitchen wearing her plush bathrobe that showed off her sexy legs. "Almost packed. Goodness, are you fixing an entire buffet?"

"A hearty late breakfast will last you until dinner tonight." Jordan winked and scooped Emmy up for a passionate kiss. Their tongues intertwined and Jordan's hands began to wander.

Out of breath, Emmy broke it off. "My, my, someone has a cheery disposition. We'd better stop before we catch fire to the house."

Jordan beamed and smacked her bottom. "If we must, but you coming out half-naked doesn't help."

"Why are you in such a good mood? You were anxious about my trip last night."

Jordan told Emmy about the events at the grocery store and the news from the sheriff. "It feels like everything is moving in a positive direction. And your trip...well, I know it's crucial to your consulting business, but I will miss you terribly."

"I'll call every day and text. The time will go by fast."

"Oh, I almost forgot, I did get an email from the state department saying my new passport will arrive soon. So next time, let's plan a romantic getaway. Now stop distracting me with your gorgeous body and go get some clothes on. Besides, you need this breakfast. Who knows what they'll serve you on the plane. You will come back to me?" Jordan's words were half joking and half serious."

"Yes, silly. Life is about more than making money. I'll be back in no time."

Jordan's hands lowered from Emmy's back to her butt. Emmy smacked them away. "If you keep doing that, we'll never get to eat, and I'll miss my flight." As she stepped away, she casually opened her robe and flashed her breasts.

"Well, if you do that, you'll never make it to Scotland because I'll keep you in bed." *God, she is hot, and her sly grin is adorable.*

Emmy's voice dropped to a sultry tone. "All right, I'll get dressed but you know I've got an affection for desserts, and I want something special afterward." Before stepping into the bedroom, she dropped the robe.

Jordan threw back her head. "You're killing me. Get dressed, and I promise you'll get your just desserts before we go to the airport."

After breakfast, Jordan checked the traffic. A bad accident had shut down the direct route to the airport in both directions, and they had to leave abruptly. On the way, the alternate route was also choked with traffic. The added stress left them with less than two hours to get Emmy checked in. The line was long and word of a computer problem filtered back through the grumbling passengers.

By the time they got to the counter, the ticketing agent had verified Emmy was on the flight, but apparently, the business class had been overbooked. The agent made several phone calls and typed furiously while apologizing profusely.

"All resolved. I'm sorry about this delay and confusion. I see you are a loyal customer with platinum status." Not wanting to inflame the situation, Emmy nodded. The woman handed Emmy the boarding pass along with her passport and turned on the charm. "I want to thank you for your business and hope that today's experience has not tarnished your view of our service. To ensure your satisfaction, I've booked you into first class at no additional charge. Do you have any further questions?"

She thanked the woman for the upgrade, and they rushed toward security. There was little time to say goodbye. That didn't stop Emmy. Near the entrance with the security line jammed with people, she dropped her bags and took Jordan's hands. "Your eyes are the most amazing deep brown, and your lips are so soft. I'm going to kiss you right here and now in front of all these people because I love you. I don't give a damn what anyone else thinks and neither should you."

Pushing her fear aside, Jordan eased into Emmy's long and sensuous kiss. The announcement of Emmy's international flight broke the moment.

With one last hug, Emmy grabbed her bags and took her place in the TSA PreCheck line, which was as long as the regular line. She shouted over her shoulder, "I'll call when I arrive to let you know I'm safe and to whisper some sweet words to wake you up."

Jordan was bursting. Nothing could wipe off the satisfied grin on her face. She wanted to yell out, "That incredible woman is mine!"

Chapter Twenty-Eight

*E*mmy spotted Calvin Thornton across the restaurant. He was a private man, extremely wealthy, yet generous and kind. It was Calvin who had boosted her career in finance when he picked her to manage his stock portfolio.

She enjoyed his odd humor and company. He could be a royal ass when he was fixated on a harebrained idea. Luckily, he listened to her advice most of the time. When he didn't, he always accepted the blame if things went badly. While he paid her well, he could be time-consuming and demanding. Now was one of those times.

Upon seeing Emmy, he rose, kissed her cheek, and immediately poured her a glass of Scotch. It was pointless to launch immediately into personal business discussions. Drinking over a delicious meal with small talk and a bit of politics beforehand was more his style. To her surprise, he did the opposite tonight.

"I bet you're wondering why I called you here." Calvin beamed at her like he held the secrets of the world. "I've run across some tips in the energy market in the North Sea. Production is expensive, and the price reduction per barrel hasn't helped the market—"

"Stop right there. You're not serious. Your portfolio has a tiny energy segment. And that is not entirely in North Sea wells, which by the way has been declining for several years. On top of that, deep sea drilling is not exactly environmentally friendly. Also, why am I here? You could have sent me the company balance sheets and statistics via email."

He leaned over, the sparkle still in his eyes. "Aberdeen North Sea Oil and Gas Company has found a field worth triple the reserves of the Forties Oil Field. It's the richest in quality to date. They've also come up with a version of horizontal drilling that is more cost effective and reduces the chance of accidents. They are looking to brief potential new investors but only in person. We have an appointment with them on Saturday."

"You're joking, right?" He sipped his Scotch with an impish grin and didn't reply. "My God, I can't believe you're serious. You don't have some crazy idea about touring an oil platform, do you? It's still winter and unnecessary. I'm sure they have excellent videos." She eyed him suspiciously.

"Ah, Lassie, where's your sense of adventure."

She rolled her eyes. The last thing she wanted was to freeze her arse off standing on top of a floating oil rig. From past boating adventures, the swaying rhythm of ocean swells made her susceptible to seasickness. Plus, storms this time of year were unpredictable and could turn brutal within hours.

"Calvin, I'll go to the company for their boring pitch, but if a visit is extended, you go alone. To do my job, I have to see the company's quarterly and annual earnings reports, a future outlook report, their earnings per share and their price-to-earnings multiples, info on the percentage of their market share, and their balance sheet. A list of their executives and bio sheets wouldn't hurt, but I need at least a couple of weeks to look everything over." She took a drink and smirked, confident that her exhaustive request would slow him down.

He reached down and grabbed a black leather briefcase. "Everything is in here."

If Calvin had already amassed this ridiculous amount of data, he was serious. Energy was not a smart move now. "So how much stock are you thinking of buying?"

"I'm looking to sell twenty-five percent of my portfolio. Three-quarters will go into Aberdeen North Sea Oil and Gas Company."

She choked on the Scotch. "That's insane. And the other amount?"

"Well, that little tech company in Glasgow you've had your eye on for the past ten years? I think you might have been onto something. They've got a new line of personal electronic devices. I saw a new laptop computer that blows away the competition, but they've hit a rough spot in financing. Our visit is scheduled tomorrow before the oil company. Oh, that info is also in the briefcase."

This one interested her. Her own portfolio had a minor investment in Campbell Computers. The company had been fairly stable even without major stock gains. Still, her head was spinning from his crazy interest in the North Sea oil industry.

"Calvin, that's a lot of your portfolio to liquidate on a whim."

He looked her straight in the eye. "I believe this is a lucky break, and I need you to formulate a plan with a couple of options. I'm bullish on both opportunities. Of course, if you want nothing to do with it, then I will find other means."

The proclamation shocked her. The contingency plans were to shift toward less risky options. The oil industry was a high-risk venture, but emotions overruled her brain. *You need him. You can't lose his business.*

"I'll keep an open mind and see what I can do to review the material and update your options. Just keep in mind that it will take some time to go through the company data."

"That's my Lassie."

Emmy methodically sipped her Scotch. Calvin was more than capable of outdrinking her and everyone else at the restaurant. She didn't know how he did it, but she could not lose control. When the food arrived, they eased into more enjoyable topics.

"So, my Lass. What have you been up to? I couldn't help noticing that you've spent extra time at your auntie's house. Anyone special in the good ole USA?" He looked at her with a twinkle in his eye.

Emmy broke into a smile as she thought of Jordan. "How is it that you always worm your way into my private life?"

"Because I'm charming, loaded, and a friend besides your number one client. I care about you, and you deserve some happiness. Who is the lucky woman?" He waggled his eyebrows. "I can see she's special. Your eyes are filled with joy and some deliriously wicked thoughts. Why don't you amuse this old friend and tell me about her? And don't leave out any details."

"I never thought I believed in love at first sight, but I'm crazy about her. Jordan's a beautiful person—stunningly gorgeous and a kind soul."

"Blond, brunette, redhead, tall, average. Spit it out, girlfriend and don't leave out the juicy parts." He winked and took a swig of the amber liquid.

"Are physical looks all you care about?"

"And sex but I know you won't reveal that. Although, I can already surmise that you've consummated the relationship. That damn look you're sporting gives it away."

Emmy shook her head with a laugh as she swirled the full-bodied, smoky, rich Scotch. She envisioned pouring it over Jordan's body and licking it off. He snapped his fingers in front of her face, shaking her out of her daze.

"Details, love. Details."

"She's taller than me, fit with silky black hair and gorgeous dark-toned skin. Her father's Spanish and she has a grandmother from

Central America. Her brown eyes and soft hands," Emmy paused, emphasizing the latter, "melt me in an instant. She's smart and talented and owns her own restaurant."

"Oh no, long hours."

"Yes but she's made time for us. Oakville is a small town with a seasonal tourist base." Emmy's face glowed, and her lips curled up into a mischievous smile. "And yes, the sex is great."

"Sounds perfect. I'm happy for you. No hang-ups? I'm sure West Virginia is not the capital of lesbian wonderland."

"She recently came out to her family and a few friends."

"Oh, my. Did it go okay?"

Emmy's smile softened. "It went better than expected except for one brother who's overly religious."

"Um. If he's anything like our religious fanatics here, I understand the apprehension. All those wankers ever do is waste precious time."

"He's a homophobe. Mostly all blow. He's brought heartache and sadness, but Jordan has stood up to him, and her mum and younger brother are brilliant. They've accepted us with open arms."

"And the rest of the family and humble townsfolk?"

"There've been some ups and downs, but many have surprised us with support."

"So how are you going to handle a long-distance relationship? Looks like your job and West Virginia are several hours apart."

"I haven't felt this way since Heather. The feelings are different but stronger. I've moved in with her. And speaking of long distance..." Her tone had become harsher, and she tapped the side of her Scotch glass. "I quit the job at the bank. They did a bait and switch on me and demanded I quit my private financial management business. I couldn't do it. The work would have killed my relationship with Jordan, and I didn't want to cut ties with you and Becca."

"I thought you already signed a lease on a flat in Washington DC."

She swallowed hard and stared into the strong Scotch. "I can do consulting by spending two or three days a week in DC and New York. After I expand my client base, Oakville will be my permanent home. If I take a hit on the rent then so be it." She gave Calvin a serious look. "I would appreciate some help. Two or three more accounts would be great. Could you please steer some of your connections my way?"

"Absolutely, my dear," he replied without hesitation. He reached out and patted her hand. "Those wankers at the London firm held you down and never appreciated your talent."

The night flowed on with brighter conversation and drink. Emmy eventually talked Calvin into calling it a night around 11:00 p.m. After calling Jordan, she experienced the blessed warmth of finding love again and fell asleep quickly.

Chapter Twenty-Nine

So far, the tour of Campbell Computers was running smoothly. Their new thirteen-inch ultraslim notebook had specs that beat all competitors, even the Americans. After going over the details, the development team let Calvin and Emmy play with the standard model. The speed and ease of the interface were like a dream come true.

Although impressed, Emmy toned down her excitement. "Tell me how you can offer it at that price?"

"Our profit margin is slim, but we've broken into the student base with the previous model. This model has an option for a high-end graphics chip for gamers and an option more aligned toward business applications. Grabbing a larger share of the overall market will increase profits over time. This is our shining achievement, and is a critical time for growth."

"You haven't lost much during bear markets, yet growth in bull markets has been lackluster. My client Mr. Thornton is considering investing a considerable amount in this company. Why should he do so?"

The company spokesperson looked toward the back of the room. A sharply dressed woman who had been sitting quietly throughout the presentation gave him a nod.

He cleared his throat before continuing. "We have been working with content providers on a new mobile app that will stream exclusive music and video at a discounted rate at record speeds. Research shows consumer costs reduced significantly. The combination of entertainment with state-of-the-art graphics, speed, and storage will make our product extremely sought after for several years."

The woman in the back of the room stood and moved to the front. "I'm sorry for coming into the briefing late. I'm Maggie Walker, Chief Technical Officer here at Campbell." She reached out to shake hands. Her manner was warm and gracious, and she met their eyes with a look of confidence. The redheaded, green-eyed beauty was young for the company's CTO, perhaps in her early thirties. While she was pressing the charm, Emmy was taken.

"I can't break ethics and give you any illegal insider infor-mation. You can only take my word for it. We have partnered with top software developers on several innovative new apps. Our negotiations with two of Europe's top content providers should be closed soon. These deals will give us exclusive rights to provide premium data at cheap rates."

"You seem awfully confident, Ms. Walker," Emmy said. "Do you always get what you want?"

"Always. I take pride in hunting down what seems elusive, and please call me Maggie." The powerful smile on the CTO's lips was nothing compared to the hungry look of desire in her eyes. Her gaze lingered.

Emmy felt like sliding down in her chair after the gaffe. *Damn, I can't believe I walked into that sexually charged innuendo. Where the hell, is my brain?* She shuffled in her chair to get more comfortable. It did no good. She could sense Maggie's eyes already undressing her.

The CTO pressed on. "You could wait until the deal is sealed, but you'll miss a larger profit. Get in before the public announcement and make a killing."

We would make a small fortune if you're telling the truth, but can I trust you?

As if reading her mind, the CTO added, "Again, I can only give you my word."

The beautiful woman's intense stare had rattled Emmy. She quickly recovered. "Mr. Thornton's large investment would help secure those deals. It seems you need us more than we need you." Emmy abruptly stood. "I'm sorry. We have to depart for another appointment. We will be in touch soon. Thank you for the presentation."

Calvin gave Emmy a funny look. Emmy could tell he was sold, but she had to keep a stone-cold face. As she rushed to put the paperwork in her briefcase, the CTO said to Calvin, "I'd be delighted if we could treat you both to dinner tonight."

Without hesitation, Calvin replied, "That would be splendid."

"Excellent. I can have a driver pick you up at your hotel around six. Would McAllister's Bistro suit your taste? They have the best cuisine along with some international favorites."

"Ah, they also have a nice Scotch selection." Calvin beamed. He was smitten with Maggie's charm.

"That they do."

Emmy knew it would be rude not to accept. "That is generous. Thank you."

Once in the car, Calvin grabbed Emmy. "Why did you act so unemotional like you weren't interested? Do you think there is a problem?"

"No, I was pleased. The tour of the company and presentation of their products were exceptional. Rumor has it they are dealing with Smyth Media Productions. The value of the company will dramatically increase if they make a deal with Smyth."

"So why did you act so unimpressed?"

"Poker face, Calvin. While everything seemed in place, I had to downplay excitement. We might get a better deal if I give them the impression of being uninterested. It got us a free dinner at one of Glasgow's best restaurants."

"Ah, I see your point."

"Now, my friend, as your financial advisor, you can't continue to act like a kid in a candy store. If you want a good deal, you've got to give them the impression that your decision hinges on my advice."

"Got it."

His cell phone rang. He chatted enthusiastically. "Yes, I remembered. Tonight at seven sharp at the pub. Fabulous, I'll see you there, James."

Emmy glowered at him. "What are you doing? You're not going with me tonight?"

Calvin shrugged. "I'm sorry, love. I forgot about my other business meeting. You'll have to go without me. Please make my sincere apologies."

"Business meeting my arse. You're going on a date!"

"You've caught me. Besides, you can play hardball with that poker face much better without me." He grinned from ear to ear. "By the way, how did you keep your eyes in your head when she was leaning over you like fresh meat and showing off her bountiful endowment? I had to silence my chuckle when your stupefied reply was, 'Do you always get what you want?' Better watch it, or she'll eat you up."

"You owe me, Calvin. And as I told you, I'm attached to a dazzling woman. I'm not a player like you. It will be business and nothing more."

Calvin chuckled. "Ah, Lassie. I know you'll be faithful. Still, it doesn't hurt to let your eyes take a holiday and have some fun."

Emmy called home before dinner. Scotland was five hours ahead of East Coast time. No time was convenient to call, and she longed to hear Jordan's voice. It rang several times and started to go to voicemail when, at last, Jordan answered.

"Hello." Jordan's voice was sharp and short, and she sounded out of breath.

"Hi, sweetie. I'm pressed for time with a business dinner but wanted to say hello and that I miss you so much."

"Hi, baby. Sorry. Things are a little crazy right now. Can't talk long, but I'm happy to hear from you." The rushed tone was almost panicky.

"Is everything okay?"

"Yep. Busy. Love ya, but I've gotta get back. We'll talk later. Gotta go. Love ya."

Jordan hung up before Emmy had a chance to say goodbye. *What the fuck was that? First, she called me baby, which I hate. Then she cut me off.* Something was wrong, but dinner with the Campbell Computer CTO awaited.

West Virginia

Emmy's call came shortly after Jordan had finished calling the sheriff. *God, it's good to hear her voice, but I have to handle this mess.* Gerry had shown up with his followers in the middle of lunch. They marched back and forth along the sidewalk with hateful signs: "Repent your sins." "Homosexuality is evil." "Don't support her lesbian ways." "Keep away from sin and don't eat here." They all chanted, "Give yourself to God or burn in hell." She had to deal with the situation now.

She headed back into the dining room. Her heart was pounding, her head was spinning, and her ears buzzed. Gerry and Robby were squaring off in the middle of the dining room among customers. *God, could it get any worse?*

"You don't care about your sister or anyone else. You're a two-bit, judging hypocrite. Get out now." Robby shoved Gerry toward the exit.

Gerry poked Robby in the chest. "My sister's soul is on the line. She needs help. She has to repent." He glared at everyone in the restaurant; they were aghast at the spectacle. "If you want to help her, leave now, and don't patronize her restaurant until she turns her life around."

Jordan stood in utter shock. Gerry's behavior was beyond even her wildest imagination. He spotted her.

"Jordan, we can get you help. Please, we love you. Emmy's evil ways have blinded you and will bring nothing but pain. These perverted actions will hurt you and others."

Robby's voice was filled with anger. "Get out now! There's nothing wrong with your sister or Emmy!"

Jordan stepped between them. "Emmy hasn't made me a pervert. I love her. I don't know who your God is, but my God is love. He doesn't preach hate." She hoped the slight tremble in her voice didn't show.

No one had noticed that Reverend Anderson from the Presbyterian Church had entered. He walked up to Gerry and placed his arm around him, speaking loud enough for everyone to hear. "Son. God's call and his love are open to all. We all must respect the dignity and rights of every person. It saddens me, but you're the one being disrespectful. Go home, son, and pray to God. Please do not harass your sister again."

Gerry looked like he was going to argue, but the sheriff's deputy arrived. Jordan recognized him as one of the Williams boys. Word around town was that he was fair.

He slapped Gerry on the shoulder. His massive bulk looked intimidating, but he spoke kindly. "Sir, let's end this peacefully.

You don't have a permit to protest, and you've been asked to leave. We've received several complaints. Please step out of the restaurant."

Before leaving, Gerry shouted, "You all need to pray. And Jordan, you can't hide from the Almighty."

Reverend Anderson drew everyone's attention as the deputy pulled Gerry outside. "Folks, it's sad that Gerry did this. I want to stress that God does not condemn two loving, committed people. God's love is for all his children. Please practice love through Jesus Christ and not hate."

Reverend Anderson moved toward Jordan, kindness in his eyes. "I'm hungry today," he said, cupping her face. "Can I please get my favorite sandwich and soup?"

"Salmorejo and bocadillo coming up for you, sir."

"Extra virgin olive oil and piquillo peppers, please."

After giving Jordan a fatherly peck on the cheek, he started chatting with folks. The reverend had defused the situation and calmed the patrons. It was as if nothing had happened. Jordan and Robby headed back into the kitchen.

"I'll get this. Go rest in your office."

The rest of the staff mumbled how sorry they were. Jo squeezed her shoulder as Jordan shuffled past. She closed the door to her office, sank into the desk chair, and thought of the quote by Persian poet Saadi. "Have patience. All things are difficult before they become easy."

Scotland

The maître d' escorted Emmy toward the back of the exclusive restaurant. Maggie Walker was sitting by herself at a table set for three. The fireplace and a window overlooking the garden made it a romantic location. This was going to be uncomfortable, and the CTO wouldn't make it easy.

Maggie was gorgeous and dressed to impress. Her hair was down and flowing. She wore a silky green dress that highlighted her eyes and showed off her cleavage. Emmy did not know whether the intention was for Calvin or her or both of them since Calvin didn't bother to call. *Damn, Calvin. You owe me.*

"Mr. Thornton sends his deepest apologies. An urgent matter came up at the last minute, but he is carefully considering the investment."

"I'm sorry to hear that. I'm pleased you came. Please sit down."

The rest of the night remained on course until Maggie shifted closer and placed her hand on Emmy's upper thigh. The provocative gesture instantly achieved its desired effect sending small tingles through Emmy's body. She delicately removed the CTO's hand and flatly responded, "I am here only for business. I will talk to Calvin, and you'll have our decision within a couple of days."

"Thank you. That's all I ask." Maggie flashed her perfect smile.

"And by the way, you're a beautiful woman, but I'm in a serious relationship."

"My apologies. You can't blame a girl for trying."

"Apology accepted. Let's keep the evening focused on business and nonpersonal topics. So, tell me how you feel about Scotland's recent attempt at independence?"

Emmy knew Calvin could go on forever discussing politics. Fortunately, the same was true for Maggie. The woman's face lit up, and the conversation wholeheartedly dove into politics. Awkward issue diffused. She never touched Emmy the rest of the night. Still, Emmy felt guilty for even admiring Maggie's beauty.

"Hi, Em. I'm sorry it's late. I needed to hear your voice." Jordan's exhaustion hung in the air like dead weight.

"I'm happy you did. I've been worried after the odd call earlier. You were curt with me. Is something wrong?"

Jordan sighed. "I'm sorry. I didn't mean to hurt your feelings. Gerry showed up at the restaurant with followers carrying signs of hate. You called in the middle of the situation when my hair was on fire."

"Oh my God. What happened?"

"They were chanting outside for me to repent and harassing people. Things got out of hand when Gerry came into the restaurant screaming."

Emmy could hardly believe what she was hearing. "I'll cut my trip short and be home as soon as possible."

"No, don't do that. We got through. Although, I thought Robby was going to punch his lights out before the deputy arrived. Also, Reverend Anderson just happened to drop by for lunch and gave Gerry a dressing down. I had a restraining order served to Gerry and his devoted homophobic groupies. They shouldn't be back anytime soon."

"Sweetie, you're hurting now, and I can't bear it."

"I'll make it through, Em. I won't let this beat me down. You've got a couple more days. Finish it up. We'll have a private celebration when you get home."

"I'll hold you to that promise. I love you and miss you."

"Me too. Talk to you tomorrow. Love you."

Chapter Thirty

The next day was the meeting with the Aberdeen North Sea Oil and Gas Company. Emmy had no real interest nor much experience investing in the energy sector. Sure she had a slice in the portfolio, but it was in solid, large companies. Aberdeen was still a midsize company, and she was more nervous about the future of energy in the North Sea.

The briefing droned on and was the most boring presentation she had ever seen. Being attentive and responsive was difficult. She thought of Jordan. Oh, how she wished she was home.

"Ms. Russo, do you have any reservations about traveling in a helicopter?"

The statement snapped her back to reality. "Helicopter?" Glaring at Calvin, she said, "No. Mr. Thornton is the only one visiting your field operations."

"Oh, Emmy. It will be fun, and we will only be out there for half of the day." Calvin mockingly batted his eyes.

Half a day, my arse. What is Calvin doing? She was getting pissed about this entire trip. Now he was putting her on the spot.

The company rep sat down next to Emmy as if to apply pressure. "I assure you the trip is perfectly safe, and the weather prediction is good for the next eighteen hours."

"Of course, she'll come. She's braver than me and loves exciting trips," Calvin piped up.

Emmy gritted her teeth. Calvin was smiling at her with his famous "I dare you" grin because he knew she didn't like to be called a coward.

"Okay. I'll join my client." She twirled in her chair. When the company rep turned away, she lip-synced to Calvin "Arsehole." At which, he only chuckled.

West Virginia

Jordan woke up renewed but was astonished that she had been in bed for almost ten hours. After calling Robby at home to say she would be in late, she noticed a text from Emmy.

The text began with a picture of the Celtic heart. *I LOVE YOU. This briefing is boring. I wish I were with you now. Calvin wants me to go on a field trip with him. In a helicopter of all things. Talk to you soon. Love, Emmy.*

After reading the text twice, she called her mom. It was highly likely that she had heard the news about the incident with Gerry.

"Oh, Jordan. My heart aches. How do you feel?"

"It shook me up at first, but I'm doing okay now."

"You've got a big heart and a tremendous amount of strength. I'm proud of you."

"Thanks, Mom. You're the best."

"Today will be a better day. Dave and I have decided to come for dinner. Could you make us a reservation for five thirty? We're in celebration mode."

"I'll save you a great table near the windows. What's the occasion?"

Through giggles, Gwyneth managed to say, "We've made a decision on our wedding date."

"So what is the date or are you going to make me guess?" Jordan listened to her mother snickering. Obviously, she wanted to drag the date out for effect, but Jordan was biting her lip. While she was happy for her mom, it was still a lot to process.

"June twenty-eighth."

"I thought you were planning an early December honeymoon in Mexico."

"We'll go another time. So, I proposed June twenty-eighth and our relatives and friends can stay through the Fourth of July holiday."

"That's great. December is too risky with the weather anyway. It's also better for planning since we've got over a year."

"We're getting married this year." Gwyneth laughed.

Stunned, Jordan didn't know how to react. "Mom, that's four months away," she blurted out at last. "How can we plan a wedding so fast? You're not planning a justice of the peace thing are you?"

"Don't be ridiculous." Gwyneth flicked her hand. "We've been sneaking around for over a year and decided to finally take the plunge. You should help Angie with planning."

Holy crap. They are serious as a heart attack. Angie did want to be the wedding planner, but she was going to be the one having the heart attack. She wondered if the kids would be out of school.

"Sounds like a plan," was all Jordan could say. Who was she to spoil their happiness?

As Jordan drove to the restaurant, the wedding consumed her thoughts. Angie would do the planning, and Jordan's restaurant would be providing the food. The timing was awful. The Fourth of July was the height of the tourist season.

She called Emmy, but the message went straight to voicemail. She recapped her mother's wedding plans and ended the message with, "The challenge is to get my mind off the recent ugliness, and focus on the happy event. Em, I love you. See you soon." She parked in the back of the restaurant.

She walked in a good half hour before they opened. "Good morning, everyone."

"You're here. Wonderful!" Jo hugged her and shouted, "Robby, she's here."

Everyone was looking at her like they had won the lottery. They were always a happy crew, but today, they were overzealous.

"Okay. Who has the happy pills? Something's going on."

They all stood with the same positive crazy looks. Robby came in and ran over to her, wrapping her in his arms and twirling her around. He was a big guy, but she was no light feather.

"Wow. I'm dizzy now. Is someone going to tell me what is going on? You all are grinning and jumping around like monkeys who escaped from the zoo."

"Did you drive down Main Street?" Robby could barely contain himself.

"Ah, no. Should I?"

Jo grabbed her by the hand and started pulling her along. "Come out front. We've got something to show you."

They walked into the dining room. Nothing caught her attention. "So, what's up?"

Robby and Jo walked her to the door and outside. Almost every shop and café displayed a rainbow flag. There were big ones, small ones, some were painted on store windows, and a few had displayed the words "Love is Love." Jordan couldn't believe her eyes. She walked out into the middle of the street. It was the same all the way down the entire length of the business district.

"News spread fast. Sherry Nelson and Neil Becker heard what happened and decided to take immediate action. They teamed up with Reverend Anderson and made it happen last night. Look down at the Lost Dog Saloon. Neil had some artists paint a huge custom flag last night on the side of the building. You can see it from two blocks away."

Jordan's eyes watered up. She didn't know what to say. She smiled through sniffles as Robby hugged her and gave her a tissue.

Sherry exited her restaurant and crossed the street. "How are you holding up today, girl?"

Sherry was a good twenty years Jordan's senior. They'd talked but never got to know one another.

"I'm grateful for the gesture. Thank you," Jordan managed to say while keeping the smile on and wiping away tears of joy.

"No big deal. It was wrong what happened yesterday. I'm sorry about your brother. I know it hurts, but sometimes you've got to let it go."

Jordan nodded. Again, unable to speak.

Sherry stood with her hands on her hips. "However, we do have another problem."

Everyone looked at Sherry curiously.

"Think about it. We've never done Pride month in June. We should start this year."

All of a sudden, Jordan doubled over in uncontrollable laughter. People didn't know what to make of it at first. She soon regained control. "I'm sorry. I didn't mean to make it sound as if I'm mocking your suggestion. I think it's a great idea. It's just that—" She snickered again. "Mom and Dave have decided to get married on June twenty-eighth. So, I guess it's going to be one busy month." Soon they were all in stitches.

After their good belly laughs had calmed down, they hugged again. For the first time, Jordan felt comfortable hugging. Times were changing, and people were beginning to stand on the right side of history.

Glowing with all the love she had recently received, she called Emmy to tell her the news. It was close to 11:00 a.m. in West Virginia and the time in Scotland was five hours ahead. She was in such a good mood that she thought nothing of the fact that it went to voicemail again.

The North Sea, Scotland

Good thing the day was gorgeous because Emmy was livid. Nowhere in the briefing did she recall the helicopter ride being a two-hour trip. She didn't think the day could get worse until Calvin talked about staying for the freaking sunset. The only good news was they should be back at the hotel in time to call Jordan.

After finishing the tour, they were in the control room with windows all around. There had been minor swells in the ocean, but the Dramamine helped her motion sickness. She walked away from the group, closer to the windows on the other side facing the helicopter pad and blocked out the representative droning on with hype and technical crap. A few more hours and this would all be over. Tomorrow, she would fly home. She thought of Jordan's sexy voice and envisioned her hands roaming over Jordan's succulent body.

In an instant, a bright light, deafening noise, and a strong hot wave of air violently knocked her to the floor. She felt pain. As she tried to focus, the ceiling lights and fans swayed and dangled in a disorderly fashion. Alarms were sounding, and a loud warning speaker said something she could not understand. Everything was muffled, and the ringing in her ears nearly drowned out the voices.

She craned her head to the window where she had been standing. It looked like spider webs all over. *Was that a hole?* She laid her head back and closed her eyes as bursts of vertigo ripped through her and her stomach roiled. When her head calmed, she opened her eyes. *Better.* She tried to get up but could not. It hurt. She touched her face and head. It was warm and sticky. She moved her fingers in front of her eyes and strained to focus. Red. Blood. The voices became more distant. *Calvin? Is that Calvin?* Her vision began to tunnel and darken. *I don't want to die. Jordan, I love you.*

West Virginia

Jordan was frantic. It was almost 10:30 p.m. in Scotland and Emmy still had not called. She was also not answering her phone or texting. In desperation, she called the emergency phone number. The man on the other end answered as Mr. Colin Brodie, Mr. Calvin Thornton's personal assistant. Jordan explained who she was and her concerns but the man sounded unalarmed.

"I'm sorry, Ms. Simón but I wasn't expecting them until late. I was told not to check in with them until tomorrow. They may have gone to dinner. Late dinners are typical for Mr. Thornton—"

"Mr. Brodie. Something is wrong, and I demand you check up on them. I asked my girlfriend to call me, and she would not be ignoring several text messages and voicemail from me. Please, Mr. Brodie!"

He promised to get back to her within the hour but did not seem serious about her concerns. She was of no use in the kitchen and sat at her desk tapping her fingers. Finally, the maître d' announced her mother, Dave, and Betty Jean had arrived for dinner. *Maybe Betty Jean knows something.*

Jordan whizzed past the usual dining room crowd straight for the table of her loved ones. Not wanting to sound too terribly alarming, she greeted them with the typical hugs and kisses. With a weak smile, she asked Betty Jean if she'd heard from Emmy.

Betty Jean immediately dropped her menu and scrunched her eyebrows. "No, dear. I haven't. That's not unusual for me. She sometimes calls me a couple times when she's traveling, but I'm not the one she's in love with. Haven't you talked to her today?"

Jordan plopped down in the one empty seat. "No, I haven't. She calls me every day, and even when we're busy, we manage to talk a few minutes. She's hardly ever late, but today is different. I'm worried sick."

There was silence. Betty Jean reached out and patted her hand. "I'm sure we will hear something soon."

At that moment, Robby walked up to the table with one of the restaurant's mobile phones. His face was solemn. "A Mr. Colin Brodie is on the phone and says the matter is urgent."

The North Sea, Scotland

Emmy strained to open her eyes. She heard muted voices in the background but the ringing was gone, and she could make out some words. *Dammit, talk louder.* Everything hurt, her mind was foggy, and her eyes would not focus. She had no clue where she was. Then the details came back. The damn oil platform trip Calvin insisted she go on. The explosion. She must be in a clinic.

She craned her neck and could make out dull metal gray walls and ceiling. She was still on the platform. Panic spread through her body and seized her brain. She could not control her emotions.

With all her power, she propped upright on one elbow, ripped off the oxygen mask, and tried to scream, but her throat hurt and the words came out soft. "What the fuck happened? Get me out of here." Calvin and a man rushed to her. The man injected her with something. The needle stung and felt huge. Her body involuntarily relaxed and she dropped back down on the bed. She managed to blurt out, "We're going to die."

"Emmy, you're going to be fine. You hit your head hard, but we all know you've got one damn hard head." She couldn't move much after the injection and could barely hear Calvin's words. He was stroking her hair. "We're not going to die. There was a small explosion, and the resulting fire was extinguished. Everything's under control. Rescue is on the way."

With tremendous effort, she slurred, "Blood. I had blood on my face."

"A piece of shrapnel nicked you. Stay calm and still because of the head injury. Please, Emmy. Just relax."

"Damn you, Calvin. I'm not going on any more crazy trips." She was still hanging in there fighting the drug as much as possible but could hear her words beginning to slur.

"Deal. Close your eyes, my dear Lassie, and I promise you we will be out of here in no time."

The man pushed Calvin out of the way and injected her again. This time, she felt more than the stinging. She could sense the drug coursing through her veins like a warm rush, and it quickly gripped her. Soon the motion of people slowed like wet paint dripping down a wall, and their voices sounded miles away. Darkness came again.

West Virginia

The air in Jordan's lungs was sucked out in an instant. She dropped the phone. Her head slumped to the table into her hands. "No, God, no. This can't happen." She squeezed her eyes so tight, but the tears burst through as her body struggled to breathe.

Betty Jean put her arm around her while Gwyneth jumped up to her side.

"Honey, what's wrong?"

Jordan heard her mother's voice like it was a thousand miles away. Her body shook with every sob as her mind spun out of control. The shallow, fast gasps were not sufficient, and wooziness crept in while thoughts of Emmy rushed through her head. *I love you. Don't leave me. God, don't take her away.*

West Virginia – Scotland

Calvin's assistant had somehow fixed Jordan's passport issue, and by the next day, she was boarding a Gulfstream G3. Betty Jean was too distraught to travel, and despite her mother's offer, Jordan had insisted she could do this alone as Becca would be meeting her in Aberdeen. Dave and Gwyneth took her to Dulles for the private flight.

Jordan walked onto the plane as best she could. The soft cream leather seats reclined for resting but she was neither sleepy nor hungry. When the stewardess offered food, she declined and only sipped water. A couple of times, she went to the washroom to cry in private.

The long flight seemed like a time warp that she could not control. Relief washed over her when the stewardess leaned over. "Ma'am, I've hung a fresh change of clothes for you in the washroom. We have about an hour before landing."

Jordan shuffled past the only other passengers on the plane. The two businessmen hunched over their laptops nodded in her direction. Their faces told Jordan all she needed to know. She looked frightful.

Inside the spacious washroom, towels of the softest cotton hung on shiny racks. Scented soaps and other amenities were arranged on the walnut shelves. A bouquet of flowers added a splash of color. All were a sharp contrast to how Jordan looked. Laying her head on the cool marble vanity top, she broke down and wept. It took time to regain her composure, but after washing, applying makeup, and slipping on the fresh clothes, she looked almost human again.

When she exited, the stewardess stepped forward. "You look better, ma'am. If you don't mind, your collar has twisted a smidgen." The young woman fixed it for her and brushed some lint off the sleeve.

"It's dark. What time is it? I've lost my bearings."

"Half past eight, ma'am."

"Thank you for your help and kindness."

"My pleasure. Please take your seat now."

At landing, a Range Rover with tinted windows pulled up while Jordan was descending the stairs. Becca jumped out. They briskly walked toward one another and embraced.

"Her status hasn't changed much," Becca shouted over the airport noise. "We can talk in the car."

Inside, the SUV was warm and quiet—everything Jordan's body was not. She pulled her coat tighter as Becca offered her a drink.

"Just water please."

"They won't let us see her until she's out of intensive care. I've secured a hotel room so we can take turns getting a bit of rest, but I figured you'd want to be near her tonight even if it's only the waiting room. My PA is at the hospital now."

"Thank you, Becca."

"Jordan, I..." Becca grasped Jordan's hand. "I was concerned when I first met you. Em had always been a city girl, and I thought she was rushing. And...I...I was a bit jealous and worried about losing my best friend. I'm sorry." She wiped away a tear. "We hardly saw one another because of our busy careers, but we always had time to talk on the phone. Over the past month, we've talked a lot." Becca teared up. "She loves you, and I know it's the real thing."

Jordan squeezed Becca's hand. "I love her so much, Becca." She took a deep breath and exhaled slowly. "At first, there was the thrill of intimacy. More than sex, the joy of having someone who would stand by me. But..." Jordan bit her lip and buried her face in tissues before continuing. "It's hard for me to say, but I had mixed feelings when I first told her I loved her. After the words spilled out of my mouth, I panicked. I questioned whether I honestly had the guts to come out and make a life with her."

"Looks like you jumped off that cliff in one piece. I heard about your older brother at the party. Can't say that I'd done it any differently if I were under the same pressure."

"As each day went by, I wanted to make a life with her and then I'd panic more. I was terrified of this trip. I thought she might change her mind...that I...I wouldn't be enough for her. But every time I'd see her smile or laugh, I'd melt. Hell, I'd do anything for her. Anything. I can't lose her. I love her. It may have taken me longer to come to my senses, but there is no doubt left in my mind. I love her."

Becca didn't say a word but held fast to Jordan's hand. She lay back in the seat and closed her eyes.

"Becca, I'm sorry. I can't imagine how you feel."

After wiping a few more tears, Becca said, "It was rough losing Heather. And I'll be damned, we're not going to lose Emmy." She squeezed Jordan's hand.

Chapter Thirty-One

*E*mmy rustled out of a deep sleep, wondering if it had been a dark dream. Sunlight streamed in through a window. Despite her blurry vision, she could make out trees against a blue sky. The view made her throbbing headache more tolerable. As she scanned the room, she thought she saw Jordan asleep in a recliner. *I must be dreaming.* She closed her eyes and faded out again.

Nighttime had descended the next time she woke. An IV and medical equipment were on one side. She sensed a presence. Turning her head, Jordan lay next to her on the very edge, and her hand rested on top of Emmy's. Safety and love washed over her and overrode fear and pain. She wanted to tell Jordan she loved her, but her mouth was so dry that only small incoherent sounds came out.

Jordan propped herself up, and the look of affection on her face was pure bliss. She leaned in and kissed Emmy's forehead.

"Let me get you some water."

Emmy immediately felt the loss of Jordan. She so desperately wanted to reach out and wrap her in an embrace, but her sluggish body would not cooperate.

Jordan brought the water to her mouth. "Slowly or I'll have to take it away." She stroked Emmy's hair. "You're recovering beautifully, but you don't want to vomit from drinking fast."

The water refreshed her and made it easier to talk. "What happened? How did you get here?"

"There was an accident on the oil platform. Calvin flew me over ASAP. Somehow, he helped get my passport pushed through. The doctors treating your head injury induced unconsciousness with medication. You need plenty of rest, but they said you will fully recover."

"How long? What day is it?"

"It's Wednesday, March the fourth. Trust me, Em, you're going to be fine. I love you so much." She continued to tenderly smooth Emmy's hair and kissed her forehead as a few tears ran down her face.

Emmy reached up to wipe away Jordan's tears. "I love you."

The nurse entered the room interrupting the conversation, which agitated Emmy. "I want to speak to the doctor."

"Yes, Ms. Russo. You've got to calm down. Being agitated is fighting the healing process." Emmy vaguely recalled what had happened the last time she woke in a panic. She remembered the stick of the needle, the swift drop in speech and vision. The thoughts forced her to calm down.

A female doctor entered the room. "So, this is our lively patient. We need your blood pressure and heart rate stable, and working yourself into a tizzy does not help. Take a few minutes for some relaxing breaths. I'll watch the monitor here, and when vital signs calm, then we will talk." Emmy nodded, and Jordan massaged her hand.

Finally, the doctor pronounced, "Good job. This is the situation. Your nasty head injury caused internal swelling with some uncontrollable seizure activity. A medically induced coma was necessary to lower the intracranial pressure and stop the seizures. Your body has responded well to the treatment with a measurable decrease in the swelling, and your overall vitals have improved. Most important," she flipped through the medical chart, "you haven't had any seizures for forty-eight hours as we eased you off the medication. In fact, we might be able to release you in four or five days if your progress continues." She intently stared Emmy down. "You should recover fully, but please follow instructions. There are no shortcuts to recovery. You need to be in a nice relaxed state. Do you understand?"

Emmy nodded, and Jordan asked, "What about follow-ups?"

"Good question. I want her in the area for at least a couple of weeks. No air travel. Bed rest and no physical exertion." The doctor glanced at Emmy over the rim of her glasses. "Ms. Russo will come back for a re-examination, and if everything is fine, then I will then clear her to fly home. Let that information settle, and we will talk again tomorrow." The doctor patted Emmy's hand. "We have a competent and caring nursing staff. I'd bet they're gentler than the panicked medic that treated you on the oil platform. No one likes shots and IVs but remember the goal. We want you to regain your strength and health."

The doctor scribbled some medical notes in the chart, and Calvin waltzed in. She wagged a finger. "Only a few minutes, Mr. Thornton. Ms. Simón, you may stay." The doctor departed.

"Hi, Lassie."

His much-too-chipper voice annoyed Emmy. She stared at him as her mouth drew to a weak smile. "Your house in Barcelona free for as long as I want? You owe me for this awful trip."

Calvin grinned. "You got it." He winked.

"I assume we didn't do the deal with Aberdeen North Sea Oil and Gas Company. What about Campbell Computers?"

"No energy deal but I did say yes to Campbell."

Jordan motioned him out of the room. "That's enough, you too. Stop talking business. Calvin, you need to go and come back tomorrow. She needs rest."

Emmy cleared her throat. "I'm lucky to be with such a loving lady, but before I rest, I want the truth. What happened out there?" Silence filled the room and Emmy could hear the hum of the medical equipment. Jordan began to mumble more about getting rest, and Emmy cut her off. "No, sweetheart. I won't rest until you two tell me the truth. If you won't tell me now then how do I know that everyone's not lying about my medical condition? If you want me to calm down, then tell me. I'm tough. I can take it."

Jordan laid her hand on Emmy's shoulder and nodded to Calvin.

"There was a pressure pump explosion. The debris somehow breached the reinforced glass window where you were standing and punched a hole in the damn thing. The blast was powerful and knocked a lot of us down, and you came down hard. The blow caused your brain swelling." He swallowed, ran his fingers through his hair, then said, "There was a big piece of shrapnel that almost ended your life. It grazed the side of your head and impaled in a support column nearby." He was pale. "A fraction of an inch closer and you would have been dead. They know that because the blood type on the shrapnel matched yours. Fourteen platform workers were severely injured, and two died. They evacuated us out late that night."

Emmy touched her head. Although she was unable to feel under the bandage, she somehow knew that one side of her head had been shaved. She could now feel the pinching sensation of the stitches.

"Well, at least I got a new hairstyle out of the event."

Her dry humor caused chuckles and relief that she would soon be her old self.

Throughout the next couple of days, she talked to various friends and family over the phone. They raised her strength and made her aware that her family circle was growing.

Six days later, Emmy was released. She didn't complain as the staff motioned to a wheelchair, explaining it was standard procedure. Outside, Calvin was standing next to a gray and black Rolls Royce limo. He opened the door for them.

"Where are we going?" Emmy asked.

He grinned. "It's a surprise. Trust me."

She arched an eyebrow, and he chuckled. Jordan shrugged.

Less than half an hour, they arrived at the Aberdeen Anderson Resort and Spa. The luxurious nineteenth-century mansion loomed over the rolling hills of thirty acres. The stone exterior with turrets and spires soaring to the sky reminded Emmy of a fortress. They were greeted by an attentive staff from the very moment they arrived.

Inside, the mansion exuded warmth and charm. Rich hand-carved wood, a coat of arms, and other antiques showed the lavishness of an era gone by. Modern tartan fabrics hung from the ancient stained glass windows and added a splash of color. Calvin had arranged for everything and insisted on escorting them to their room.

Several bouquets of double-flowering rose lilies adorned their suite. The fragrance of the rich rose-pink petals was soothing. The living room's high ceiling, wainscoting, and traditional mahogany furniture tied to days long past. A fire had already been started in the massive fireplace.

They followed the bellhop into the spacious bedroom. Its modern décor was the opposite of the living room. A chandelier hung over a king-sized bed. The deep purple duvet contrasted against a plush light gray carpet with a faint geometric pattern. There was another fireplace. Bouquets of lavender double tulips, Blue Bird roses, lavender orchids, and pink Godetia were placed around the room. The corner suite had many vantage points and views of the landscaped gardens below.

Emmy mumbled, "Wow. This is a gorgeous suite. It's enormous."

"And don't worry about one little thing. I'm paying for it. The staff has been ordered to attend to your every need. It's the least I could do." He bounced on his toes.

"Calvin, thank you for the suite and for the flowers. Jordan and I appreciate the kindness."

"I know how much you love flowers, my dear. And the suite is booked for sixteen days, but say the word, and I will make it longer." He bowed. "I know you two are dying to lie in one another's arms, but remember the doctor did say rest. No activity that would significantly increase your blood pressure."

Emmy gave him a mischievous smile. "I think we can manage."

"Well, you must make sure that you're decently dressed by six. A romantic dinner will be served in your suite tonight." He winked and started to leave but spun around on his heels. "Oh, I did leave you some lesbian porn on top of the TV, but you should probably wait until you're medically cleared to that level of exertion. Ta-ta, ladies. Enjoy your stay."

Emmy was not fazed by his risqué humor. She had been used to it for so long. Jordan was another matter. She flipped through the DVDs so rapidly they almost flew out of her hands. Her face contorted in shock. "These look like porn for guys with a harem of girls."

Emmy chuckled. "He has no expectation of us watching those crude movies. His humor with me is over the top. He's always trying to raise the volume with me. Once he realizes that he has gone too far for your sense of decorum, he will be apologizing to you." She grabbed the DVDs and threw them in the trash. "Tomorrow, I'll hand him the waste can, movies and all." She paused and picked up the can. With a facetious look and a coy voice, she said, "Unless you think we can gather some insights watching them."

"Oh, I can't believe you said that."

In a seductive voice, Emmy said, "Well, research does show that visual stimulation can help a couple maintain the spark."

"Maybe so but having Calvin give them to us makes my skin crawl. And I definitely don't want a man in any damn film. Now let's get you tucked in. Otherwise, I will give you a good tongue-lashing." Jordan turned an instant crimson when she realized the double entendre. "I didn't mean that like it sounded. It's just a stupid American phrase for scolding."

Emmy's eyes twinkled. She cocked a brow, and her grin spread from ear to ear as she stood with her hands on her hips. "If you say so, but I'll take a rain check just in case."

Jordan spooned against Emmy's backside. The lingering smell of the flowers filled the suite. She smiled remembering yesterday, the best day ever. After a delicious meal, they talked about how lucky they were. Lucky to be alive, lucky to be in love, and lucky to have caring families. Hugging, holding hands, and laughing never felt so good. She carefully unwrapped from Emmy and slipped out of bed.

Emmy stirred several minutes later. Pulling the covers up over half of her face with only her eyes peeking out, she groaned in protest. "I miss your warm, soft body pressed against me. Come back to bed. Please."

"I'm stoking the fire and ordering breakfast." Jordan tucked another blanket over Emmy.

"I think you'd be enough for breakfast," Emmy softly said.

"Rest. Don't fight the prescriptions. They may make you drowsy, but they will help you heal. Close your eyes, and we will eat in a couple of hours."

Jordan placed wood on the glowing embers. As the flames grew, Emmy slipped back to sleep, and Jordan settled in an oversized chair between the fireplace and the bed, curled up in a blanket. She listened to Emmy's breathing and occasional soft snore. Her sound was like a gentle background noise that often helped lull Jordan to sleep. She loved this woman, snores, quirks, and all. Sex was fantastic, but the snuggling was the best.

I've never loved anyone more. I'm never going to let her go. As the words flowed in her mind, her heart swelled, and tears of joy and determination filled her eyes. Yes, they had said those three precise words several times, but now "I love you" took on a deeper meaning. With Emmy well on the way to healing, Jordan felt contentment, happiness, and an intense desire to make a stronger commitment. She wiped away the tears.

When the knock came on the door, Emmy's eyes fluttered open.

"I'll bring breakfast in here." The dishes clanked as Jordan wheeled the heavy cart into the room. Emmy sat on the edge of the bed, and Jordan stopped and admired her. "You're stunning."

"Ditto, Ms. Sexy."

"Don't get me going." Jordan laid out the hot food on a small round table next to the fire. "We have oatmeal with golden currants, eggs, sautéed mushrooms, sausage...I mean bangers. And pita bread with lots of butter?" Jordan picked up the plate to eye the dish.

"Tattie scones. It's a mashed potato griddle cake. You did well, sweetie."

Emmy rose and kissed her cheek while Jordan poured the tea. They both were hungrier than they realized. Between bites, Emmy talked about Calvin's ideas for expanding her consulting business.

"I'll have to spend at least three days in DC and travel to Europe as well. It will be challenging at times. I'd really like for you to be with me on some of the trips."

"Em, slow down." Jordan's hands caressed Emmy's fingers intently before she looked up. "At first, I was worried you'd change your mind about our relationship and stay in Europe. There are a lot more lesbians and parties here than in little Oakville. Then the accident ripped my heart out."

"Jordan, don't you know you rock my world? I love you." Emmy gripped Jordan's face. "I choose you. I'm happy with you."

"I promise to take more time and travel with you."

"You better because business trips are dull and I could never be happy leaving you for more than a few days."

Jordan's eyes misted. "I was going crazy from the moment I heard. I thought you might die."

Emmy leaned over and hugged her. "This near-death experience has made me appreciate life and every little detail. We have both been through a lot, and we're stronger for it."

"I don't know how to say this." Jordan took some deep breaths. Her nerves caused her to pause, and she saw Emmy's facial expression change to one of confusion. She needed to get this out and hoped for the best. "I can't imagine going forward without knowing that you'll be by my side. We've only known one another for four months, but will you marry me? I admit it sort of scares me. A wedding that is. No, that came out wrong. The crowd at a wedding scares me. But I love you. I need you, and I want to be there for you. I want us to build a life. I know Oakville isn't the center of culture but Emmy, please be my wife. Please." Jordan pleaded.

"I didn't know anyone could speak that fast." Emmy smiled and put a peck on Jordan's lips. "Nor did I expect that question but yes."

"So, yes, you'll marry me and live with me in Oakville?"

"Positively, my love. Why do you look so surprised?"

Jordan let out a sigh of relief. "Are you kidding? You're smart, gorgeous, and a terrific person. You make me laugh and"—she brushed Emmy's check with the back of her hand—"you don't take anybody's crap, even mine."

Emmy laughed. "Why thank you. And you are equally a lovely catch. I think we're a smashing couple."

Jordan hugged her, and they rocked in one another's arms. Comfort and exuberance consumed Jordan. Then a snicker rose from her throat and soon turned hysterical. She could not control it.

Emmy leaned back. "What's so funny?"

"Just don't say June."

"Why? You have a strange look on your face." Emmy squeezed and gently kissed Jordan's hand. "Life is short. Jordan, I know you're a planner, but we can keep it small and private."

"Then you definitely don't want to get married in June."

Emmy cocked her head. "Because?"

"I guess you didn't get my text or messages about Mom since it was the day of the accident."

"No. What's up with your mum?"

"She and Dave switched their date. They're planning a big wedding on Sunday, June twenty-eighth."

Emmy's eyebrows shot up. "How big of a wedding, and how's Angie handling this?"

"So far, the list is over two hundred. Angie's hanging on but consuming a lot of caffeine. I've made it well known to Mom and Angie that I have no intention of wearing a dress. I've got my eye on a satin-trimmed tuxedo." They both laughed. "I suggest we quietly plan. There's too much whirlwind around Mom's nuptials."

"Agree."

"Mid-to-late October would be nice. The leaves are turning gorgeous orange, red, and gold, and the weather is cooler. Perfect for snuggling. Do you fancy a large wedding?"

"I'll be your bride either way but will your family push you into a large wedding? You know they love loud and large gatherings."

"You've got a point. Let's keep it a secret until we're ready."

"There will be a few complications to overcome."

Jordan scrunched her eyebrows. "Complications?"

"Is our last name going to become Russo-Simón or Simón-Russo?"

"Anything you wish." Jordan laughed. "Let's get you back to bed. You need to rest."

"Only if you snuggle with me."

"Snuggle time with the most beautiful fiancée in the world. Nothing could be better."

Chapter Thirty-Two

Two months later – West Virginia

Emmy's hair fell over her pale shoulders as she leaned down to softly kiss Jordan. She peered intently into Jordan's smoldering gaze before her fingers and eyes moved down Jordan's torso. Her fingertips stopped to circle and pinch perky nipples before moving on to tease Jordan's lower abdomen. She stroked the delicate skin between the belly button and Jordan's curls.

"Em, you're driving me crazy."

"Hush. My craving is to meticulously examine your body before I devour it. So soft. Such a beautiful brown. You're like a caramel that I can't get enough of."

She replaced her fingers with her mouth. Kissing the belly button, she moved upward with her tongue, teasing the breasts with smooth strokes and occasional flicks. Only when Jordan begged did she fully take the nipple and suck. After lavishing one, her tongue made a broad leisurely swath across to the other.

Jordan's gasps were ragged. "Please. More."

With her mouth feasting, Emmy's hand moved through the curls to stroke the folds before she slipped two fingers into the core. As her strokes began to build in intensity, Jordan moved her hips up to match the thrusts. Emmy took pleasure in feeling Jordan's muscles constrict around her fingers, and she enjoyed the quivering of Jordan's body and her moans. After pleasing her lover, she inched up to watch the rise and fall of her chest. She loved simply giving.

But before Jordan had calmed, her eyes popped open. "I want you."

Emmy followed the gestures and straddled her. Jordan cupped her ass and guided her over her hungry mouth and took her with vigor. Emmy held the bed frame trying not to crush her, yet gently rocking. As the climax built, her knees and thighs weakened and she cried in pleasure. "Oh, sweetie. Oh, yeah!"

Jordan didn't let up, and her frenzied tongue slowed to soft lapping. Emmy rode every wave until she couldn't take it anymore. She rolled off exhausted.

Jordan rose on one elbow, kissing her forehead. "Satisfied?"

Emmy laughed. "Very. You can take me like that anytime."

Jordan scooped Emmy into her arms. "I have to confess. I wasn't sure how our dynamics would change after you moved in. Some people freak out when they see the other's idiosyncrasies. But it keeps getting better. Well, all except you can't cook worth a damn."

Emmy playfully punched her. "Watch your criticism, or I'll make you beg harder next time. I also have something to confess. Your cooking and hot body are two of the mouthwatering reasons why it has been bliss. Yet, what nails me is your zest for life. Do you even realize how much you've grown? I can clearly see positivity flowing out, and nothing is hiding below the surface. Even when you do an ordinary activity, you look more relaxed and at peace."

"So, I guess you're glad you took a chance on me?"

"It wasn't hard to do. I saw a determination in you to make the leap and how desperately you needed and wanted to do so. While I gave you a gentle nudge here and there, it was all you."

"And don't forget, plenty of sweet kisses helped."

"Yes, they are good medicine for both of us, but you never answered my question. Jordan, do you realize how much you've grown?"

"I do, and my next step is for you to be my wife. I'm not going to waste any more time. What are we going to do for our October wedding? I will do whatever pleases you."

"I always wanted the fancy dress and dinner. I know the crowd makes you a little nervous and the family's likely to kill us if we unleash another extravagant event. Even with the immediate family, it's going to be its own force of nature by the sheer number of relatives. That doesn't take into account their personalities and spirit."

Jordan chuckled. "We have to make some decisions this weekend. The clock's ticking." Maybe, we should go downstairs, sticky note options to the basement wall, and throw darts."

"Uh-huh. I'm all for simplicity but not that far."

"I checked out some dates for the resort lodge and cabins. There are a few still available. If we stick to immediate family and friends, the cabins will do. We're going to have to book them within the next week. Otherwise, they'll be snagged up by the tourists coming for the fall festival."

"Speaking of decisions, how's Angie holding up since your mum's plans keep changing?"

"She's running from predawn until way after the kids go to bed, but she makes it look effortless. Poor Carter tries to help when asked and stays out of her way when she's spun up like a twister."

"When are we going to announce our engagement? The news is going to spread like wildfire through town gossip if we file for a marriage license and don't tell our families. Your mum and Betty Jean will be hurt if they find out that way."

"Yeah, you're right. Never thought about that. It only takes one day for a license. If we marry in October, we could tell everyone in July. It would give them time to recuperate from Mom's wedding."

"Guess that will work. By the way, a simple wedding is fine, and I can do most of the planning with a little help."

"That's a possibility, but it's getting late. Let's take time and figure it out tomorrow. Right now, I'm still horny." Jordan captured Emmy's mouth giving her a long, hungry kiss while her hand slid down her body. It would be well after midnight before they collapsed into sleep.

"How was the coffee with your mum and Dave? Sorry, I couldn't go, but I'll be ready to go in an hour for the big BBQ this afternoon," Emmy shouted out over her shoulder while typing on the computer. When Jordan didn't respond, she spun around in her chair.

Jordan was propped up against the wall and looked flushed. "Are you okay?"

"Sort of but not when you get your hands on my neck."

"Why? What did you do?"

"I mentioned our engagement to Mom."

Emmy shook her head and gave a small grin. "Last week, we agreed not to say anything until after their wedding, but that was your idea. It's no big secret. She's your mum. You should share."

Jordan still had not come unglued from the wall and remained across the room.

Emmy rose, closed the distance with Jordan, embraced her, and gave her a tender kiss. Jordan's muscles began to loosen, but she was still a little tense. Emmy separated and took her by the shoulders. When Jordan diverted her gaze down, Emmy brought her chin up with her finger. "Sweetheart, I'd marry you tomorrow or even tonight. You're the one who's a little timid about a wedding. I can't figure out if you're worried about the planning or if you're getting cold feet."

Jordan's eyes widened. "I'm not getting cold feet. I want to announce to the world that I love you. I just...ah...Dammit. It's the whole formality of a ceremony, particularly in this town, is a little scary. We made a lot of progress with friends and family, but there are still nutcases out there."

Emmy sighed. "Did the restaurant get another phone call?"

"I think Gerry's church buddies have calmed down. The gas station episode last month shook me up. I can handle almost anything, but the threat to hurt you scared the living crap out of me. I couldn't bear it if anything happened to you."

"Change can be frightening to people, and some people never want anything to evolve. I think their hot air is a scare tactic to try to quiet us, but I'm not backing down. I'm not giving up my rights to happiness and equality. I refuse to hide and live my life in the shadows."

Everyone knew about the stranger at the gas station shouting hateful rhetoric and putting a dent in the hood of Jordan's SUV with his fist. The guy had grabbed his crotch and said, "I've got something to make your girlfriend straight." The sheriff's department had been called, and it made the papers. The judge ordered him to pay damages and sentenced him to jail for a week followed by community service.

As for the phone calls, only Robby and Jo knew. People would spout off and slam down the phone. They were the same harassing lines shouted by Gerry's group months ago, and the numbers on the phone bill also matched the church protesters. Emmy had talked Jordan into installing additional cameras at the restaurant and around the house perimeter and along the driveway.

Jordan kissed the palm of Emmy's hand. "I want to marry you, and I don't want our love locked away. I thought a small ceremony with only family wouldn't stir the pot so much. But some people just can't keep their mouths shut. Some will always make comments."

Emmy was curious now that a lopsided grin had replaced Jordan's worry lines. "So what has you upset and scared this time?"

"Mom scares me. Any chance we could run away and do a Provincetown weekend wedding?"

Emmy playfully swatted her arm before kissing her again. "No. A wedding with family, formal dress, and cake in our home as you agreed. Sure, I'd relish a bigger ceremony where we party the night away, but I'll settle for a small wedding. You promised. What did your mum say? It can't be that bad."

"Before or after she told Dave or after she called Betty Jean?" Jordan swallowed.

Emmy raised her eyebrow. "You are her only daughter. She's excited for you. I can see her telling Dave but why call Betty Jean? Not that I mind if she knows. What did she say exactly or shall I say what plan is she hatching with Auntie?"

Jordan visibly swallowed. A light knock at the door interrupted their conversation. "Brace yourself. If it weren't morning, I'd fix us a drink."

Emmy crossed her arms. "I doubt it's that bad, but curiosity has the best of me." She eased her stance and gave Jordan another kiss. "Go sit down before you fall down, and I'll answer the door."

Emmy stifled her laugh and put on a pleasant face. "Gwyneth and Dave! What a wonderful surprise. Please come in."

Hugs and kisses were exchanged, and they joined Jordan in the living room. Good thing Jordan was sitting because she looked frightened. Emmy got a kick out of Jordan's personality. She could be brave one moment but sensitive and shy in another. Even when she was upset, her actions were always considerate. She took others' feelings and safety into account.

Gwyneth and Dave sat across from Jordan and Emmy.

"Jordan told me the wonderful news. I can see how much you make my daughter happy, but I'm afraid my wild idea sent

Jordan running out the door. It was only a thought, but I will respect and honor what you all wish to do."

Jordan moistened her lips. "I know, Mom. I want Emmy to be happy. We will talk it over. It's not a bad idea. We don't want to be a distraction, and honestly, the formality of such a large audience is a bit much."

With those words, Emmy suspected what Gwyneth had proposed. Yet she needed to know exactly what was going on. "So, bring me up to speed. Jordan hasn't told me, but we have no secrets." She glanced at Jordan and squeezed her hand. "You obviously felt strongly about this idea, Gwyneth, and in a sense, you're like a mum to me, too. So, what's this idea? We haven't made any solid plans other than having the family at the house."

"Well, dear, everyone's going to be at our wedding."

Emmy began to smile. *Oh my God, I know exactly where you're going with this. No wonder Jordan is petrified, but I like the idea.*

"So with everyone coming to our wedding, it would be no bother to add more guests and expand the festivities. We could send out another invitation, that's no big deal. A double wedding would save money in the long run. Of course, it might be difficult for your European friends and family to make it on such short notice."

"It's an intriguing idea. As for my European relatives, most are older and don't travel, and I'm not close to my brother."

Jordan shot Emmy a questioning glance saying to her mother, "I know you mean well, but it's your special day. We can't take that away from you."

Dave looked deep into Jordan's eyes. "You would not diminish our special day. It would add to our joy. Your mother and I were talking a couple of weeks ago how you and Emmy were such a loving couple."

Jordan's mom quickly added, "We laughed over dessert and coffee about how it would be such a fun whirlwind if we had a double wedding."

Dave swung his arm around Gwyneth. "Well, there is a bit more." He sported a goofy grin. "Betty Jean was there too. We were just fantasizing. Now that we know you two are planning to marry, we thought, 'Why not go for it?' But, we also understand this is all so sudden. We won't push."

Gwyneth squeezed both their hands. "Yes, honey. I understand if you and Emmy want a separate wedding, and we both respect that. I'm sorry I scared the daylights out of you by bringing it up."

Emmy wanted to know more. "Jordan mentioned you also said something to Betty Jean. Does she know about the idea or only about our engagement?"

"Yes, I did call her today. I apologize. It was not my place to tell her."

"No apologies necessary. I know you meant no harm. Jordan and I have been talking about a small wedding, but we will consider the idea." She felt Jordan's hand squeeze harder.

"I'm sorry. Again, I didn't mean to frighten you. We should get going and let you enjoy the rest of the morning."

After their departure, Emmy took Jordan in her arms. "We need to talk about what each of us wants."

After several minutes of discussion, Jordan bit her lip and cracked her knuckles before looking Emmy in the eye. "Over two hundred people are attending the June wedding. It's anything but simple but as crazy as it sounds, I think we should do it."

"Wow. Why the change of heart?"

"Mom's right, it would save money and time. And you're right. We should not adjust our lives to please someone else."

"You sure you're not just trying to please me?"

"I've wasted too much time being scared. No more. I want to marry you, and I'll be damned if I will let anyone influence me as to when and where. That's why we should do it now. It will make a loud statement that we deserve to be together and to be happy. So, what do you want?"

"I want you. Period. I can adjust to anything with you by my side. I will marry you in June. But, I have one condition." Emmy rubbed Jordan's hands. "We have to tell someone about the phone calls."

"There haven't been any since the gas station incident."

"Yes, but they could start again at any time. And I know it is more annoying than threatening, but that could change. I'm not suggesting you alarm any of your family. I think we should tell Reverend Anderson. He can give us support, and I believe he would reach out to the other church. They may not be perfectly in sync when it comes to beliefs, but I'm betting he can quietly calm the situation. Plus, it's only fair to tell him since he is the minister for our wedding. Next, we need to tell the sheriff. I figure it's better to be safe than sorry."

Jordan slouched on the sofa and closed her eyes. "You're right again." Emmy noticed a new determination when Jordan opened her eyes. "I'll call and see if we can meet with them together. It would be best, and easier on my nerves, to tell them at the same time."

"Deal." As Jordan reached for the phone, Emmy said, "By the way, are you going to fix that tangy cucumber salad for this afternoon?"

Jordan grinned. "Ah-ha, now the truth comes out. You only agreed to marry me so I'd become your own personal culinary slave."

"You got it, luv." Emmy winked.

Chapter Thirty-Three

God, she's gorgeous even without makeup, Jordan thought to herself. Emmy was propped up on one end of the sofa sipping her tea and contently reading a romance novel. Her feet lay in Jordan's lap.

Jordan was not a morning person, and it normally took an hour to hit her stride. In contrast, Emmy was productive the minute she rolled out of bed. They embraced each other's quirks and made it work.

They were content, and Jordan couldn't be happier. All her worries disappeared when she looked into Emmy's eyes, and she was actually looking forward to their big wedding day in less than a month. She was about to turn off the TV when the announcer spoke. "Join us tonight at six for a special news segment on the growing public opinion and activities surrounding the Supreme Court's impending decision on gay marriage. A panel of experts will tell us what it means to our community."

"It should be marriage, not gay marriage. Can you imagine if *Loving v. Virginia* had not passed? Why do some people somehow feel threatened by two people in love?" Jordan was silent for a few moments. "The Supreme Court has to provide a constitutional right to marry. If they don't and kick the decision back to the states, it will be chaos. It would threaten our marriage. The

October 2014 Fourth Circuit Court of Appeals ruling could be invalidated, and West Virginia would likely go back to banning same-sex marriage."

Emmy sat and scooted closer. "If somehow we lose, then we'll worry about it and fight. Regardless of a piece of paper, we love each other and are married in our hearts."

The muscles in Jordan's jaw tightened. "But it will also embolden the yahoos around here to start harassing us again. Reverend Anderson stopped them a couple of times, but I doubt he can hold them back if the Supreme Court upholds treating us as second-class citizens."

"Put the worry out of your mind. What matters is our love for one another and our family. No matter what the decision, our wedding is going to be a wonderful time. It will be filled with love, friendship, and good old-fashioned fun, especially with your Poppa picking out 1950s dance songs." Emmy kissed her before taking Jordan's hand. "Let's get our morning walk in before getting ready for work."

Jordan managed a weak smile but felt queasy. Conservatism ran deep, especially in the eastern panhandle. She prayed that hard-fought fairness would prevail. If not, she and others would be looking over their shoulders worried about their safety. Even if marriage equality passed, the so-called religious freedom bills were taking root around the country. These laws were discriminatory and aimed at taking away LGBTQ rights. Indiana Governor Mike Pence was a scary figure. He had signed the first such discriminatory law back in March. The Indiana legislature only modified the bill under national pressure. She shuddered. Despite all the progress, much more work was ahead.

Jordan arrived at the restaurant before anyone else. The quiet of the office and book work were her go-to distractions the past couple of days. She had been a ton of nerves since the Supreme Court had added another date for official rulings to be read. They had selected today, June 26. Not just any ole day in June. This date was special to all LGBTQ as a beginning toward equal rights. Back in 2013, the court had struck down the Defense of Marriage Act as unconstitutional in the *United States v. Windsor* case and also upheld same-sex marriage in California in the *Hollingsworth v. Perry* case. Could it be that the court wanted to intentionally announce another historic decision? She glanced at the clock. The world would likely know within the next couple of hours. Would Emmy be her legal wife in two days or would the court leave it up to the states and a patchwork of conflicting legislation? She paged through invoices and nibbled on a pastry. Soon, Robby and Jo walked through the back doors.

"What the hell, Jordan. Why are you here so early? Jo and I have the restaurant in hand. You're not chickening out, are you?"

"Sorry, Robby. You're good, but word around town is everyone misses my cooking."

He wadded up a towel and threw it at her. "In your dreams."

Jo snickered. "I bet you're weaseling out of the last-minute wedding plans."

"Guilty as charged. Oh my God, I can't believe we have gotten this far in one month. I watch Angie, Mom, and Emmy and my head spins. I'm glad they seem to be having fun. I knew weddings were a lot of work, but it's been so crazy. Now I understand why there are honeymoons. It's necessary to keep a couple from dying of total exhaustion."

"So running off to work and doing bookkeeping is soothing? How long have you been here?"

"About fifteen minutes."

Jo tossed an apron her way. "Well, make yourself useful. We're closed this weekend for your wedding, but there's plenty to be done right now. Help us then get your butt home after lunch."

"So, where's the menu?"

"Here." Jo handed her a small placard.

"No, not today's. Where's the one for the wedding?"

"Sorry, hon but I've got it password protected on the computer."

"Cough it up."

This time, Jo picked up a towel, wound it tight, and snapped it, cracking sharply on Jordan's upper thigh.

"Ouch!" Jordan rubbed her muscle. "That hurt."

"Did it? Sorry, boss but you need a snap back to reality. You'll have to have Emmy kiss it when you go home." Jo smirked as she walked over to the walk-in cooler.

Robby laughed. "Got to admire that twenty-something generation," he said, pointing at Jo. "They unapologetically speak their mind, and you and Emmy did agree to the menu being a surprise."

"Yes, but thank God she's one of the hardest-working millennials. I'm glad you talked me into hiring her. She's been a real asset."

"Yep and she has worked splendidly with me on the meal for your special day. Her creativity is amazing. You will be pleased. You do know that she looks up to you as a big sister, don't you?"

"Yes. I'd take Jo as my little sister any day. Now let's get to work."

The day flowed as she helped Jo with lunch preps and a new dessert recipe. They had talked about everything from family pets to movies. During the conversation, Jo changed the satellite radio from a music channel to a news channel. The move had not gone unnoticed by Jordan, and she glanced at the clock. It was 9:50 a.m. Ten more minutes for a possible Supreme Court decision. She swallowed and went on with the preps and listening to Jo as if nothing had happened.

The radio droned on with commentary from an announcer with a British accent. Jordan tried to be attentive to Jo, but her mind soaked up the radio commentary, and Jo's voice drifted away. By now, Jordan was aimlessly staring at the baked bread cooling and hadn't noticed that Jo stopped talking.

"Today could be a historic turning point for LGBTQ rights in America. The gay community hopes this will be a joyous occasion. Hundreds are gathered here on the steps of the US Supreme Court. Same-sex marriage became legal in the Netherlands over fourteen years ago. Great Britain approved gay marriage in March of 2014. Will the United States be the twentieth country to legalize marriage equality nationwide? We're possibly a few minutes away from a potential answer. Signs are everywhere. Anti-gay protesters are in attendance, but the crowd has been civil for the most part. I'm standing among the LGBTQ supporters. There's a nervous but positive feeling among this group. Here are the interns running with the decision. We will find out momentarily."

The announcer paused. The crowd's energy grew. A shout in the background pierced through. "Marriage. It's marriage. Love has won!" The crowd erupted in cheer.

"As you can hear, the crowd has gone wild. People are jumping up and down celebrating. It's a five-four decision. Marriage equality is now the law of the land throughout the United States!"

Jo turned down the volume. Jordan teared up. A lump formed in her throat and her voice cracked when she finally spoke. "I can enjoy my wedding."

"You sure can." Jo hugged her tight.

Robby hugged them both. "I'm so happy for you."

Relief and joy continued to wash over Jordan as the three cried tears of joy. Soon, her cell rang.

"Hi, sweetie. Did you hear the news?" Emmy's voice sounded so soothing to Jordan.

"Yes, I did. Jo had the radio on. What a month it's been. I get to marry the love of my life, my best friend, and one of the kindest people in the world."

"I love you so much, sweetheart." Emmy's words were partially drowned out by yelling in the background. "As you can hear, everyone is ecstatic at your mom's house. When are you coming home so we can celebrate?"

Suddenly, her mom's voice burst over the phone line. "Jordan, get your butt home and be with the woman you love. Or I swear I'm going to drive down there and throw you in the car. Why on earth did you go to the restaurant today?"

Jordan was wiping tears from her face with her hand, but there were too many. Although choked up, she said, "I'll be home in record time. Love you all."

Never in her life had Jordan imagined the law would change allowing her to marry the woman she loved. A big smile crossed her face knowing their marriage would not be dissolved simply by crossing state boundaries. The warmth of love surrounded her. She and Emmy were blessed.

Like interracial marriage in the past, there would be some rough spots for the country. The fight for civil rights legislation would continue. Protection from employment and housing discrimination had to be next. Adults might be free to marry nationwide, but there were still places where a person could be evicted or fired for being LGBTQ. Married on Sunday and fired on Monday.

She thought about how far her family and hometown had come and hoped that more hearts would eventually open. For now, she savored the victory of love over hate.

Chapter Thirty-Four

Jordan stretched her muscles. The light of day was poking through the sides of the blinds. She rolled over and caressed Emmy's arm. It was going to be a hectic day.

"Wake up, sleepyhead. You're usually the first one up." Jordan gently prodded her.

"Umm, you wore me out last night. I want to lie here for a few minutes."

"I'll fix us breakfast." She laid kisses on Emmy's cheeks before bouncing out of bed to greet the day. Today was their wedding day, June 28, 2015, and she felt like doing somersaults.

Wrapped in her robe, Jordan floated on air and began singing the song "Shut Up and Dance" by Walk the Moon. The infectious joy soon had Emmy in the kitchen dancing and singing along. After a breakfast of scrambled eggs and fruit, they stood on the deck looking out at the mountain. Jordan was behind Emmy with her arms wrapped around her. They swayed back and forth.

"Are you ready for all the hoopla today?" Jordan nuzzled Emmy's ear.

"Hoopla?"

"Slang for all the excitement."

Emmy laughed. "It's going to be tiring for sure, but I can't wait to call you my wife. How do you feel?"

"Like I want to go back to bed and make love to you all day."

"I'd love to hear that any other day, but your mum would kill us if we're late." She snuggled into Jordan and faked a pout. "Besides, the dresses are fabulous."

"Oh yes, the dresses that you, Mom, and Angie spent days, no weeks, going over half the East Coast to find."

Emmy turned and playfully pinched her bottom. "You'll be in awe as we take your breath away."

"I'm already in awe."

"I love you, sweetie. You've worked hard to stand up for your integrity and for us."

"You're worth it, Em. And you will be in awe when you see me in my tux."

Jordan kissed her tenderly and ran her tongue along Emmy's lips. Their tongues intertwined and the kiss intensified and consumed them. Jordan's hands slipped down Emmy's ass, pressing Emmy hard into her, and Jordan's lips moved to her neck. Emmy gasped and groaned as Jordan was caught up in the moment kissing, nipping, and sucking.

Emmy pushed her back. "If you give me a hickey, it will ruin the pictures, and the entire family will tease us throughout the evening."

"Let them."

"You're forgetting—"

Jordan drowned out Emmy's words with a fiery kiss on the lips while one of her hands moved to cup Emmy's breast. The sounds of pleasure escaped from Emmy's lips in tiny moans.

Emmy broke off the kiss. "Oh, sweetie. What time is it?"

Jordan ignored her question and kissed her passionately again.

"Good morning! It's time to get going. Where are you two?" Carter's voice boomed.

They quickly disengaged and straightened their robes.

"There you are. Why aren't you ready? We gotta go," he said, bouncing on his toes.

They tried to look casual, but Jordan could tell when the moment that reality dawned on him. His face was the reddest she had ever seen.

"Sorry," he mumbled. "I thought you knew Angie changed the time I was supposed to pick you up."

Emmy tried to ease the awkward moment. "She did. I forgot to tell Jordan. I'll get dressed. Be right back."

Jordan nodded as Emmy walked away. The two siblings stood for a while then both broke out in laughter.

"Emmy's a wonderful person. You're one lucky person, sis. Go on and get ready while I try to block out this memory before it scars me for life. By the way, I've never done any such thing on the deck." His eyes held a wicked gleam. "At least, not for several years since the kids were born."

He winked, and Jordan left him chuckling.

Jo ripped off the plastic protecting the freshly pressed tux. "Jordan, let's get you spruced up."

"Hey, Jo. There's something I've wondered about."

"Yes?" She picked up Jordan's shoes to polish them one last time, but Jordan laid a hand on top of hers to get her attention.

"There were times you appeared to be the only one who understood me. That night at Lost Dog. The text. You knew I was falling in love with Emmy."

"Well, I've always been good with my intuition."

"Did you always know I was a lesbian?"

"I suspected, but I didn't know for sure until that night at Lost Dog. Women are better at figuring out subtle distinctions. Robby was your wing pilot in the business and a teddy bear of a friend but didn't have a clue." She put the shoes down and grasped Jordan's shoulders. "And thank God, you woke up from the hurt inside. You are a terrific person, but every now and then, I could see a flicker of pain. I may not know everything you've been through since you are stubborn and don't share feelings."

"Not to mention I'm your boss."

"Yes, but you've got to have friends. You've got to let some people in. And if you don't then well, we will worm our way in because we care about you. That text I sent you at Lost Dog was to make you get off your ass. Remember one thing." Jo shook her finger. "Love provided the spark, but the fire was you. Accepting and loving yourself was what made the embers blaze and catch. But don't forget, how you arrange the wood affects how long the fire will last and the amount of heat it gives off."

Jordan was stunned. "How did you become such a wise old kindred soul in a twenty-eight-year-old body?"

"Thank you for the compliment. Think about it. So many people, no matter what their age, focus on the trivial crap. In the end, it only winds them up tighter. People need to learn to relax and live their lives. Emmy is good for you, and any fool can see how happy you are."

"I've always been amazed at your never-ending energy."

"The key is positive thinking. Can't go wrong if you count your blessings." She went back to polishing the shoes. "Come on! Widen that smile and put on that tux because today Emmy becomes your wife."

"So when are you and Ted getting hitched?"

Jo stopped and slowly turned. "I enjoy the play and Ted's a good guy. We split around New Year's. Still friends." She shrugged. "Everything happens for a reason."

As Jo went back to fussing over the outfit, a thought hit Jordan. "Jo?"

"Hmm?"

"Jo, look at me." Jordan hesitated then said, "Was the woman at the courthouse more than your friend?"

As Jo's watch alarm chimed, she said, "Time's running short."

"I'm sorry for being rude. I shouldn't have assumed."

Jo fiddled with the watch. Her facial expression was mixed. "It's okay. She's moving away for a job. I cared more about us than she did. That's the way it goes sometimes."

Jordan embraced her. "She's crazy. You know that, right? Anybody would be lucky to have you."

A frisky expression slowly replaced the frown. "Don't worry. I'm not giving up. I like the chase and variety."

Jordan laughed. "Fun and happiness do go hand in hand."

"Absolutely. Now get busy. Holler when you're dressed, and I'll come back in to make sure you're all spiffy."

Emmy heard the long low whistle and turned to see Becca with her arm around Olivia.

"What a dress, Em. Jordan's eyes are going to pop out of her head."

"Yes, you're simply glowing," Olivia added.

Emmy wrapped her arms around them the best she could then patted Olivia's tummy. "You look splendid in your dress with that tiny baby bump."

"Thanks to you for talking some sense into Becca." She warmly looked into her wife's eyes.

Becca's happiness was clear as she kissed Olivia's hand. "My arm might have been twisted, but you are so cute, and you're going to be a fabulous mother."

"We are going to be fabulous mothers."

Emmy admired their warm embrace and silently chuckled at Becca's change of heart.

As they departed, she gave Becca a warning. "No revealing the details of my dress. It's bad luck."

"I wouldn't dare risk your wrath. See you in a few."

It was a gorgeous day, partly cloudy with small puffy clouds in the bright blue sky. The temperature was near seventy-five degrees. There was no hint of rain, and the breeze was gentle and refreshing. The chairs were arranged with a small pedestal holding fragrant flowers at the end of every other row.

As Reverend Anderson faced the guests, Dave was to the left with his best friend and Aunt Elizabeth. Jordan stood on the right with Robby and Becca. Both Dave and Jordan wore light gray tuxedos with teal vests, bow ties, and accent pocket squares. Dave winked at Jordan as they stood awaiting the arrival of the brides.

Once the idea of a double wedding took root, there was no turning back. And Angie, Emmy, and Gwyneth were unstoppable. The grandeur of the event grew with each passing day. Jordan never dreamed such an enormous affair could come together in such a short amount of time. Now here they were in front of 260 guests. Yet all that mattered was Emmy would legally be her wife within the hour.

The processional began with Canon in D, Pachelbel, played on classical guitar by a friend of Emmy's. Looking down the aisle, she was stunned by the beauty of Emmy and her mother. There was no doubt, they did indeed take everyone's breath away.

Gwyneth wore an A-line ivory silk wedding gown adorned with glimmering metallic lace appliqués, and Emmy wore a chiffon sheath dress with scoop neckline and sparkling crystals embroidered at the waist and along the shoulders. Both had their hair up with flowers. Jordan was rocked to the core with their beauty and grace.

What truly made Jordan's chest burst with love was their grinning escort. Poppa Lange had been over the moon with

Grammy's idea of escorting both women. After his revelation about his brother, he'd had several conversations with Jordan, and they had grown extremely close. She thought the actions were just as cathartic for Poppa as they were for her.

When each bride stood next to her chosen companion, it was time for the seriousness. Reverend Anderson began in a loud, rich voice. "Friends and family, we are gathered here today to witness and celebrate the union of David and Gwyneth and the union of Jordan and Emmy. They stand here in front of you and in the presence of God himself seeking the gift of being united in marriage. A ceremony that serves to magnify life's joys by joining their hearts and securing strength in the power of the love, faith, and devotion they show to one another. Let us first begin with David and Gwyneth. Will you please turn and face one another, join hands, and recite your vows."

Jordan played with the collar and her bow tie, knowing they would be next. She had never been this nervous in her life, but she was not going to let it spoil the day. Lost in her thoughts and trying to calm herself, she lost track of the ceremony until Reverend Anderson announced, "David and Gwyneth, I now pronounce you husband and wife in marriage. You may seal the union with a kiss."

Jordan's heartbeat raced. When the crowd settled down, Reverend Anderson caught Jordan's eye and nodded. "Please turn and face one another, join hands, and recite your vows."

Jordan swallowed. Sweat trickled under her arms and rolled down her back. Her head was light, but she was determined. When she faced the stunning woman who had captured her soul, Jordan's worry melted away. Although her hands were slightly shaking, Jordan's voice didn't falter.

"Emmy. You are my companion, my best friend, and the love of my life. I promise to respect and cherish you. You have my hand, my heart, and my love forever as we join together. I will be at your side and support you through whatever sorrow, joy, or adventure comes our way. I love you." Emmy's smile and glistening eyes told Jordan she had done well.

"Jordan. I look forward to us walking hand in hand wherever this journey leads us. You have made me so happy. I pledge my love, devotion, and faithfulness to you. I will honor and respect you. With my whole heart, I promise to love and care for you, always and forever."

Reverend Anderson smiled broadly. "The rings, please."

Jordan slid the platinum diamond-encrusted band onto Emmy's finger. "With this ring, I thee wed. In the name of the Father, and of the Son, and of the Holy Ghost, amen." Emmy beamed as she repeated the words.

"Jordan and Emmy, I now pronounce you wives in marriage. You may seal the union with a kiss."

This was another moment that had Jordan nervous. She leaned in, but Emmy took charge, grabbed her by the collar, and laid one on her long and deep. Everyone erupted in applauding and whistling.

After the ruckus died down, the reverend announced, "Couples, please face your family and loved ones. Ladies and gentlemen, please welcome the new couples as they begin their journey in blessed union."

It was not ordinary clapping at this point. This was West Virginia. They were hooting and hollering like at a championship football game.

Emmy shouted in Jordan's ear, "My Lord, good thing no one passed out noisemakers."

They stood several minutes at the makeshift altar waiting for the lively guests to calm. Finally, the guitarist was able to play the recessional song "Close to You" by the Carpenters.

"Good thing he used an amplifier," Jordan said.

Emmy's eyes sparkled. "Ready to escort me down the aisle, my charming wife?"

Wife—hearing the word from Emmy filled Jordan's heart with joy. She motioned for Dave to lead the way. As they stepped down, Jordan looked over at the first couple of rows with all her relatives. She saw Grammy, Betty Jean, Sam and Gina, and Angie and Carter seated together. The kids were jumping up and down. She was bewildered why Carter had insisted on Robby taking his place at the altar. It was a good thing they rented a tux for Robby at the last minute. She had no idea what had changed Carter's plans until she looked who was seated next to him. Her heart ceased to beat for a split second and air caught in her throat. Anne and her two oldest children were next to Carter and Angie. Anne gave a small smile, nodded, and mouthed congratulations. Jordan still could hardly believe her eyes. Anne was a conservative, but here she was.

As the procession began, people waved and smiled, almost drowning out the guitarist. Some reached out to pat them on the back. Some gave thumbs up and winked. It was surreal and full of love.

After surviving the rowdy well-wishers, they gathered for photographs.

"What's going on with Anne and Gerry?" she blurted out a little too loudly to her mother.

"Anne and I had a good long talk. She wanted to attend. I thought it was best for her and the children to sit with Carter and Angie so she would be comfortable. I'm sorry I didn't tell you, but we were all worried that you would have a panic attack. She is here to wish us all happiness."

Jordan lowered her voice. "And Gerry?"

Gwyneth's smile faded, and she gave a heavy sigh and leaned over so as not to be overheard. "As I mentioned, he wasn't invited, and he's not likely to be around anytime soon. He is not welcome if he insists on hateful language. In fact, he and Anne are separated. They don't believe in divorce, but she's staying at her parents' house with the children and calling it a break."

Jordan's mouth hung open for several seconds. "Does he know she came to the wedding?"

"She said he only huffed a bit, but they did have a big fight once he realized Gerry Jr. and Margaret were accompanying her. They wanted to come, and in fact, Gerry Jr. stood up to his dad when he was yelling at Anne."

Jordan's eyes bulged. "Holy cow."

A few tears arose in her mom's eyes. "I also got to talk with the other children over the phone for a bit, but apparently Gerry doesn't want them around me. Anne and I are planning a get-together after the honeymoon. After another screaming match, Anne took out a restraining order. I don't know everything, but apparently, a psychologist wrote a letter saying it would be best. I hope Anne will tell me more details later. Maybe, there was something I should have done."

They all jumped in with telling Gwyneth that she was a fantastic mom and was not to blame for Gerry's actions. Dave hugged her and bathed her in tiny kisses. Emmy lowered her head on Jordan's shoulder and squeezed her tight.

After some moments of silence, Dave said with gusto, "Time to celebrate. We can't let this spoil the mood. Let's get these pictures done and get the party started. There is lots of fun to be had tonight. Lots to celebrate. One is that I am now a stepfather who is very proud of all his children, especially you, Jordan. That is if you'll have me as a dad."

The sincere words warmed Jordan, and she smirked. "Absolutely, Pops!"

"That makes me sound old, but it does have a nice ring to it."

They began to line up for the photos. Of course, Gwyneth and Emmy insisted on several angles, and it took some time with the Lange clan.

In the banquet tent, Jordan was relaxed through the customary toasts and speeches. The positive energy had made her swell with pride. People gathered to pass by the couples to express congratulations before the music and dancing began. Carter and Angie approached with their children. Anne and her oldest, Gerry Jr., seventeen, and Margaret, fifteen, were right behind them. Jordan was happy but anxious and wondered what Anne would say. Her head swirled, and she fought to relax her body. Anne had spoken religiously but respectfully at Jordan's birthday party. Still, she had no idea what was coming next.

"Congratulations to you both." Anne leaned in and lightly hugged them. "I know we have different views, but I have no ill will toward either of you. Only God can judge people, and only God can see your true heart and feelings. You gave an oath today pledging your love to one another. I wish you both peace." Anne looked at her children before returning her gaze back to Jordan and Emmy. "I want my children to grow up confident in their beliefs but willing to see the point of view of those who think differently. I don't want them to blindly follow. I want them to listen to God and think for themselves. Through God's love, I am confident we will find the right path. We may disagree, but we don't have to be ill-mannered."

Anne hugged them each again, and the kids stepped up and did the same. Margaret smiled wide but said nothing. Gerry Jr. was a pensive and serious teenager. "I wish you well," he said softly. To everyone's surprise, he cracked a smile. "You always were one of the most adventurous relatives, Aunt Jordan. I admire your courage."

Jordan was overtaken by his words, and the tears welled up in her eyes. While she tried to brush them away, Gerry Jr. removed a linen handkerchief and held it out to her. At that point, the emotions hit a high point. She hugged them all again and let the tears flow.

As they began to walk away, Anne stopped and returned. She leaned in so close that Jordan could feel her breath. "I never knew about the phone calls until Reverend Anderson stopped by to talk," she whispered. "I'm sorry that Gerry again chose to harass, but I hope you can forgive him one day." She took a deep breath, and her hands tightened around Jordan's arms. "He has a few problems, but deep down there is still some good in him. We're getting him help."

As she walked away, Jordan had a sense of sadness. She didn't know where Anne found the strength to go on with the marriage, but she had to admire her dedication.

Emmy rubbed her shoulder. "Let's have some fun. I've been longing for our first dance together as a married couple."

The entire evening was a whirl. Jordan had never received so many hugs and kisses. The festivities, dancing, and liquor flowed into the night. Dave and Gwyneth bid goodbye around nine, but no one would let Emmy and Jordan leave. Although exhausted, they were easily talked into more dancing. After another hour, Emmy announced to the crowd, "I'm tired, and my feet are killing me. Plus, I really want my sweetie to take me home."

Folks hollered, and several patted Jordan on the back as they tried to make their way through the crowd. Laughter erupted as someone yelled, "Jordan, better take her home before she changes her mind."

Jordan grinned and gazed at her lovely wife. *Simply exquisite,* she thought and leaned over to nuzzle her and caress her cheek. This caused louder howling and cheering. It took them several minutes to walk through the partygoers.

At home, Jordan passionately kissed Emmy before Emmy broke away and giggled. "Are you going to take my virtue in the vehicle or inside?"

"Um, let me think a minute." She leaned in to kiss her again.

"As I recall, you once pointed out the bedroom offered more maneuverable positions."

Jordan hopped out of the SUV like she was on fire and ushered Emmy into the house. "Welcome home, Mrs. Russo-Simón. After you."

"Why thank you, Mrs. Russo-Simón, especially for being my wife."

Emmy kicked off her shoes first thing and faced Jordan. Her look was seductive, and her voice flowed like honey. "Can you help me get out of this dress?"

Jordan kissed her neck while unzipping the dress. "I know we're fatigued, but I'm going to take you to bed, send you over the edge of pleasure, and caress you to sleep in my arms. First, close your eyes."

Emmy gave her a puzzled look but did as told and Jordan gently took her beloved's hand and guided her to their bedroom. As they entered, the sweet scent of roses wafted through the air.

"Open your eyes."

Several vases of roses and candles were arranged around the room, giving off a heavenly scent.

"Welcome home, my wife. I love you."

About the Author

Addison M. Conley grew up in central Illinois, moved to the east coast in her twenties, and now lives in the eastern panhandle of West Virginia with two fur babies. For many years, her writing was strictly business reports filled with facts, but the yearning to write fiction never left.

Falling for Love: A West Virginia Romance is the second edition of her first published novel. Other work in progress includes a military action/romance, now in edit, and a contemporary romance set in Rehoboth Beach, Delaware; which just happens to be her favorite East Coast beach town. The military novel will be released in the spring of 2019, and the contemporary romance is set for late 2019 or early 2020.

When not writing, she enjoys playing cards and board games with friends. Other hobbies include music and concerts, traveling, photography, reading, and working with stained glass.

Addison would love to hear from you.

Email: Addison.M.Conley.Author@gmail.com
Facebook: www.facebook.com/AddisonMConley.Fiction.Author
www.facebook.com/people/Addison-M-Conley/100017653029093.
Twitter: twitter.com/NeoTrinity13

Yeah, Addison's a die-hard fan of the original movie *The Matrix.*

Novels in Progress

Beyond the Checkpoint, estimated publication date spring of 2019.

Intelligence officer Ali Clairmont is looking to get out of debt and joins her agency's deployment program. She's openly gay because it's not a punishment in the federal workforce. Air Force Major and NSA SIGINT officer Lynn Stewart is deep in the closet because DADT is still in effect.

Over ten years, they cross paths three times – twice in Afghanistan and finally at home. In 2008, they attempted to keep everything professional, but add a little coffee and close quarters and the attraction ignites. A near death experience brings them closer together, but Lynn ends up breaking Ali's heart. In 2010, a spy is selling secrets. Lynn is brought into the investigation but ordered to keep Ali in the dark. Once again, mission above all else takes a toll.

As the years go by, neither can forget the other. Ali isn't happy when Lynn walks into her life again as her new civilian supervisor in 2017. Then Ali's cousin arranges for a lesbian to help with her home renovations. When Lynn shows up, the fireworks go off. Eventually, the ice begins to melt. But is it too late for love? Is a cordial friendship all they can hope for?

Beyond the Checkpoint is a combination of military action, suspense, and romance. While a work of fiction, the novel is based on the author's experience during three deployments. Through the story and characters, the author has tried to relay what it is like to be a soldier and a civilian in Afghanistan – the emotions, the challenges, the achievements, and the setbacks.

Contemporary Romance, yet to be titled, expected release date late 2019 or early 2020.

Nineteen years after leaving to attend college in North Carolina, Maddy moves back to her hometown of Rehoboth Beach, Delaware. She's in the middle of a divorce, and all she wants is to get her life in order, help her son, and move on. No one suspects she's gay, and she'd like to keep it that way until after the divorce. She bares her soul to her best friends, who keep her secret. Things turn ugly when her husband and father-in-law uncover a past lesbian affair, but there are a lot of skeletons hiding in their closet.

Jessie is a mysterious, motorcycle-riding, soft butch who be-friends Maddy. The complication: Jessie is like a daughter to the woman dating Maddy's grandfather. As the friendship grows, so does the attraction. They remain respectful of boundaries while silently hoping for more. But Maddy finds it difficult to put a lid on her simmering feelings, and Jessie isn't sure how Maddy identifies.

The two women come together as the divorce draws near, but their bliss is interrupted by the exposure of Jessie's troubled past. In a flash, that quickly becomes the least of their worries.

Reviews

Reviews are especially helpful and greatly appreciated by the author. Please consider leaving a review on Goodreads, Amazon, Smashwords, or another vendor site. Also, reviews posted to your website/blog, Twitter, Facebook, Tumblr or another site of your preference are splendid.

Below are excerpts from a few reviews of the first edition, *Falling for Love: A Winter Romance*, which were posted on Goodreads at www.goodreads.com/book/show/36170647-falling-for-love

Kitty Kat on Goodreads, Kitty Author on Amazon, rated it five stars. "'Falling for Love' is a beautiful, emotional, surprising and uplifting love story that had me totally gripped... The story is about coming to terms about who you are, but there was so much more. It went in directions I did not expect at all and had layers that caught me unawares. The romance was intense and very sexy, but ultimately it was the love between the two main characters that had me shedding tears of joy. I loved it."

Laure Dherbécourt rated it five stars. "WOW!! I dived deeply in the story and wasn't able to stop my reading. The plot is quite simple but powerful and very efficient!!! Both strong and fragile at the same time, Jordan and Emmy are two very touching characters ... I also really appreciated their consequent age difference and the fact that they are 40+ years old... I highly recommend this sweet and tasty novel and confess that I'll be delighted to read Addison's next books."

R. rated it five stars. "*Falling for Love* is a story about facing fears, rejection, and inner turmoil for the sake of love... The characters are intriguing, but I think the best part of this story is witnessing the emotional and social growth of Jordan as she battles and conquers her fears in the name of love. She seems to be on an emotional seesaw throughout the story, but the author effectively allows other characters, besides Emmy, to give Jordan balance, stability, and welcoming protective arms. Overall, this is a good story and relevant in today's ever-changing society."

Ameliah Faith rated it four stars. Review excerpt: "I enjoyed this beautifully descriptive later in life coming out story very much... I loved the nice, slow build-up of the sexual tension and the very sexy lovemaking. I did feel the ending was too rushed, but everything was tied up so nicely and neatly for a true HEA that I really didn't mind. This is a perfect book for curling up on the sofa while winter snows fall or on the patio while getting some sun on a warm summer's day. I think you will like it!"

Loek Krancher rated it five stars. "A fascinating story that deals with a lot of devastating situations. It includes social issues that are, unfortunately, still very alive today. An unforgettable, heart-wrenching story of love and strength. I was deeply touched by Jordan's story and the unconditional support of the most important people in her life. It is beautifully written, and I strongly recommend it."

Rocío rated it five stars. "As it is well and perfectly said in the blurb of this book, *Falling For Love* is not just about romance, but also about family, friends, and forgiveness... Unfortunately, we can find something very common nowadays, homophobia. But fortunately, we can also find people who stand for each other, who stand for other people's rights. And there is all of this in the book... It is an excellent way of starting a writing career. Addison has done a great job."

Mirtha Siblesz rated it five stars. "Very good debut novel. The plot development was flawlessly done. The two main characters had tons of chemistry. The supporting characters were all charming and fun. I hope the author would consider a story about Jo. Her character was very intriguing."

A.W. rated it three stars. "I especially enjoyed the journey the author took me through with regards to Jordan's character growth... The minor characters were well written, Betty Jean was a hoot and quite possibly stole each scene she was in."

In regards to the three stars, A.W. has a variable scale. I sincerely appreciate the honest review. Even the giants in LesFic have gotten a three-star from time to time.

An author always tries to improve while stretching the boundaries with plot and character diversity. Every bit of commentary and constructive criticism helps. Thank you all!

www.ingramcontent.com/pod-product-compliance
Lightning Source LLC
Chambersburg PA
CBHW020253200626
46816CB00001BA/263

* 9 7 8 0 9 9 9 8 0 2 9 6 0 3 *